KATHY LEE SUMNER

Kathy Lee Sum

2014

Captiva Island

A NOVEL

ISBN: 1-4392-4910-5
ISBN-13: 9781439249109

Visit www.booksurge.com to order additional copies.

Dedication

This one's for you, Dad.

Nothing makes us so lonely as our secrets.

-Dr. Paul Tournier

Prologue

ust a few turns off Peachtree Road in the heart of Atlanta,
Georgia, sits a grand ole home in the posh neighborhood
of Buckhead that my grandparents had built as newlyweds.
After fifty-some faithful years of marriage, they both got summoned to a better place, Grandpa Ashton making the journey
just months before Grandma Peg.

Close friends knew that I had inherited the estate, and
those not-so-close friends...well, I just let them assume that
the family column Julia Parks wrote for the Sunday edition of
The Atlanta Post shucked out the bucks. *Tips from the Domestic
Trenches* had been running for about ten years, a cropped shot
of my blonde head beside headlines ranging from "Cheerios
and potty training—ready, aim, fire!" to "Flirting with the
soccer coach can lead to marital suicide."

As a little girl I'd dreamed Grandma Peg's place would
someday be mine. I used to climb the dogwoods that lined
the brick-paved driveway and look back at the sturdy white

columns that anchored the wraparound porch where countless barbeques and Christmas parties had brought the embracing house to life. A white picket fence surrounded all that was there and its lush lawns—a Norman Rockwell-esque scene viewed by all who stood on the outside. That fence did a fine job of protecting all our secrets, until early last spring.

Grandma Peg died two weeks before my wedding to Darrell Parks, and on her deathbed, at my mama's insistence she signed the house over to me. Mama told her that she already had a nice house in nearby Marietta. "I don't need another house to keep clean." Thanks to their gracious decision, Darrell and I had a handsome nest to land in after our nuptials.

That was fifteen years ago.

Starting our lives together in my grandparents' happy house *had* to be a good omen. I wrapped myself in that fuzzy thought, certain that nothing would ever throw Darrell's and my happiness off course. The blessings multiplied when our children, twin boys (the result of a honeymoon in the Bahamas), came into the world. We never did have much time to do the naked-newlywed dance around the house.

A month after they were born, a heart attack took my daddy and Mama came to live with us—said she hated that empty house in Marietta. Funny how she wound up living in the same house in which she was raised. It was a good thing for me though. Without her help babysitting, I never could have launched my career so early, and with twins, we certainly needed the money.

Yep, that's right. Darrell and I, in this wonderful house in all its glory, were strapped for cash. Between my meager income from writing and Darrell's salary—he was a professor of American history—we barely kept up with maintenance and property taxes. We had to put our kids in public schools rather than private. When other mothers in the neighborhood turned up their noses at the idea, I told them that learning other "cultures" would enlighten my boys. They all bought it, figuring I must be a liberal working at the paper and all. We struggled through, all the while enjoying the upper-crust façade we'd created. If I told you that status did *not* bring us happiness, you might be surprised. Some live to attain that high society label no matter what the cost. But what about something as simple as honesty? That's where it got complicated.

So Mama watched after the boys while I stayed busy with the paper and Darrell taught classes at Emory University, which is where we'd met. A student teacher at the time, he wooed me during a series of tutoring sessions that began with states rights and the Articles of Confederation, proceeded to Miller High Life and ended with anatomy. A B+ and an engagement ring resulted. It was quick; love had slapped us both silly.

We might have stayed silly, but after years of grueling schedules mixed with the demands of parenthood, the in-love part began to fade. Who in the hell wanted to make time for romance?

I did.

Now I admit, when the twins were little, there were days I didn't have time for a shower let alone even speak to my husband. But once the boys went to grade school, I returned to the living. Darrell didn't seem to notice. It got to the point where I could count on one hand the times we'd made love in the previous twelve months. As the years passed I began to wonder if gravity was sneaking up on me, the old downhill ride toward forty. But when I studied myself in the mirror, it struck me that my package still shimmered in the right light. Why, just a few months before our mess of secrets was disrobed, a gentleman standing in line behind me at a Starbucks asked if I was an aerobics instructor at the Atlanta Fitness Center. Yes, it was cheesy, but I basked in that compliment for days. Too bad it wasn't the man in the coffee line that I needed.

Umpteen times I asked Darrell if he still found me attractive. "Wha*t*?" he'd answer, putting stress on the *t*. Then he'd shrug and shake his head. "You're being ridiculous, Julia."

A woman can only ask to be touched by her husband so many times before she grows desperate.

I grew desperate.

Late one night about a year and a half ago, Darrell ran to get a cappuccino from his favorite coffeehouse near the campus. He always did this when he fell behind grading papers. While he was gone I made sure Mama and the twins were asleep, then went to Darrell's study and draped myself across his desk clad in nothing but garters and stockings and a swath of red silk from Victoria's Secret. I couldn't believe I was being so provocative—lil' ole modest me. When my husband returned, puzzled, he rubbed tired eyes and then stroked the stubble on his chin.

"Not tonight, honey. I've got to get these midterms graded." With that, he bent over and kissed me on the forehead. What a consolation prize—one of many I'd been rejected with over the course of our marriage. I left the study that night with nothing but a checkmark on my ass from the red grading pen I'd sat on, and a dagger in my libido. *I can't do this anymore.*

Of all people, it was my own mother who had given me the idea to make a trip to Victoria's Secret. A retired hippie and born-again Christian, she told me that visual stimulation was the key to catching my husband's eye again.

"Ya gotta jazz it up every now and then," she'd said one day over lunch, between bites of a chili cheese dog. "Maybe he's tired of the same ole same ole."

Mama and I were at the Varsity drive-in for our monthly grease fix. It's one of the few places we talk without Darrell or the boys disturbing us.

"We're not even having the same ole same ole," I replied. "He doesn't touch me anymore unless it's to get me to pass him the remote."

"Your father and I went through the same thing, God rest his soul."

"You did?" I said, wrinkling my nose.

"Of course we did. All couples go through this. I promise you, sugar, if putting on a sexy little getup doesn't stoke his fire, either something's wrong with the equipment, or maybe, and I hate to say this—," she looked down and stirred her chocolate shake, "maybe he's getting it somewhere else. He does spend an awful lot of time away from the house, considering he only teaches twelve hours a week, and then there's that campout..."

That thought had crossed my mind. The third weekend of every month for the past few years Darrell had met with The Brothers of the Confederacy for a campout in the lower Blue Ridge Mountains. By no means is Darrell prejudiced, it's just a group of guys proud of their Southern heritage. They dress in Confederate garb and have paintball wars out in the woods. No women allowed. Funny thing was... I'd noticed a few times that he'd forgotten his uniform.

After the failed Victoria's Secret ploy, I feared maybe Mama was right. What husband in his right mind would pass on his wife when she's all dolled up in garters and stockings and a little patch of red silk?

He didn't want me.

That was when I did the other thing that was out of character. I began looking at the *The Atlanta Post's* new assistant sports editor in a whole new light. BRUCE CRAWLY at my service...aims to please. Oh—my—God!

I continued to keep mine and Darrell's lives on autopilot, tortured by a secret that would eventually need telling. This was uncharted territory. I was the *good* girl in school!

Then one night, just after I'd finished watering all the houseplants (my Wednesday routine—"W" was for Wednesday and water both) a call came that served as the catalyst for all that needed unraveling.

Chapter 1

After a decade of faithful service to *The Atlanta Post*, my editor granted me one month's leave to prepare for my newest assignment as long as I filled my column space each week. Thank goodness Julia Parks kept a small stockpile of "rainy day" stories.

It never occurred to me while studying journalism at Emory that someday a famous romance novelist like Helen Van Buren would want me to write her long-awaited biography. When her nurse Isa called Wednesday night after I'd watered the houseplants, the excitement left me tongue-tied.

"Helen Van Buren, *the* Helen Van Buren?" I kept repeating. She insisted that I stay at her beach cottage in South Florida to boot!

Nurse Isa said there were to be no cameras or big names involved, and my whereabouts were to be kept hush, hush. She told me that Mrs. Van Buren, a former Atlanta resident, loved my column on the endless trials and tribulations of married life and raising children. Not even Barbara Walters could get an interview with this renowned author. And she wanted me? I had no idea why but it didn't matter. This would catapult my career to the next plateau.

The night before the trip I double-checked my briefcase to make sure I had plenty of pens, notepads, and backup batteries for my tape recorder. Darrell came up from behind, startling me. I swirled around and saw him with something tucked under his arm.

"I figure a serious writer needs the best tools of the trade."

He watched me slip a silver bow off the laptop computer that I'd been holding out to buy. With the boys' braces to pay for, and our extra cash going toward some stock that Darrell insisted we invest in, I'd thought a luxury like that would have to wait at least another year. It was the first time he acknowledged my career as something serious. Usually his career dominated our conversation, day after day discussing his students, half of them sorority girls who I could imagine gazing at him with big eyes, chin in palm, swooning over his Jimmy Stewart-like lankiness and charm while he lectured from the podium.

"You're always saying that you'd love to write sitting in a lounge chair on the beach and now you can."

"But Darrell ... can we afford this? I thought you wanted to invest all our—"

He put two fingers over my lips. "Shh, you deserve this. I've arranged my schedule so I can drive you to the airport in the morning."

He smiled and brushed my cheek with his fingers, the way he did when he wanted more than a kiss. My skin went numb to his touch. We hadn't been intimate in months. And then there was that damn Bruce Crawly that'd come to work at the paper six months ago.

"You all right?"

I blew it off and said, "Just need to get to sleep early tonight…big day tomorrow."

Before I knew it, five AM glared on the digital clock. I roused Dylan and Ryan from bed early.

"Come on guys, up and at 'em," I said, the morning refrain they'd heard since the age of two.

"Go away," Ryan waved as I threw back his covers.

But Dylan sat up and smiled, flashing a mouthful of braces at me. "Mornin', Mom," he croaked. I couldn't tell if my young teen was sick or just having a hormonal blowout through the vocals.

Sitting at a desk wedged between their beds, I said, "Ya'll know I'll be gone for five days and—"

"We know, we know," Ryan said, peeking out from under his pillow, "don't drive Nana crazy." They called my mama Nana.

"That's right, don't drive Nana crazy. No soccer in the house and no junk food after eight."

Dylan climbed out of bed and sat on my lap like a sack of potatoes. "Why can't we go to Florida, too? We could stay somewhere else with Nana. We promise not to bother you."

Ryan sat up. "Yeah, this Captiva Island place sounds awesome. We could go snorkeling and skimboarding. It'd be sweet!"

"Come on, Mom," Dylan begged. "We don't have school next week. It's spring break, remember?"

"That's right, no school. With all this cold weather we've been having, it's hard to believe that the first day of spring is only a day away. I've had how-to-write-a-biography on the brain ever since that call came from Mrs. Van Buren's nurse and making plans for the break just slipped my mind. Maybe ya'll can come down with Nana for some fun after I'm finished with the interview."

"About this lady, um, Van Durum?" Ryan said.

"You mean Helen Van Buren?"

"Whatever, Nana said Great-Grandma Peg knew her. Is that true?"

"Nana told you what? She must be mistaken. Helen Van Buren is one of our country's most famous romance novelists. We still have all of her books down in the study, most of them signed at book fairs when she'd come to town. Maybe Grandma Peg met her at a book signing, but I doubt she knew her, she would've told me for sure."

"I heard Nana say it too," Dylan seconded. "Last night when she came to tell us goodnight she said that this was a special trip because it would help your career and that it would've made Great-Grandma so proud."

"I'm sure that's all she meant, that Grandma Peg would've been proud to see me write about Helen Van Buren. She's an icon! Now up and at 'em, boys! Breakfast in twenty."

My three guys sat at the kitchen bar top shoveling pancakes in as fast as Mama could flip 'em out. Ducks in a row they were, each with sandy brown hair casting off in five directions. A half foot more and the boys would reach their father's six feet. Mama and I had the distinction of being the small ones of the family. When asked we'd claim to be five feet, and that was stretching it. I have no idea why we got the short end of the stick when it came to height. My grandparents on both sides were tall people.

After breakfast the boys sped upstairs to get ready. I kissed the twins goodbye before they left to catch the cheese wagon, as they liked to call the school bus, but five seconds later Dylan poked his head back in the door.

"Mom, get out here. We got rolled again."

"Last weekend was one thing, but whose mother lets them out on a school night?"

"I bet it was one of Ryan's girlfriends."

"Shut up!" Ryan said, swinging his backpack at his brother.

I stepped outside to survey the damage. Each of the twelve dogwoods that lined our redbrick driveway was draped with white streamers of toilet paper, not to mention the fountain in the courtyard. Poor St. Francis of Assisi, friend to the animals, sat atop the two-tiered fountain like a mummy.

"He'll be papier-mâché if we don't clean him up before it rains," I said.

Mama came out in her purple foam curlers, Darrell trailing close behind, shaking his head and laughing.

"Papered again," he said. "Not to worry, honey, that just means our boys are popular with their peers. I'll have 'em clean it up after school."

While I let out a frustrated roar, Darrell loaded my stuff into the back of his Escalade pickup, and I hugged Mama good-bye.

"I'm so excited for you," she said, one of the foam curlers smashing my ear. "Now don't you worry about a thing. I've got those boys under control, all three of them," she joked, glancing at Darrell.

"Ha, ha, very funny," he teased back, and then his coat pocket chimed like a bell—his work phone. He carried two phones, and his personal line played "I Wish I was in the Land of Dixie." The University insisted that he have a separate phone that was specific for school. One of them seemed to always be ringing...

His amber eyes swirled around in his head as he listened to whoever was on the other end. "I'm sorry, Julia," Darrell said as I was climbing into the car, "that was our department head. I've got to take a class for Dr. Randall. He phoned in sick. I'm the only one who's familiar with his syllabus."

"I should've figured something would come up."

"I guess I'll go get dressed," Mama said, padding in her pink slippers back to the house. She hated driving through downtown, especially on overcast days. To top it off, on this particular day the weatherman had called for sleet.

"There's never time for me anymore," I said to Darrell, unable to conceal my bitterness.

"Don't take it like that," he said. "I'll make it up to you. I promise. Here," he handed over the keys, "ya'll take the Escalade so you don't have to reload the luggage."

"Gee, thanks."

He leaned towards me. "Quick kiss?"

"Aren't they always?" I put my cheek to his lips and shrugged off his superficial hug.

Thank goodness the rest of my morning went well and the air traffic gods got my plane off on time. I didn't want any kinks as I winged my way to Captiva Island in south Florida.

A few minutes after takeoff I sighed in relief, thinking of the worries I was leaving behind. I knew damn well that I had to end the affair with Bruce if I wanted to keep my marriage intact. So far my efforts to save it had been minimal—a few marriage counseling sessions with Darrell, first to cope with stress after the twins were born, then to learn how to communicate better. We obviously needed a session on sex therapy, too.

The flight attendant hadn't even brought out the drink cart when a man in the aisle tapped my shoulder. I looked up from some notes I'd been reviewing and gasped.

"Bruce!"

"Surprise!" he said, leaving his hand on my shoulder. "I've got work to do in Florida, too."

"Bullshit," I whispered.

"No really, I do." He looked at the middle-aged lady sitting next to me. "Mind if we trade?" he asked her with an irresistible smile. "My seat's 10-A, in business class."

He didn't have to convince her and my plans for sex therapy with Darrell quickly receded as Bruce's alligator boots did a side step in front of me and he wedged into the seat. He smelled of Irish Spring and mint gum, which he chewed to camouflage the smell of smoke, and it aroused my senses, conjuring up our activity the previous Monday night. We didn't say anything for a moment, just stared at each other.

A little bit about Bruce...a former outfielder for the University of Miami's baseball team, seemed like every girl's dream, which is why I was dumbfounded to find that he had remained single. Our desks at the paper were just across from each other, and conveniently, nothing separated us but glass walls. Every time I looked up from my computer there he was, luring me with those dimples and light eyes, the kind that look to be outlined in black ink; penetrating. He'd catch me looking at him, and I'd snatch up the phone as if I had someone important to call.

The flirtation had started out harmless enough. A little wink here, a playful pat on the butt there—that's how Bruce came on to me, and my responses just egged him on. But I never intended for it to go anywhere. It was simply a test of my ability to attract not just the average Joe up on the rafters of a construction site, but a man the single girls of Buckhead clamored to sidle up to during happy hour. I passed the test with flying colors.

Bruce was a vivacious twenty-nine-year-old and I was almost ten years his senior, but who cared? The way he carried himself lit my fire: broad, erect shoulders, a confident bounce to his walk. He had strong thick hands and no wedding band, which meant, no baggage. He looked at me as if he wanted me, something Darrell hadn't done for years. I even found his early receding hairline appealing. My knees quivered. My face blushed. I thought about him no matter where I was or what I was doing. Making spaghetti, weeding the yard, sleeping... No matter how many times I taught Sunday school or offered volunteer time with the PTA, I couldn't shake his image from my mind. These domesticated ventures had no power to pull me out of the vortex of lust.

Initially, I thought all I would need was a nibble to satisfy my hunger.

The first time Bruce got into my personal space we were in the basement at work. I was looking for archives not yet entered in the *Post's* database. Though he pretended to have been smoking a cigarette out in the stairwell, I was convinced he'd followed me down there from the office.

The jungle of shelves housing old file boxes towered over my head, and worn-out office equipment cluttered the aisles, obstructing the path of anyone coming through. The fluorescent lighting was dim that when I initially ran into him, it took a few seconds for his face to come into focus.

"Fancy meeting you here," he said, looking down at me. He was so close I could feel his breath.

I smelled peppermint gum on top of tobacco. "Out having a smoke again?"

"Guilty."

"Better than the wacky weed."

"Hey, that was in college and..." he bit his lip, realizing I had only guessed about his experimentation.

"You, the quintessential athlete, smoke pot? I'm highly disappointed."

"It was only a few times," he said, eyeing me up and down. "I got caught up with the wrong crowd while I was still in Miami working the sports beat for *The Herald*. I swear that's all behind me now."

"So," I said, stepping back, "are you looking for something in particular down here?"

"I saw you coming down the stairwell when I was sneaking a smoke, thought I'd ask if you'd like to have lunch today."

"Lunch?" I blurted out, and then with barely a pause, said, "Yeah, I'd like that." I looked down at my hands and fiddled with my wedding band, knowing where a potentially innocent lunch could lead. But it felt so good to have a hunk give me the time of day.

The awkward stare we exchanged was broken by the soft kiss he planted on my cheek.

"Sorry," he said. "I guess you're married."

"*Very* married."

"It's just a kiss, right?"

"Yeah, and nothing more," I assured him.

Trouble was, I thought about that kiss for the rest of the day. I wanted more but couldn't come right out and say so. Then one Monday night after a PTA meeting I left it up to fate. I called him on my way home, telling myself that if he answered, having more of him was meant to be.

He answered after one ring.

The consequences of risking my secure, sanctified marriage didn't cross my mind during that first glorious climax we shared, the passion gripping us on his kitchen table. I kept saying to myself, "Just this one time, Julia, and that's it." Little did I know how hauntingly addictive he would be. To feel those urges again! He brought me back to life.

One night while en route to his house I called Bruce on my cell phone. "What if it's like a bag of chips, and we can't be satisfied with just one?"

He laughed and said, "Munch away, darlin'."

It turned out to be a super-sized bag of chips, me never missing a single Monday night PTA meeting. Darrell never asked where I'd been. It had been my habit, prior to meeting Bruce, to go out to dinner with some friends on the PTA, and he just assumed that's where I was, at a restaurant with the girls.

But it got to the point where just one bag wasn't enough. I needed Bruce. I ached for the attention. The devil and the angel perched on my shoulders argued about it from the time I woke up in the morning to the moment my head hit the pillow at night.

Week after week I continued this addictive cycle, horrible I know. Meanwhile, I wanted nothing more than to fix my marriage and go back to the days when Darrell's touch made me shiver. But how?

"You sly devil," I said. "Same flight, same place. What's going on?"

"You know Mike, that new guy in sports?"

"Yeah?"

"Well, his wife is about to have a baby so I took him off this story and put myself on it."

"And what story might that be?"

"Major league baseball training. A handful of teams go to Fort Myers every year in the spring. I get to write up the Red Sox, and I'm not due to meet with them until Monday so that leaves you and me some time together at the Doubletree. Plus I might visit some old friends in Miami." He put his hand on my thigh.

"I thought you didn't associate with those old friends in Miami anymore."

"Not all of them were dope-heads."

"No, this isn't happening," I said, trying to get my head straight. "My whereabouts this week are confidential. Helen Van Buren is a respected novelist and I want to abide by her wishes to keep this biography a secret until it's time to release it. You're not supposed to know where I am, remember?"

He frowned. "Then you shouldn't have told me about it the other night in my hot tub."

"Maybe we shouldn't be doing the hot tub thing anymore." I pushed his hand away.

"What are you saying, Julia?" He grabbed my hand and stroked it with his thumb. "We've got a good thing here."

I couldn't bear to look at him. The dimples that framed his smile would suck me back in for sure. I fiddled with my wedding band and said, "Not this trip. My career's on the line here."

He dropped my hand, and when I finally looked up at him he was pouting like a child. "Please come see me, Julia. Captiva Island is just across the bridge from Fort Myers."

"We'll see. But whatever you do, don't call me, I'll call you."

"We'll see." He winked.

The flight lasted another hour, and with every passing minute my frustration at being crammed next to him mounted. I'm extremely claustrophobic. At last the captain's voice came on saying that we'd be making our final descent to Southwest Florida International Airport in twenty-five minutes.

When the plane made a hard turn I saw the Gulf of Mexico just over the right wing. The warm sun reflected brightly off its waters—a welcome change from the sleet we'd left behind. The landing was smooth and I prayed the rest of the trip would follow suit.

As we stepped off the plane and onto the jet way, Bruce asked me if I wanted to share a rental car.

"Not on your life," I said, knowing that the car would drive straight to his hotel. "There's supposed to be someone picking me up at baggage claim."

"Well darlin', I'll say my goodbye here. Call me later?" He kissed the top of my head, and I rolled my eyes at him. "Think about it," he added.

I reached up and brushed a piece of lint from his lapel. "Doubtful…"

❦

After passing a long string of stores peddling golf bags, bathing suits, "I Love Florida" t-shirts and shells, and wedging through the crowd around the baggage carrousel, I retrieved my red suitcase and found my ride—a silver-haired fellow holding up a sign with "JULIA PARKS" scrawled in bold black letters.

"That's me," I said, extending my hand.

"Pleasure to meet you," he said, tipping his golf cap. "I'm Stephen Donovan. Mrs. Van Buren says to tell you hello and sorry that she couldn't be here. Sometimes the ole gal needs a morning nap," he chuckled. "Look who's calling who old— my hair's whiter than hers is." He jovially winked.

"Will she be up when we get there?"

He checked what looked to be a diamond-faced Rolex as we walked toward the parking lot, him rolling my suitcase behind him. "Oh sure, Mrs. V usually just catnaps. You two can begin your talks over tea," he said gesturing his pinkie like a lady at tea. "She likes to have tea in the afternoon."

"That'll be perfect."

"Three more cars down," he said, pointing.

"The old-timey car?"

He raised his eyebrows. "She's not old, she's just mature. The 1926 Chrysler Imperials are hard to come by nowadays."

"What a beauty," I said, admiring the baby-blue paint job, buffed to a high sheen. I wondered what Mrs. Van Buren would look like sitting in the backseat. It was hard to picture because she was a renowned recluse. Only two officially sanctioned photos had ever been published of her: one accompanied by a wedding announcement in *The Atlanta Constitution*, and a profile shot in *Life* magazine after one of her best sellers, *Two Souls in Paradise,* hit the shelves in 1955. Seventeen novels later—the last released in 1988—and she'd only been spotted in public a handful of times. All other media photos of her had been taken by tabloid photographers. The pictures I'd come across while doing research always showed her wearing a scarf draped around her head and tied under the chin. Rumor had it that a growth or scar of some kind blemished the once porcelain-like skin on her face.

It was striking how quickly the metropolis turned tropical only a few miles from the airport. A series of bridges came before us, each stretching over water as blue as the sky, and traveling at a speed no faster than forty miles per hour, the vintage engine chugging away beneath me, I had plenty of time to take it all in.

When Stephen stopped at the toll before the Sanibel Causeway, he put in a Sinatra CD.

"We had one of those specialty car shops put in the CD player and A/C, updating the ole girl without taking away her charm."

"I Get a Kick Out of You" started playing. "That's one of my favorites," I said, leaning back and closing my eyes.

"Favorite old songs are like old friends. They take us back to that special place or time we once loved."

"I know what you mean," I agreed. "Every time I hear Peter Gabriel's 'In Your Eyes' I'm back at the college dorm making out with the man who's now my husband. Oops, maybe that was too much information."

He let out a chuckle. "You're fortunate. You'd be surprised how many married couples never have passion to begin with."

He had a point there. At least Darrell and I could claim that.

"Are we getting close?" I asked as we approached the end of another bridge.

He turned down the music and said tour-guide-like, "That's Sanibel Island just ahead. Then we cross over to South Captiva Island. North Captiva comes last and can only be accessed by ferry or small plane. No cars there, only bicycles and golf carts. We'll head north, a few miles up Sanibel, cross over Blind Pass Bridge, and then we'll be on South Captiva where Mrs. V's place is."

"Oh, I'd love to take the ferry over to North Captiva some time, maybe after I'm finished with the interview."

If an old guy could be adorable, Stephen was him. His right cheek dimpled every time he grinned, which was often.

A golf glove laying on the dash made it obvious where he spent his days off.

"How about I take you over the next time Mrs. V needs a nap? She takes at least one a day. Remind me to tell you the story about how Captiva got its name. It's more fun to tell while floating across the water."

"You bet. So how long have you been Mrs. Van Buren's driver?"

He laughed. "I wouldn't call me her driver, per se. She likes to consider me a good friend that gives her a ride now and then. Isa takes her around at times, but usually she's too busy taking care of the house or running errands. But to answer your question, I've been helping out since the doctor told her she couldn't drive anymore. Let's see," he rubbed his white stubble, "I guess it's been about a year now. I just recently sold my condo in Fort Myers and moved over to the island. It made sense to be closer so I rented a guest house just a small hike from her place."

We small-talked ourselves over the bridge and onto Sanibel. The main drag, Periwinkle Way, curved around an assortment of seafood restaurants, quaint shops and small family-owned businesses. After a few slowly driven miles, the road turned residential and I could see water again. We crossed Blind Pass Bridge onto South Captiva. The one road that ran along the island's west side had crumbled in places from hurricanes lashing it, and we had to zigzag forward, avoiding the destruction. Other than the shoreline, every inch of the island laid canopied in shade from massive banyan trees and Australian pines. With strained eyes, I caught glimpses of cottages as we passed bird of paradise plants and bougainvillea vines climbing up coconut palms.

Stephen eased the Chrysler Imperial onto a road that was barely more than a shell path. Banyan branches swept the windows as the old car bounced over the uneven ground. Up ahead I could see an apple-green cottage with pink trim and a two-story porch with a spiral staircase. Four potted ferns hung under the awnings, swaying in the breeze, and white wicker rockers sat in pairs both upstairs and down, accompanied by teak end tables.

The nurse, Isa, greeted us at the door in a starched chambray shirt dress and white apron. On the phone she had come across as soft-spoken, and I was surprised to find her so tall—at least six feet, a good twelve-inch advantage over me.

She shook my hand with both of hers and said in a slight German accent, "It's so good to finally meet you in person, Mrs. Parks. You're much blonder than the picture next to your column."

"Please, call me Julia. I had my hairdresser do me a shade lighter since I was coming to the tropics." The stained glass door slammed behind Isa, and we both jumped.

"Sorry about that." Isa opened the door again. "The gulf breeze is overpowering at times. You can see the view better upstairs from the sunroom. Mrs. Van Buren is waiting for you there." Isa's chestnut hair, feathered with gray, framed her face in a bob like the one my mother used to wear in the sixties.

The house was bright and airy and smelled of spring flowers, a bouquet of which greeted me in a cut crystal vase in the foyer. Floral patterned rugs reached across oak floors, and

Tiffany-style lamps sat on either side of a pink-velvet loveseat in the living room. I followed Isa back to the kitchen and up a staircase to a room that burst open with light. The whole west side of the house breathed salt air through two open sliding glass doors. The gulf shimmered beyond the figure of a woman standing in the foreground, an ivory-handled cane in her hand.

Slowly she turned toward me, the cane tapping two times. "Mrs. Parks, or may I call you Julia?" she said, smiling and extending a worn warped hand. "Come sit next to me on the sofa. I feel as if I already know you after reading your column for the past ten years."

Strangely, there was something familiar about her too, as if I'd known her in another life or something crazy like that. The feeling didn't just come from reading her books or doing umpteen hours of research about her. It was a warm, spontaneous connection.

"It's such a pleasure to finally meet you, Mrs. Van Buren."

Even inside, she wore a scarf wrapped around her head and tied under her chin. It was turquoise, like the water, and semi-sheer. I could make out some discoloration beneath the fabric on her left cheek, but quickly averted my eyes when she noticed me looking.

"How was your flight, dear?"

"Quick and smooth."

"It takes no time at all to get here from Atlanta nowadays." She put on her glasses, which hung around her neck from a multicolored beaded chain, and got a better look at me.

"I remember when my late husband and I made our first drive down from Atlanta in the early forties. It took two full days."

To the left of her desk was a bookshelf filled with her works along with stacks of magazines and newspapers. On the top shelf a copy of *Gone with the Wind* stood alone, displayed on a wooden plate stand.

She saw me notice it and said, "It's a signed copy. Go ahead, you can look inside."

With loving care I took it down and opened the cover.

> *To Miss Helen Anderson:*
> *Best wishes from one booklover to another.*
> *Sorry I missed you.*
> *Margaret Mitchell*

After placing it back on its stand, I nodded toward the shelf below it. "Are all twenty-one of your novels here?"

"Yes. You've read a few?"

"Yes, all of them, and so has my mother and Grandma Peg. Grandma Peg was an especially avid fan. Your work is timeless. Why did you stop?"

"Stop what?"

"Stop writing novels."

"After my last book came out in eighty-eight, I felt drained. Writing novels can be exhausting because you have to live through the characters as you write. And the onset of arthritis made putting my thoughts to paper more challenging. So I dabbled in short stories when I could, but the one thing I've always wanted to get back to was a novel I started years ago."

"You mean there's another work that you're hiding from the world?"

"I wouldn't say I'm hiding it, perhaps just hanging on to one last piece of me."

Isa brought in a tray with loose tea leaves, dainty teacups painted with daisies and some shortbread cookies.

"I'll be down in the kitchen if you need me," she said. "Stephen said he'll be back at six-forty-five. Your reservation is for seven."

I was surprised that we'd be going out to dinner. Could Mrs. Van Buren even stay awake past seven? "Please don't feel as if you have to take me to dinner. I can help Isa cook up something in the kitchen if you'd like."

"I wouldn't hear of it, dear. I'm looking forward to getting out tonight." Once Isa was downstairs Mrs. Van Buren said, "She's been my right arm for years. Isa never had children. She came to the States with her mother after World War II. I'm like her child now, always needing something—when I'm not sleeping, that is. My alert hours are few, that's why I wanted you to be here for a few days. When my energy is up, we can talk about me. That sounds so self-centered…talk about me. I've never been one to talk about myself."

"Oh, don't you worry, you'll do fine. Which reminds me…" I retrieved some legal documents an attorney friend of Darrell's had put together for me. "This is a release for our interview. Since this is a private agreement between you and I and not the newspaper, my editor advised me to have this drawn up."

"Of course, dear." She started to call for Isa to bring her a pen, but I handed her one from my purse. "Did you know I knew your grandmother way back when?"

"Really?" So the twins were right when they mentioned Mama saying Grandma knew her.

"Sure did. She used to come in the bookstore where I worked in downtown Atlanta, before I married."

"I'm surprised she never mentioned it, being such a fan of yours and..."

"It was long ago when I was a nobody," she said, waving the pen, cutting me off. "Besides, my books weren't published in my maiden name, and I never had my photograph in any of them. Anyway, I feel good karma from you as I did from her. You either get it from people or you don't, and it usually comes with first impressions."

"Yes, Grandma Peg had a way with people, all walks of life." I bit my knuckle as she paged through the legal documents. "I hate red tape. But thanks for understanding and letting me get this out of the way."

To my surprise, she signed without hesitation. Relieved that that was over, I spooned some sugar in my tea and asked, "Would you mind me asking where we're going for dinner?"

"The Bubble Room," she said, her eyes lit up like a child's. "It's just around the bend. I enjoy their food, but it's the cluttered nostalgia that's on display there that I relish. I've had a morning nap so I'm rearing for an outing this evening."

"Sounds like an interesting place," I said, wondering when our interview would begin. "Can we talk there or would you like to do all of our interviewing at the house?"

"Of course we can talk there, but let's make it light, no notepads or recorders. Have some wine with me while we're there. They have a wonderful selection. Do you drink? I just assume you do after reading your story about the time you told your son the morning after a big party to bring you the green bottle from the kitchen, but he showed up with a bottle of Tanqueray gin instead of the green Excedrin bottle. Nothing like a little hair of the dog."

She laughed and it thrilled me that I'd brought her some joy through my column. "Yes I do drink occasionally, but to-night I'll be on my best behavior."

"Then we'll just have a glass with dinner. Anyway, I've told what few friends I have here on the island that my niece is coming to visit, so best behavior would be fitting."

"Your niece?"

"I certainly don't want anyone thinking I'm giving an interview after turning down everyone in the business. Let them read about me after I die." She looked up soulfully, then closed her hazel eyes and shaking her head, said, "Lord, take me soon."

After tea Isa showed me to my room, which was just off the sunroom, and like the rest of the house, blazed with color. Mrs. Van Buren and Isa both had rooms on the first floor. I set my suitcase on the yellow matelasse bedspread, leaned against the open window and admired the palm-framed view.

No wonder Mrs. Van Buren had stayed tucked in this corner of the world for so long.

The next five days would be intense, not only extracting Bruce from my pores, but flushing out this mysterious woman who had a treasure lurking somewhere under her gingerbread roof.

Chapter 2

*J*ust when I thought something couldn't be pinker than the trim on Mrs. Van Buren's cottage, the Bubble Room came into view. Patrons were spilling out the door of the lit-up three-story shack, waiting to be seated. Stephen drove up to the awning-covered entrance, offered Mrs. Van Buren her cane, which she took, and led us through the crowd to the hostess' stand.

A round-faced woman with a likeness to Mrs. Clause greeted us. "Good evening, Mrs. Van Buren. We have your favorite table ready and waiting."

Mrs. Van Buren took Stephen's arm and we wedged through the crowd. The trip to our table was an experience in itself, accompanied by tunes from the Big Band era. I'd never seen so much thirties and forties memorabilia in one place, most of it carrying a Christmas theme. Small red and green lights twinkled around several movie stills hanging on the walls. Mrs. Van Buren pointed out a mechanical snowman and vintage Coca-Cola ads. The hostess directed me to a seat against the wall so that Mrs. Van Buren would face me and be less conspicuous. Stephen winked at me as he helped Mrs. Buren into her seat.

"We'll call you when we're ready," the dowager directed him.

Once seated, she removed the blue scarf and let it drop around her shoulders. Trying not to stare, I noticed a shiny raised scar across her left cheek. It zigzagged about three inches down her face.

"I can see why you like to come here," I blurted out when she noticed me looking. "Did you and your husband frequent this place?"

"No, I'm afraid the restaurant wasn't here then, but I think Henry would've liked it."

"Henry," I said, and thought how cute—Henry and Helen. "How long were you married?" Her eyes wandered off to a corner of the room and her perky apple cheeks sank. "Is everything all right?"

She kept staring.

"Mrs.Van Buren," I said, raising my voice slightly.

"Yes dear?" She looked back at me and the corners of her mouth found a smile again. "It's hard to think of him sometimes. We would've been married over sixty years if he were still here."

"That certainly would have given you bragging rights."

The waiter came and announced the specials of the evening. We both ordered the red snapper. Halfway through dinner, I finally asked about the unpublished piece that I assumed was lurking somewhere in her house. She blotted the corners of her mouth, mystery dancing about her eyes.

"It's tucked away, always close beside me, but I rarely pull it out anymore. It's three-fourths of the way done, no ending yet. A love story, of course, the first novel I ever wrote. Well, I guess it's more like a novella, most of it written in forty-nine."

"That long ago?" Imagine that, one of her works sitting lifeless for over fifty years. "What's it about?"

"Ah, my dear, in due time. I'll let you take a peek soon."

Just a peek!—I wanted to read the whole damn thing and spill the news of it in this long-awaited biography I was about to write.

"How about you, Julia, how long have you been married?"

"Thirteen years and five months," I said quickly. "I don't know why I added the five months. The kids have entered their teens and my hours at the paper are longer than ever, now that they've added assistant feature editor to my duties. Don't get me wrong, I love my work, but it leaves me a lot less time at home. My poor mother does so much for me and I wish I could help with everything. And Darrell..." Now it was my eyes that fell to the corner of the room. I collected myself. "I'm sorry to ramble on about me, Mrs. Van Buren. This is supposed to be about you."

She reached across the table and gently squeezed my arm. "I understand," is all she said. But I could tell she meant it.

Mrs. Van Buren insisted on dessert, a red-velvet cake that the restaurant was famous for. "It's almost as good as Margaret's," she said, as if I was supposed to know who Margaret was.

"Who's Margaret, if you don't mind me asking?"

She paused. "Margaret was my roommate in college."

"Wesleyan College in Macon, Georgia, correct?"

"I see you've done your research," she said. "Yes, Wesleyan. Oh, what glorious days those were! Margaret boarded in a room at our house on Rivoli Drive. We were thick as thieves."

"Did you like attending an all-girl's college?"

"It was wonderful, no boys around to interrupt our studies. But don't you worry, we had our social functions. With Mercer and Emory so close, there was a nice crop of young men to pick from."

"My grandfather graduated from Mercer Medical School... Ashton Ryan sound familiar?"

"Doesn't ring a bell," she said with a yawn. "There were so many students... If you don't mind, I think I'll give Stephen a ring to come and get us."

Mrs. Van Buren assured me that we'd get started with our formal interview first thing in the morning. I thanked her for dinner and retired to my lemon yellow room with daisy trim. Isa had turned down my bed and placed a chocolate mint on my pillow as if I were staying in a fancy hotel. The bathroom was spacious and equipped with a large porcelain tub as well as a bottle of bubbles for a bath. I giggled, wondering if Mrs. Van Buren had a bubble fetish.

While luxuriating in the frothy water, I called home to check on Darrell and the boys. Mama answered. "Hey Mama. Everything okay up there?"

"We're all just fine. How 'bout you?"

"It's postcard perfect here." I went on and told her about my dinner at the Bubble Room. "Did you know Mrs. Van Buren was at Wesleyan Collage the same time Grandpa Ashton was at Mercer?"

"Isn't that something. Did she say she knew him?"

"Said his name didn't ring a bell."

"Hmm, go figure. My father said he used to date girls from Wesleyan. That's where he met your grandma."

"Grandma Peg went to college?"

Mama paused. "Didn't she ever tell you that?"

"No, and neither did you," I said, a bit peevishly.

"Well, maybe she never mentioned it because she didn't finish. She was always embarrassed about not finishing."

"Is Darrell around?"

"No, he decided last minute to go camping with the Brothers of the Confederacy."

"But they're not due for a campout till next weekend. Hmm... Do me a favor, will you, Mama?"

"What's that?"

"Go check the storage closet under the staircase and see if his Confederate uniform is still hanging in there."

"Julia! You don't think he lied to me, do you?"

"I don't know. I hope I'm wrong and that gray wool uniform has gone to the mountains with him."

"Why don't you call him yourself? See if you hear forest sounds in the background."

"That's no good. He always turns off his cell phone while he's out there because the reception is horrible. Just go look under the staircase for me, please."

"Oh, all right, hold on…"

In the minute it took Mama to go look, I envisioned Darrell having dinner with some blonde twenty-something student. Why was it that his cheating seemed worse than my own?

"I checked the closet."

"And?"

"I'm sorry, sugar, the uniform's still in there."

My chest sank deeper into the bath water until the phone almost submerged. "I hope there's some reasonable explanation for this."

"I'm sure there is."

Before I could ponder the matter further, Isa called from the bedroom door.

"Yes?" I called back.

"Mrs. Van Buren would like to see you if you're not too tired."

"Did you hear that, Mama? I've got to go. I'll call you tomorrow. Kisses to the boys."

"I'll be right there, Isa," I said, hopping out of the tub.

"She's propped up in bed. A chair by her bedside is waiting for you."

I pulled on my drawstring PJs and a matching robe, crossed through the sunroom and downstairs. The bi-fold louvered doors squeaked as I knocked and entered Mrs. Van Buren's room.

She smiled, pushing herself up against her bolster pillow. Her long white hair was arranged in a loose bun. "Noisy doors, aren't they? The hinges on those darn doors have squeaked since the day I moved in. That salt air gets to them no matter how much silicon spray Isa puts on them. Come, come," she waved, "and shut the doors behind you."

"How long have you lived here?" I asked.

"Since forty-nine. Before that Henry and I had a cute little place near the downtown district of Fort Myers. It's still there...I think it serves as a law office now."

If my room was full of daisies, her room was bombarded with roses, mostly pink. Blossoms covered the wallpaper, the bedspread and shams, her bolster pillow, even the robe she had on. A familiar perfume bottle sat atop her vanity. The container looked like a mini wine glass, and on the lid "Shalimar" sparkled in blue letters against a gold backdrop.

"My Grandma Peg used to wear Shalimar to church every Sunday. She kept a small bottle in her purse and used to let me have a squirt. Is this vintage?" I tapped the lid.

"Vintage?" she laughed. "Well, I guess so. Does that make me vintage, too?"

"Why, of course, like a fine wine."

"All right then, I'll take it. I'm vintage." She giggled— more like a cackle, with her aged vocal chords. "Now come sit. I've got something here to read to you."

As I settled into a pink-velvet wingback chair, Mrs. Van Buren reached for her bifocals on the bedside table, exposing her left cheek beneath the reading lamp. The scar tissue, thicker than I'd realized, looked like a stretched-out capital M turned on its side. With her shaky, gnarled hand, she opened the drawer and pulled out a brown leather binder with a lock. A musty aroma wafted from the drawer when she shut it.

"I was going to wait and show you this tomorrow, but I just couldn't wait. It's been locked away for so long."

My heart fluttered.

"Julia dear, sometimes words of fiction need to mellow with time, like a fine wine. I wasn't sure that the women of my day would accept this delicate story back then, especially those ladies from the Bible Belt where I grew up. It's filled with adultery and unwed pregnancies. Writing this first manuscript made me realize that I wouldn't be happy doing anything else, but I knew my debut novel had to be a winner if I wanted to be published."

"And your debut *was* a winner, *Love Lost and Found!*"

"Well, now you know that that was really my second novel. *This* was my first." Her old hands lovingly stroked the binder cover.

"Why didn't you give the first manuscript to your publisher once you were more established as a novelist?"

"First of all, I hadn't finished it, and second, my gut feeling was that he'd toss it in the waste bin. It wasn't like the others he'd published under my name, all of them prim and proper happily ever after's."

"What about *The Great Gatsby*? It was well received with its affairs and such."

"A *man* wrote it," she answered. "Stories like the one I'm holding in my hands weren't often written by women, and when they were, the readership could be brutally critical. The television had couples sleeping in separate beds, for goodness' sakes. Remember those twin beds in 'I Love Lucy'? Most publishers of romance wanted fiction about fresh young virgins who idolized their men and rode off into the sunset with their white gloves on. It only took a few years of my own marriage to realize that that was a bunch of malarkey."

"I can relate," I said, and we shared a chuckle.

"I suppose that since I've finally made my peace with God about some things in my past, it's high time to share this story, but first with you. Are you ready?"

"Please begin!"

"Now being a writer yourself, you have to cut me a little slack. This was, after all, the first story of substance I ever wrote."

I nodded eagerly, pulling the wingback chair closer to the edge of the bed, hugging a needlepoint throw pillow in the shape of an angel.

"I would start by reading the title, but I haven't discovered one yet," she said. "Maybe after we read it over the next few days, you can help me think of one."

"I'd be honored."

She adjusted her bifocals and began…

Chapter One

The stock market crashed the week of my eleventh birthday, as did my adoration for my father.

My name is Haley Bernice Anderson. The Haley came from my mother, who thought I was an angel, *halo* and all. I still don't know where the Bernice came from, probably Papa's side, which Mother rarely mentioned.

Lester Anderson, that would be Papa, was a respected architect in the small Georgia town where I grew up. The stately columned homes he designed still stand, brick-and-mortar reminders of him dotting the quaint streets and avenues of Macon.

That cool day in October of 1929, Papa walked out the front door of our two-story brick house with a suitcase in one hand and a present tucked under his arm. I was playing jacks on the front porch waiting for two o'clock to come. That's when my party was scheduled to begin. I bounced the small red ball one more time before glancing up at him.

"Where're you going, Papa? The guests should be arriving at any minute."

He rested the brown suitcase by the porch swing and sat down on the step beside me.

"I'm going to find peace, Haley. This gift is for you," he said through bearded lips. "Go see the castle for both of us someday, okay kiddo?"

He'd used old blueprints to wrap the flat package and fastened a red bow on top. After tearing off the paper, I couldn't believe my eyes. It was one of the original renderings of the historic Breakers Hotel in Palm Beach, Florida. He'd found it at an auction before he'd married Mother. The castle picture, as I called it, was his treasure. It had hung over his drafting table for as long as I could remember.

"Who built this again?"

"Henry Flagler, the railroad tycoon. He said he'd build the grandest resort on the east coast, and I think it's the grandest place in the country. The twin Belvedere towers were patterned after the Villa Medici in Rome, a spectacular piece of architecture...and to have such a romantic setting kissed by the great Atlantic Ocean—what a vision!"

"But why are you giving this to me, Papa?" I paused. "Where are you going?"

Papa brushed my wispy brown bangs to the side. "Sometimes grownups don't have an answer for every question, Haley. Just always remember that I love you, and keep this safe. Let it be your vision for living happily ever after. I *have* to go now."

He kissed my brow and never looked back. As I watched him get into the Ford Model-T, the red ball I'd been squeezing popped out of my hand and went bouncing down each of the three porch steps, landing under a shedding maple tree.

That day guests came and went, Mother and I never letting on that anything had gone awry. We both wanted to believe that he'd gone off on an extended business trip, that we would see him come back through the front doors real soon.

A month later I worked up the courage to ask Mother why he had left.

She sighed. "Maybe it was me, maybe it was the stock market, but it certainly wasn't you, Haley, and don't you ever think that." She held me close and stroked my cheek. "Now I've bought you something that might help you express all those emotions you've been hanging onto. My father always told me that writing things down can sometimes take the hurt out of your soul. So here's a journal. Write in it whenever you're feeling down. Tell it when you're happy. Tell it when you're sad. Or make up whatever you want. Just write out those frustrations, and don't ever wear them on your sleeve."

For years I did just that, writing short stories, incorporating imaginative friends into my daily entries, creating another place where I could run and hide and be safe. Mine were stories of kingdoms with happy families, housed in castles that resembled that exquisite structure on the Atlantic shore that Papa had bequeathed me. If writing stories could ease one ounce of my emptiness, I would write for a lifetime.

My mother, Joyce Anderson, was a petite woman. What she lacked in height she made up for with a fiery determination to succeed as my sole provider. At one point she carried two jobs: one as an evening sound effects person at the local radio station, and another as a secretary at Wesleyan College, the girls' school located in our little town of Macon.

By the time I turned sixteen, even with the Depression lingering, Mother had squirreled away enough money for my college tuition at Wesleyan. We never would have been able to afford it had Mother not worked there. They gave us a reduction in tuition on account of her employee status.

She told me, "This is a privilege for you to continue your education. These days only the high and mighty can afford to go to college."

The summer before my classes started, she quit her job with the radio and put an advertisement in the newspaper for a boarder. People in our neighborhood commonly took in boarders, since we lived just a few blocks from the school.

It didn't take long before a young lady answered the ad, and Mother accepted her sight unseen. One week before the fall term began we heard a delicate tap on the front door.

"Hi, I'm Margie Harris," a girl said to Mother. She had a smile as wide as the Mason-Dixon Line. "I believe you met my parents last week before they left for Paris? I hope I'm not too early."

"Not at all," Mother said, pleased. "Haley!" I was spying from the top of the staircase. "Come and meet our houseguest, Miss Margie."

My thick-heeled shoes tapped down the wood staircase, catching the hem of my long wool skirt. I skipped the last two steps and greeted Margie with a bang.

"Whoops, sorry about that!"

Margie covered her laugh with long slender fingers. "Very nice to meet you, Haley," she said.

Mother took Margie's hat, coat and gloves, and I told her driver to put her things in the daisy room upstairs.

I clapped my hands and hugged myself. "This is gonna be like having a sleepover every night! I've always wanted a sister. Mother says you're from Atlanta."

"Yes, born and raised," she said proudly. "Ever been there?"

"Each year Mother takes me and we shop at Rich's Department Store. We don't buy much cause we can't afford it—," Mother delivered an elbow to my ribs, "—but it always got us in the Christmas spirit."

Our new boarder nodded. "Aren't the decorations lovely that time of year?"

"Why don't you show Margie to her room while I finish preparing dinner," Mother suggested.

I took Margie's hand and skipped upstairs to her room. "This is where you'll sleep, and the bathroom connects our rooms here." I opened the door to the right of a Chippendale dresser.

"How nice," Margie said, walking through to my room. "It's like a mini-suite, my room with daisy trim, and yours with roses. Did you paint the borders yourself?"

"Yes, me and mother. Have you ever stayed in a hotel suite?"

"A few times," she said. "My father's in the lumber business and does quite well, despite the Depression."

That was more than obvious, what with the chauffeur, her gloves shimmering like silk, and the brand new coat she had handed to Mother.

"I don't mean to sound spoiled," she said. "I'm not. My mother taught me how to sew with scrap fabric during the worst part of the Depression because she wanted me to appreciate what we had. Most of my clothes I still make because I enjoy it. I just finished this last week." She spun around in a fitted violet knit dress with large tortoise buttons. It hugged her curvy form in a figure eight.

"Sewing is something I could use a little help with," I told her.

"Maybe I can help you."

The door squeaked and Isa's head appeared in the crack.

"Julia, your purse is playing 'Für Elise.' Shall I bring it to you?"

"Oh, it might be my husband. I'd better go get it if that's okay with you," I said to Mrs. Van Buren.

She closed the brown binder. "Go and talk to your husband, dear. We can continue in a few minutes. Family always comes first. I'll get Isa to help me to the bathroom."

I rushed upstairs to my room, and the phone started a second cycle of rings. The number calling was not home, but I knew it well.

"Hello," I answered, stepping out to the sunroom, purse still clenched in my hand.

"Hey, darlin'," Bruce's voice twanged.

"I told you not to call me. This interview is supposed to be kept under my hat. It's a big deal."

"I know it is. But can't you get away for just a little while tonight? Surely it's past the old lady's bedtime."

"First of all, I have no means of transportation, and secondly, if Mrs. Van Buren finds out that I told another reporter where I was going she might withdraw the interview."

"Aw, come on. How 'bout I come throw pebbles at your window and we can share a blanket on the beach later. Just tell me which window is yours, and I'll be right over."

"Nope, out of the question." As long as I could keep him out of sight, he'd stay out of my mind.

"Come on, darlin'."

"You and I definitely need to see each other, but only to have a little talk."

"You know we can't be alone together and just talk!"

"Just a talk. And not till we get back to Atlanta. Agreed?"

"Atlanta! But I want to see you before then."

The rejection in his voice weakened my stance, especially as the thought of Darrell with some blonde bimbo swirled through my head, but in the end I stuck to my guns.

"Nope, not till Atlanta."

This time when I approached Mrs. Van Buren's room, the bi-fold doors had been left open. She was propped up again, leather binder across her chest, her head to one side. The gulf breeze coming through the open windows, rustling her rose curtains, had lulled her to sleep.

This is what peace sounds like, I thought.

As quietly as I could, I tiptoed across the floor. An old black and white photo of Mrs. Van Buren sat on what must have been Henry's bureau. Dark wavy hair, full painted lips and transparent eyes, a fur stole around her shoulders. A true beauty.

What was she hiding in that frayed brown binder lying across her chest? It was hardly a coincidence that her character Haley had lived in Macon and gone to college at Wesleyan. My gut told me there was a lot more than fiction hiding between those tattered pages.

Isa startled me from behind. "I'll tuck her in," she said. "Once she's out, she's out like a light. How early should I wake you tomorrow?"

"What time does she usually get stirring?"

"Around seven-thirty or so."

"Six-thirty would be great."

When I get old, if I need assistance, I think I'd want an Isa, too. Genuine concern radiated from her eyes. You could tell she really cared about Mrs. Van Buren.

"Can I help you with breakfast or anything?"

"Sure, I'd like that," she said gladly. "We'll make blueberry muffins. They're her favorite."

"Till morning then," I said, and took one last look at Mrs. Van Buren sleeping peacefully.

Chapter 3

"Julia," a voice gently called.

I opened an eye and caught a slice of Isa on the other side of the cracked door. She wore a brilliant shirt dress, a tangerine hue as cheery as her smile.

"Yes?" I said in a raspy voice.

"Julia, your purse is conducting a symphony again. I found it lying on the couch in the sunroom. Oh…and it's six-thirty."

"Thank you, Isa. I'll be in to help with those muffins in a jiff."

"Take your time," she said. "I'll put on some coffee."

I whipped off the covers, marched out to the sunroom and fished around in my purse for the phone. "Where is the damn thing?" Frustrated, I shook it upside-down and everything spilled onto the sofa, from tampons to the cork from the last bottle of wine I'd shared with Bruce. The number on the display was Darrell's cell phone. I quickly flipped it open.

"Where are you?" I snapped.

"Good mornin' to you too, honey. I thought I'd drive a few miles from camp where there's better reception and give you a call, make sure you had a good flight."

"When did you plan this little trip? I thought the Brothers of the Confederacy weren't due to meet again until next weekend."

"We are, but we decided to have a bonus weekend for Confederate Flag Day."

"So you're there till Sunday morning?"

"No, I'll head back today. The boys have a soccer game tonight at five."

"Oh, that's right. It'd be a good thing to be there since you are their *coach!*" My voice effortlessly ramped up. I didn't know if I was madder at myself for having given myself to Bruce or at the possibility that Darrell could be having his own affair. "So you're really out camping with the boys?"

"Of course, where else would I be?"

"I don't know. Mama said you must've been in a big hurry because you forgot your Confederate uniform."

He paused. "Yeah, the guys are all giving me grief about that. So what's the Van Buren lady like?"

Hmm, quick transition into something else...

"She's delightful," I answered hurriedly. "I gotta go."

"Whoa there, honey, you have a train to catch? Talk to me."

I explained that I had to make some muffins before settling in with Mrs. Van Buren for our first official day of interviews.

"Are you sure everything's all right? You sound upset about something."

I tried to bite my tongue, but it lashed out on its own. "You want to know what's wrong with me, Darrell? You, you're what's wrong with me!"

"Huh?"

"Remember about six months ago when I dressed up in all that kinky stuff from Victoria's Secret and all you did was say, 'Sorry, Julia, got papers to grade'? Well, from that day forward I've felt nothing but rejected by you. Always the shove off, you're too tired or you've got to work late. There's always something more important than us, and I'm tired of it!"

"What about the night before you left? It was you who gave me the shove off. Remember?"

"You can't expect me to be all over you after the rejection I've felt lately. God Darrell, I can't even remember the last time you hugged me when you walked in the door from work. You used to do that all the time until this past year."

"I'm sorry, Julia, work's taken its toll on me. And as for the Victoria's Secret night, I really did have to get those papers finished, and you know I'm out for the night after a roll in the, well, on the desk. I'll make it up to you, I promise."

"Like you really mean that," I barked.

"Scout's honor." I could picture his fingers raised in a "V" like he did with the boys.

I eyed the brass wall clock over the bathroom door. *Six-forty.* "I don't mean to rush off, but my career is waiting for me this morning. I'll talk to you later tonight after the boys' soccer game."

After hanging up I pulled on some capris and a white polo shirt, swabbed my lashes with a bit of mascara, swiped my lips with gloss and swept a brush through my hair. I've never been one for heavy makeup. I have my daddy to thank for that. He once caught me sitting at Mama's vanity stool—a blonde, green-eyed eight-year-old with lipstick the color of red licorice all over my face.

"What on God's green earth have you got all over your face?"

"Don't I look pretty, Daddy?" I said, smiling into the mirror, him squatting down behind me.

"You don't need all that." He got out his handkerchief and wiped off what he could, then held my chin and said, "As my grandfather told my grandmother years ago, 'A woman with powder and paint makes that woman what she ain't.' Don't ever try and cover up the real you, people might think you're trying to hide something."

With the way things had been going lately, I should have been slathering my face with latex paint.

Just before seven o'clock, loaded down with my laptop, tape recorder and several notebooks, I made my way down the sky-lit staircase and into the lime-sherbet kitchen, the aroma of fresh coffee tugging me.

"Here, let me take that for you," Isa said, depositing my equipment on a wicker swivel stool beneath an old rotary phone mounted on the wall.

Things were kept orderly in the windowed cupboards, and I eyed a white mug with pink trim for the coffee I desperately needed.

"I'll pour that for you," she insisted, taking the cup from my hand. "Cream and sugar?"

"Yes, please."

"Have a seat." She motioned to a small white-washed table and chairs against a narrow window. A crystal vase with pink and yellow fresh-cut roses greeted me. The window overlooked a charming courtyard receiving the morning sun.

"Mrs. V loves her herb garden and her roses," Isa said.

"These are from her garden?" I leaned into the roses and breathed in their fragrance.

"They sure are. She has the lawn crew keep a hole cut through the banyan branches overhead so they can catch the morning sun."

"By the way, does she prefer to be called Mrs. V?"

"She's never really said. I picked it up from Stephen."

"It's catchy," I said.

While Isa got out mixing bowls and the few ingredients we needed for the muffins, I asked her how long she'd worked for Mrs. Van Buren.

"Eight years this June," she answered. "Then Stephen came to help out with the driving last year"

I stood up and rinsed the blueberries. "He said the doctor told her to limit her driving. What does she have, if you don't mind me asking?"

"Rheumatoid arthritis."

"Is that all?" I asked. "I don't mean to sound insensitive, but she seems in such a hurry to get her biography done that I thought it was something more serious."

"Well, I guess the cataracts give her trouble, too. But really I think Mrs. V is just ready to speak out."

"Is the arthritis why she doesn't want to be interviewed on television?"

"That's part of it. But mostly it's the scar, which I'm sure you've noticed."

"Yes... Do you know how she got it?"

Isa fell silent for a moment. "It's not my place to tell."

I changed the subject. "So where in Germany are you from?"

"A small town in the Bavarian Alps. My father was killed in the war. Mother got us to the States by the time I was three or four. We settled in Fort Myers where my father had a cousin named Roland. The original plan was that my mother would continue her work as a nurse and midwife, but the language barrier stumped her for awhile. Roland had heard that a widow on the island was looking for live-in help...housekeeping, cooking and the like. The pay was decent and it would give Mother time to improve her English. The widow had indicated that she was busy with her writing, didn't want to be hindered by chores and ferry rides to the mainland for groceries and writing supplies. But I think she was lonely, too."

"Are you referring to Mrs. Van Buren? I thought she was married for almost sixty years..."

"No. Didn't you know she was widowed at a young age?"

"I knew she was a widow but not for that long. When did Henry die?"

"In 1948." Isa stopped stirring for a moment. "I should let her tell you the rest."

How had this important slice of information gotten past me? I thought I'd raked through everything about her life. "I never saw anything about Mr. Van Buren's death."

"I recall her telling me it was a simple burial in Athens, Georgia, where he was laid to rest alongside his parents. I think she only had the obituary run in the Athens paper."

"Where I never would have looked for information. So she never remarried?"

"No. She married her work. Writing became her passion. Some days she didn't even make it downstairs. She said chapters came to her in dreamlike visions, and she couldn't rest till she got them onto paper."

"Is that so?"

"Mother and I were so blessed to live with her as long as we did. The fact that she was willing to take me in, too, was a godsend. We had the downstairs bedrooms. The one Mrs. V is in now used to be my room. She stayed in the upstairs room so she had the view of the water and could be close to the sunroom and her piles of papers and books. When her mobility went downhill, she had me move her downstairs. But back to growing up on the island…even though there weren't many other children on Captiva, I had God's playground outside my front door. I still have my shell collection, boxes and boxes. Some days when Mrs. V had writer's block she'd help me search for shells while my mother was busy with chores.

"I lived here until I was about ten, at which point Mrs. V was busier than ever with three best-sellers sweeping the nation. She kept a second home in Atlanta where she spent the summer and could be a flight away from New York and her publisher. She and Mother decided it was time for us to move back to the mainland. The Fort Myers hospital needed more nurses on the maternity ward, so with Mother's English highly improved, she took a job there, and it gave me a chance to attend a better school. Like my mother, I went on to study nursing and then took a job in Tampa."

"Ever marry?"

"No. Lots of suitors, but never found Mr. Right. Maybe my height scared them away. Anyhow, I kept busy for years in Tampa until Mrs. V called eight years ago. I could hear in her voice how sad she was about losing her independence from the arthritis. At the time her joints were painful enough to keep her from doing simple tasks like tying her shoes and pruning the rose garden. My mother had passed away and I was the only person Mrs. V trusted…that is, other than Stephen. But he had his wife to tend to. Even though she pays me well, it wasn't about the money. I owed her. She's been like a second mother to me."

I looked again at Isa's starched tangerine shirt dress, just like the chambray one she'd worn the day before. I brushed the white apron with my fingers. "If you don't mind me asking, if you two are so close, why do you look like what I would call formal help?"

"She wanted me to look professional for your stay since you are, after all, from one of the most elite areas in Atlanta. You both being southern belles, Mrs. V thought you'd appreciate the formality."

"If she only knew the truth," I whispered to myself.

Isa turned off the faucet. "What'd you say 'hon?"

"Oh, nothing, just that if she only knew not to go through all this trouble. I'm just elated to be here and if you're both more comfortable being…well, comfortable, please do so."

Isa and I simultaneously laughed. "Yes, I thought it was a silly idea, too."

"By all means, please resume your leisurewear."

As our laughing subsided she asked me to get her a basket from the pantry. When I opened the door, to my surprise, it wasn't a pantry at all. Behind what I'd thought was the pantry door sat a small elevator, maybe three by three feet—just big enough for one person.

"Cost a small fortune to put that thing in," Isa said. "Mrs. V wanted to make sure she could get up to the sunroom without assistance if need be. Never wants to put anyone out if she doesn't have to."

"Oh my, I wouldn't have known it was here. I'm terribly claustrophobic. What if it got stuck between floors?"

"There's a switch inside for battery power and lighting in case of an emergency, but so far we haven't had that happen."

Isa and I resumed our muffin making, standing elbow to elbow, her measuring out the flour and baking powder while I whisked the eggs with the oil and the sugar. By seven-forty, a two-tone chime rang through an intercom next to the wall-mounted phone.

"A visitor this early?" I asked.

"No, that's Mrs. V." Isa wiped her hands on a checkered dishcloth. "She's awake and ready for me to help her dress. Some mornings the arthritis is so bad she can barely move. Would you mind mixing all this together and putting the muffins in at 400 degrees? I've already set the table upstairs on the balcony. Mrs. V loves to start her day overlooking the water."

"Not to worry, Isa. I'll take care of it."

I hoped Mrs. V's mental joints were functioning because I was rearing to get the interview started. The discovery that Henry had died so soon after they'd been married made me more curious than ever to dig up the how and why. To write such beautiful love stories... What a lonely life she must have had after his death.

While the muffins cooked I took my laptop, notepads and recorder back upstairs. I should have known better than to bring them down in the first place. In the sunroom where Mrs. Van Buren spent most of her waking hours was a walnut roll-top desk and an old wooden chair just a swivel away from her view of the shimmering gulf. Books and newspapers were stacked to the left of the desk at least four feet deep, overspill from the bookshelves lining the wall. I recognized my picture in the section at the top of the pile. Thumbing through the first few inches, I found what seemed like a year's worth of my column chronologically stacked, with last Sunday's edition on top, "Confessing Infidelity: To Tell or Not to Tell." I'd written that one thinking it would somehow help me untangle my situation, but all it did was add to my guilt.

I sat at the desk and spun a full circle, taking in each wall of the room. The chair squeaked like the old ones down in the basement at the newspaper where Bruce and I had shared our first kiss. The rest of the sunroom was fluffy and comfortable, a bright floral print on the overstuffed chair and the sofa, lined with throw pillows in a rainbow-sherbet array of colors. There wasn't a room in the house that couldn't cheer a person up. I suppose living half a century as a widowed recluse would make one crave color.

Catty-corner to where I sat was a dainty curio cabinet about three feet high, hand-painted with pansy flowers. I walked about ten steps across the room and found the cabinet filled with ceramic Hummel figurines, a symphony of little angels holding horns, bells, harps and flutes. I couldn't resist opening the cabinet and handling the one with the harp. As I did, the rest of the angels began to rattle.

"Uh oh, the elevator's coming." Hastily I returned the angel to her place and closed the cabinet door, then remembered what I was supposed to be doing.

"The muffins!" I shrieked, and ran downstairs in three leaps, passing Isa on her way up. Thank God the muffins weren't burnt. I dumped them into the napkin-lined basket Isa had placed on the counter and made it back up just as Mrs. Van Buren was coming off the elevator.

"Good morning, Julia," she said, smiling ear to ear, clutching the brown leather binder under her arm. "Sorry I faded out on you last night."

"I'd be lying if I told you I wasn't disappointed, but it gave me a chance to review my questions one last time before bed." I extended the basket. "Muffins…"

She looked inside and gave them a sniff, then waved away the wheelchair Isa had ready for her. "I think I can cane it from here. Thank you anyway." Isa helped her to a small bistro table set up on the balcony where soft wind chimes jingled. "Quite a breeze up here this morning," she said, tying the same turquoise scarf from the day before around her snowy hair. "Help me into the rocker, Isa. I'm going to rock with what little energy I have. Yes, rocking is good for nervous energy."

"Do take it easy, Mrs. V. You had a time getting out of bed this morning and your medication won't kick in until—"

She squeezed Isa's hand. "I'll be fine."

"Please don't feel nervous on my account," I said.

"It's not you, dear. It's digging up the past that makes me nervous, but it'll be good for both of us."

For both of us?

She rocked steadily. I joined her on the opposite side of the table. Isa excused herself, went back to the kitchen and returned with a pot of coffee and a carafe of orange juice.

"Will there be anything else, Mrs. V?"

"We're fine now. I'll yoo hoo if we need anything."

"Would you prefer that I call you Mrs. V?" I asked.

"Whatever makes you comfortable."

The brown leather binder sat at the edge of the table and my curiosity sat at the edge of the rocker. "Are you ready to continue reading this morning?" I asked, tapping it.

"In a bit." She nodded over the balcony, toward the rippling waves. "Don't you just love that sound?"

We both stopped buttering our muffins and listened to the gently lapping surf and the seagulls squawking. The gulf practically abutted the cottage; it lay some thirty yards away, nothing between it and the cottage but a narrow beach sprinkled with an abundance of shells, sea oats and giant banyans. Closing my eyes, I breathed in humid salt air and released it with a long sigh. When I opened my eyes, Mrs. Van Buren was studying me.

"Penny for your thoughts?" she asked.

"My grandmother used to say that," I said in fond remembrance.

"You look as if you've got something weighing on you, dear. I know that look all too well."

"Is it that obvious?" I didn't want to burden her with my issues, but her eyes showed real concern and I owed her a real answer. "Home life, work life, married life... pick one."

"Don't let it bog you down, dear. There is a healthy balance to be had. You just have to find the right mix." Her warm knotted fingers patted my arm. "Don't try so hard."

Not wanting to talk about me, I pushed my muffin aside, got out my notes and pressed record on my mini-recorder. "If you don't mind, I'd like to start the interview. Could I ask you some questions about your childhood?"

"Sure, go ahead, but I'd prefer to do this the old fashioned way...no recorders," she said.

"All right then...off it goes. So you were born in Macon, Georgia, 1918."

"That long ago?" she teased.

"Do you remember much about the house you grew up in?"

"Why certainly," she said, cheeks aglow. "My papa had it built as a four-year-anniversary present for my mother back in 1920. He was an architect and did quite well. Our house was right along the main drag, red brick with a wraparound porch and indoor plumbing, too. The house had four bedrooms because Papa anticipated having a big family, but Mother miscarried three times after me. I never saw a sibling. So he made the downstairs bedroom into his study and the other spare was for guests."

"That must have been hard on all of you," I said, reminded of the story the night before.

"Papa was ornery about it. He couldn't get that vision of the perfect family out of his head...two boys and two girls. Mother was on a permanent guilt trip, and by the time I was eleven he was gone."

"Like Haley?"

She gazed at the gulf for a few seconds before answering. "Yes. A lot like Haley in the story."

"How and when did it come about that you knew you enjoyed writing?"

"Shortly after Papa left, Mother bought me a journal and I've been writing ever since."

"Do you still have any of those journals?"

"I'm afraid not. They must have gotten lost in the shuffle when I moved from Macon to Atlanta after college."

"What was your major?"

"English, of course."

Isa came up and gently cut in. "Stephen called and wanted to know if you would be needing him today?"

Mrs. Van Buren thought while she chewed the temple of her glasses. "Tell him if I do, it won't be till after lunch. I'd like to show Julia the old Sanibel lighthouse."

"You'll enjoy that, Julia," Isa told me as she cleared the table. "It's just a jog to the south from the main bridge." She paused and looked overhead at the dark clouds gathering. "I smell rain, Mrs. V. Would you like me to help you inside?"

"That would be a good idea."

Inside, Isa placed a yellow afghan on Mrs. Van Buren's lap.

"Would you mind shutting the glass doors, too? These early spring rains sure put a chill in the air."

With the room sealed shut, the wind chimes grew faint and the pitter patter of rain lent a soothing, hypnotic beat to our interview.

I decided to ask Mrs. Van Buren how long she'd been married to Henry, just to stir the pot a bit and see what I'd get.

"Eight years, almost nine," she answered.

"That's all?" I pretended to be surprised.

"When I met Henry, it may have been love at first sight for him, but not for me. I knew he was what my mother wanted for me and that he'd take care of me. He was quite a bit older."

"Distinguished?"

"Yes, quite. I desperately needed to feel that security after Papa leaving. So I guess you could say that I settled for a safe harbor rather than a passionate river." Her eyes slid to the angels in the curio cabinet. "He gave me those angels, one each year as an anniversary gift."

I stepped over to the cabinet, angel eyes following me as I got closer. "Eight angels," I said. "They must have been a happy eight years."

"Unfortunately, I had miscarriages just like Mother, five in all, before I simply gave up and considered myself barren. Then Henry went off to war. He served as a lieutenant in the Navy, chief engineer on a battleship in the Pacific. I thought for sure I'd conceive after he came home, but I didn't, and I so much wanted a family. He was distant after the war and consumed himself with his work at the power company. So I consumed myself with writing a cooking column for the Fort Myers *News-Press*."

"Yes, I recall seeing a copy of it on microfiche. You wrote restaurant reviews too, didn't you?"

"Sure did. That was a bonus. I loved dining out, and I got free meals from some of the area's quaintest restaurants and bistros. That's when I met him."

"Him?"

Mrs. Van Buren took her glasses off and with a faraway look, whispered, "Stephen."

"Stephen who?"

"Stephen *Don*ovan!"

She looked at me as if I was supposed to know who she was talking about. I shot her a perplexed look.

"The Stephen who brought you here from the airport."

"Oh! *That* Stephen?"

"Uh huh."

I sat back in my chair, digesting my surprise. "Okay... So you've known Stephen for a long, long time then. You're good friends, right? He told me so on the drive over. He said that he wasn't your driver per say, just a good friend who gave you a ride when you needed one. But I can see in your face that he's been more than a friend, yes?"

"Much more, but we've had to stay apart for reasons out of our hands. It's still hard for me to talk about it. It all happened so many years ago."

"You don't have to. Remember, this is your biography. I'll only write what you approve."

"Well I certainly approve of Stephen, so you go ahead and ask what's on your mind."

"Were you ever in love with him?" I said, chewing on my pencil.

She paused before answering. "You have to understand, dear, Henry made me feel safe, and I thought that would be enough, but then Stephen came along and, not to sound cliché...he swept me off my feet, made my heart sing. Until that moment, no one had ever done that. Feeling safe with Henry was never enough."

The word *safe* rang through my head like a Baptist church choir trying to sing me to salvation. Life with Darrell had been safe until I fell off the Goody-two-shoe wagon and got sucked into the vortex of lust with Bruce.

I released the bite on my pencil and reiterated, "So you say you felt safe with Henry? Did you ever love him?"

"You know, Julia, I'm feeling a bit tired. The rain has a way of soothing me to sleep. Would you mind giving me an hour or two? I promise I'll get back to where we left off from last night after a short nap."

"Of course!"

I helped her out of the rocking chair and onto the sofa, where she laid down. The peach sherbet pillow gave way under her head like a marshmallow.

"If the rain lets up," I said, "I might go for a walk on the beach if you don't mind."

"Take your time, dear. Tell Isa to get you a raincoat from the foyer closet and to wake me in an hour."

Chapter 4

*W*hen the rain let up and the breeze softened, Isa lent me a yellow raincoat with matching hat, and I strolled down the crushed shell driveway donned like a Paddington teddy bear the twins had years ago. What clouds still lingered spit rain at the floppy brim, making a sizzling sound like bacon frying.

In a blink my baby boys had grown into lanky teens, so alike on the outside, polar opposites on the inside. Those two towheaded rascals had held hands their first day of preschool. We stood in front of their classroom door where Big Bird and Elmo welcomed them to the wonderful world of learning.

Dylan clutched the Paddington bear in his free arm and shouted, "I'm not going in there!" He squeezed his brother's hand with all his might, "Don't go in without me, Ryan." His scared cocoa eyes darted up at me. I wanted to scoop him up and run home, but I knew better. This was the next step through the journey of his little life—his first little speed bump. He had to take it. I hated to think that one day those bumps would get bigger, painful; I wouldn't always be there to help boost them over. But then I remembered something my dad had taught me... "our struggles make us stronger in the end."

Ryan pried his hand loose from his brother's and skipped into the classroom without him. No fear. Dylan didn't budge. He clung to my leg so tight I thought he'd never let go.

But he did.

They both did. And over the years their bright hair dimmed as did their voices. Sometimes I felt like their hearts had dimmed when in my presence. "I don't need your help," one would say, and the other, "Just leave me alone." Mama assured me it was all just a phase. Phase or not, feeling unwanted by your husband layered with being pushed aside by your children hurt. I foolishly thought the affair would heal that wound.

Once I reached the shoreline the rain had stopped, and I took off my sandals and squished my toes into the water's edge. The gulf was like a sheet of glass—not a white cap in sight, even with the passing storm. Short of the horizon a small Sunfish sailboat came zigzagging toward the shore in an attempt to catch the dying breeze. It made me think of the trip Darrell and I had taken for our ten-year anniversary to the Bahamas. We stayed at the Atlantis Resort where we rented a Sunfish similar to the one I'd noticed. Neither of us knew what in the world we were doing. The brilliant aqua and red sail had caught my eye and it became a must on my to-do list.

"Let's sail it across the lagoon to that small island," I'd said, pointing to a mound of sand and shrubs. "Maybe you'll get lucky behind the sea oats."

"You're nuts," he said. "Someone might see us."

"I promise you won't be sorry."

Spontaneity had become a thing of our past. But after a few nibbles of his ear, I finally convinced him, and we sailed over our inhibitions and made love behind a small dune. At that moment I knew all wasn't lost.

I missed the hugging and soul gazing we'd shared in the Bahamas during that vacation and tried many times thereafter to rekindle them, the failed Victoria's Secret incident being the straw. As each year rolled by, tapping back into those feelings got harder and harder. The hand that pushes you away eventually finds all zones off limits.

Soul gazing was something Bruce was not capable of. Lust gazing better fit our exchange, though at times I tried to tell myself I could love him so the sex didn't seem so wrong.

Once the rain stopped, I took off my silly yellow hat and unbuttoned the raincoat. While my mind had been with Darrell and the boys, my feet had walked me north about a quarter mile where I noticed a man fishing. I stopped in front of a small bungalow that sat beside a larger one just like it. Both wore white stucco with green shutters, the smaller obviously a guest house. The man standing out front was Stephen. He'd positioned himself in knee-deep water, casting a fly rod back and forth, slow rhythmic moves.

Once his line was out and resting on the surface of the water, he peered over his shoulder and said, "Shhh..."

I instinctively whispered, "What is it?" in the quietest husk possible.

"Sir Snook is about to nip at my line," he whispered back. Within seconds, the fish bit, the line spun, and Stephen's powerful old hands reeled as fast as they could. "Oh, boy, that's a nice one," he said, pleased. "Fish for dinner for sure. Do you like fish, Julia?"

"What does Sir Snook taste like?"

"White and flakey like pompano or grouper...deeelicious."

"I like it fried with lots of lemon, thank you."

"I'll remember that when I fix dinner for you all tomorrow night. Mrs. V wants the two of you to come for a visit at my place."

"I bet she does," I said under my breath.

"Come again?"

Avoiding an answer, I waded over to see his catch. The Snook pouted at me as Stephen removed the hook. The fish was over two feet long, silver with a white belly and a black stripe running down its sides. "Looks like he has racing stripes."

"Yes he does, but don't change the subject. What was that you said, 'I bet she does?' Now how do you mean by that?"

"It's not appropriate for me to talk about the interview."

"Ah, hell, you can't tell me anything about Helen that I don't already know. We've been friends for a long, long time." He dropped the Snook in a large bucket of water, set his pole against a wood piling and grunted as he squatted down to his tackle box. "She's a special lady."

"She seems to think you're pretty special, too."

He shut the tackle box and sat silent for a moment. "Sounds like she's really going to tell all, even about me, huh?"

"You tell me."

"It's been a long time that this has been in the vault. After my wife died last year, Helen felt it was long overdue to get a biography done. News people have been pestering her for years now. She didn't want any of the fancy-named T.V. people to come, nope, no cameras. She wanted someone that would not make a big hoo ha, yet would still get the job done. She needed someone she could relate to and trust, plain and simple, you see?"

"But why me? I write about how to get your kids to eat their peas or how to get your husband to buy you roses again. I mean, I think I'm a good writer and all, but I've never taken on such a huge writing task. Don't get me wrong, I am truly excited to be here."

"I could see that in your face when I picked you up yesterday." He motioned for me to follow him up to the small bungalow. Once there, he put his gear inside the screened-in lanai and placed the Snook on a filet table. "You're not squeamish, are ya?" he asked, reaching for a filet knife in a drawer under the table.

"Sometimes...I'll just look out at the water if it bothers me." The squeak of the knife ripped beneath the scales, and my eyes darted back to the gulf where a few pelicans soared just inches above the surface. "So do you mind if I ask some questions about you since you know Mrs. Van Buren so well?"

"Sure you can ask about *me*, but I'll let her answer all the questions about us. I'm just her driver, remember?" He winked and grinned like he'd never tell even if I begged.

After filleting the fish he stuck it in a plastic storage bag and placed it in the mini-fridge at the end of the lanai. He held the screen door open for me and suggested we walk to the other side of the property where a small red motor boat sat docked at an inlet that filtered out to the gulf. He held out his tan, freckled arm, waiting to assist me aboard.

"Are we going somewhere?"

"I promised you a ferry ride and the story of how Captiva got its name, but the next ferry to North Captiva doesn't leave for another hour. So here's your ferry, compliments of my son, Josh. Don't worry I'll have you back in time for lunch."

"Does Josh live here, too?"

"He lives in the big house. I rent the bungalow from him since I sold my place in Fort Myers last year."

"Where is Josh now?"

"He's in South Africa. Our family has had a diamond mine there going on three generations. We supply a few jewelers in the area with some choice stones. We use to have a store downtown. Been doing it all my life, but I'm retired now. Josh's kids are grown and gone, and his wife left him a few years ago."

"Why don't you live in the house with him? Aren't you both lonely?"

"Ha! Too much commotion up in the big house when he's home. He brings home a new woman every time he goes out. It's amazing what can happen when you tell a woman that you're in the diamond business. He's in his fifties and still brings home girls half his age."

"What about you, do you ever join him…look for anyone special?" I teased

"Hmm," he rubbed his stubble, "seventy-nine and out on the town."

"You know what I mean."

"Nope." He turned the ignition, and exhaust blew right up my nose. I coughed out my next question.

"What about Josh's mother? She was special and you loved her, yes?"

Jolting the boat into gear he said sourly, "I had to love her, right? She was the mother of my son."

I decided to stop with the questions for a while.

The clouds cleared and the sun's rays stretched around a few puffy clouds. A motor-powered wind blew my raincoat open which I took off and stuffed in a cubby hole under the console where I found a sheer pink scarf like the turquoise one Mrs. Van Buren had worn earlier.

Stephen killed the motor as we approached a manatee and its calf.

"Sea cows," he said, pointing over the bow of the boat. "Some boaters have no regard for these creatures. Look at the gouges on the mother's back. They have no known enemies. The only problem is that they move so damn slow, like me now," he laughed.

"It looks kind of like a walrus."

"I suppose, but they are actually related to the elephant."

"Get out!"

"Really… look at the skin."

I leaned over the bow and inspected the creatures—frighteningly large, yet gentle. The tip of my finger grazed the mother's back.

"Thoreau once said something that I like to relate to these gentle creatures. He said, 'No humane being, past the thoughtless age of boyhood, will wantonly murder another creature which holds its life by the same tenure as he does.' Manatees can live up to seventy years if man doesn't interfere. That's why it makes me so mad when boats fly through here and don't kill their engines when these guys are crossing. You'd kill your engine if you saw a human crossing."

"They don't seem to be afraid of us, like they just want some company."

Stephen got out an ore and paddled us a safe distance away before starting the motor again. For a man of his age, he certainly kept himself fit. There was still definition to the muscles above his topsiders, and his trim waist was cinched by khaki shorts and a braided belt.

"That island over there," he pointed, "is North Captiva. Captiva and North Captiva used to be one big barrier island. But a hurricane in 1921 split it in half."

"Wow, I would have never imagined since the gap is so big."

"And hundreds of years ago the island was occupied by the Calusa Indians who were eventually run off by the Spaniards. Now somewhere in between all that is how the island got its name, you see. Pirates used to seek refuge on the island where they would repair their war-torn ships. And any female captives they had stowed away would be left on the island so they could come back to them later for...well, you know, or hold them for a handsome ransom. Anyway, thus the island's name...Captiva."

"By the looks of it I don't think I'd mind being held captive on Captiva. The beaches are still so pristine, and there's nothing commercial that I can see from here, only cottages and mangroves."

"We ought to head back now if I'm going to get you to lunch on time."

"Thanks for the ride, Stephen. I don't know what I enjoyed more, the ride or the story."

When we arrived back to the small dock I couldn't help wondering what he had meant by saying that he *had* to love his wife. Before we parted I felt comfortable enough to dig for some more information about where he'd met her.

"You say your wife died a year ago?"

"It'll be one year this May."

As he tied the boat down, I retrieved Isa's raincoat from under the console along with the pink scarf I'd seen earlier.

"Shall I take this to Mrs. Van Buren?" I asked, smiling, dangling it in my fingers.

"Now how do you know that's hers?"

"Just a hunch."

"Pshaw...go ahead."

I tied my hair into a ponytail with it and casually asked, "So was your wife from down here?"

"Paula was from a small farming town east of here called La Belle. Her Daddy farmed tomatoes, but was known around town to be quite the con man, and like they say...the apple doesn't fall far from the tree. Anyway, Paula used to come into Fort Myers and window shop, and spent a lot of time eyeing the window case in front of my father's jewelry store where I worked every summer. As a child I spent summers here, and during the school year, college included, I got my education in South Africa, not just reading and writing, but I also learned about mining diamonds. My education was mediocre, but I got what I needed to help run the mine and the store in town."

"When did you first meet her?"

"Paula sat front and center outside a display case one day while I was filling the velvet pads with new inventory. Her eyes sparkled at the stones and especially at me. She gave me a seductive look through the glass that indicated that she wanted to do more than just window shop."

He paused, the hesitation setting his eyes up in wonder.

"What is it? Come on, you can tell me anything."

"You ever just had that animal-driven instinct to want someone so bad, but you don't even know them?"

"Honestly...yes," I said, and continued to listen intently.

"Well, when a young man of twenty-one gets the green light for some action, he jumps on the opportunity, quite literally. As soon as my father locked up for lunch and went to Jessie's Grill next door, I brought Paula in through the back door, and it was all we could do to make it to the office where a loveseat sat along the wall across from my father's desk. This went on for a few weeks. Pure lust it was. I had nothing in common with her other than what went on in the office. Two months after I met her, she was pregnant. We married right away because it was the right thing to do. It never occurred to me that she might be the white-trash daughter of a con man looking for a way to claw her way up the social ladder. But when your hormones are raging at that age, common sense gets thrown out the window."

"You must have at least grown to love her if you stayed together as long as you did."

He did a humph and pouted his lip out. "There's only been one true love in my life."

I caught his jade eyes and mouthed the words, "Helen Van Buren."

He nodded a firm yes. "Like I said before, Mrs. V's something special. Now you'd better get going so you're not late for lunch."

Stephen and I shared a patted hug, and I picked up my sandals and walked back up the beach, the raincoat and hat tucked under my arm.

As I got closer to Mrs. Van Buren's place the familiar image of a man dressed in rolled-up chinos and a button down came into plain horrifying view. With alligator boots off and by his side, he sat smoking a cigarette, staring straight at me.

"Oh my God," I said, mouth gaping. "How in the hell did you find this place?"

Bruce stubbed out his cigarette in the sand, shot me a sly-devil smile and stood up with open arms.

Once in reach, I pushed his arms down and said, "Like hell I'm giving you a hug. I thought I made myself clear last night that we weren't to see each other until back in Atlanta."

He brushed the hair out of my eyes, then tugged on the pink scarf in my hair. "Nice touch, very feminine."

"Don't touch me," I waved his arm away. "Someone might see. It's Mrs. Van Buren's scarf, but you won't be meeting her because you are leaving. I told you she thinks no one other than my editor and my family knows my whereabouts." I grabbed his hand and pulled him up toward the main road. Craning my neck, I asked, "Where'd you hide your rental car? It's gotta be around here somewhere."

"I parked up at the house."

"Oh my God! You've been to the house?" My arms waved overhead in disgust.

"Of course, what did you think? That I guessed you were out here walking on the beach? Had a hell of a time finding this Buren lady's address."

"It's Van Buren," I said, continuing forward, kicking sand up with each step. "And to think I'd just earned her trust and here you go screwing it up."

"I didn't screw anything up. I told the lady that answered the door, um, Tisa?"

"You mean Isa?"

"Yes, Isa, I told her that I was a colleague of yours and that I'd cleared it with your editor to get your help on the story I'm doing here."

I stopped and faced him. "You lied to her?"

"No, not totally, I really could use your help."

"But I don't write about sports!"

"Ah, I factored that into my explanation. I told her that I needed a family angle to my story, about how the players' wives deal with their husbands' hectic schedules. Anyway, she bought it hook, line and sinker since family writing is your specialty."

"You had this planned all along, didn't you?"

He stopped and gripped my shoulders. "Calm down. Nobody suspects a thing about us, and I didn't jeopardize your interview if that's what you're worried about."

"Did you see Mrs. Van Buren?"

"No. Isa said she was upstairs just waking from a nap so I told her I was going to look for you and meet Mrs. Van Buren when I got back."

"You're not going back," I sternly said.

With the raincoat still hung over my forearm, I grasped his hands and took them off my shoulders. While still squeezing his right hand, I continued to pull him along behind me till we crossed the narrow road and got a few yards down Mrs. Van Buren's driveway where a tropical curtain of greenery hid us from view. Bruce stopped me again, picked a red hibiscus flower and seductively bit down on it.

"This is for you," he said playfully, eyes fixated on me, "but you've gotta come and get it."

"You don't get it, do you? I've come to the realization that we need to stop doing this."

"Stop what?" He let the flower drop to the ground, and I tried to continue on to the house until he forcefully pulled me into his chest. "Isn't this what you want?" he asked, groping my ass and kissing my neck. "Usually this is always what you want."

"Stop it!" My open hand hit his face.

He froze.

"I'm sorry," I said. "I didn't mean to—"

"Yes you did."

He stared me down with a vengeful eye and shook his head. "You need me, remember?" He gently cupped a hand under my chin. "You need me bad, and don't ever let that happen again." He rubbed his cheek where I'd left a mark.

His command startled my sixth sense which told me to never get alone with this man again. "You should go now," I said.

"But that would be rude after I specifically told Isa that I'd be back to meet Mrs. Van Buren. Wouldn't you agree? Then they'd think less of you."

I continued down the driveway without him.

"Oh, come on, it'll be fun," he said, his attitude again playful, a spring in his step to catch up.

He followed me up to the house where a silver SUV sat parked right in front of the five stairs that led to the stained-glass front door.

"Did you have a nice walk, Julia?" Isa asked while trimming the hanging ferns.

I put on my everything-is-fine mask and draped the raincoat and hat over the wicker rocker. "It was lovely. And thank you for letting me borrow these. I heard you met my colleague Bruce Crawly."

"Yes, hello again," Isa said. "Are you still going to join us for lunch? Mrs. Van Buren said it would be fine as long as you keep your visit here hush, hush."

I shot Bruce a paranoid glare. "Oh he'll keep it hush, hush. Won't you?"

"Mum's the word." He buttoned his mouth. "My needs here are strictly for Julia's expertise on the family so I can give my story a domestic angle. That is if it's okay with you and Mrs. Van Buren if I borrow her for a few hours this evening."

Isa waved her hand in the air and said, "Not at all. Julia and Mrs. V will have all afternoon and the early evening to continue the interview. Bruce mentioned earlier that he could come back for you at eight-thirty. Was that right, Bruce?"

"That's right. I'll be ready for her by eight-thirty."

My innards knotted into clumps of worry, fear and regret while my eyes burned a hole through his manipulatively seductive eyes.

Chapter 5

*I*sa showed us to the kitchen where Mrs. Van Buren sat at the small breakfast table. Three place settings accompanied her along with a plate full of finger sandwiches and a bowl of fruit salad.

"Thought we'd dine inside since the balcony is still a bit wet. You must be Mr. Crawly," she said, adjusting her scarf.

"Yes ma'am." He stuck out his hand. "Pleased to meet you."

"Staying for lunch are you?"

"Yes, if that's alright with you, ma'am."

Mrs. Van Buren raised her eyes up to Isa who nodded yes. "I suppose, as long as you promise to keep your visit quiet. Isa said you couldn't get through to Julia's mobile phone?"

"That's correct. I tried a few times to call but her network said there was no service. My time's limited here so I decided I'd just stop by. Hope that's alright."

That lying son-of-a-bitch, I thought, trying not to look angry. "Who knows, maybe the satellites weren't lined up right when you tried to call."

"Maybe so, anyway, I love your place, very rustic." Bruce pulled out a chair for me.

"I see your mama at least taught you a few manners, Mr. Crawly."

"Call me Bruce."

"Alright then Bruce, how did you find out my address? Did Julia's editor give it to you?"

"No," I blurted. "I mean yes, that's the only way you could have found me. Gee, it's such a surprise to hear you need help on an assignment." I laughed nervously. "He's such a talented writer."

Mrs. Van Buren chewed the corner of her glasses, a hard stare in Bruce's direction. "So may I ask what type of assignment couldn't wait till she was finished here?"

"The Red Sox will begin their spring training this Monday, and I've been assigned to do a feature story on them with a side bar about the family life of a pro player. Who knows more about family features than Julia? So I called her editor to see if she could help me, and he said she was already down here working on an independent biography. So go figure...what a great coincidence."

Mrs. Van Buren looked at me suspiciously. "Did your editor call and inform you about this, Julia?"

"I'm not sure," I lied. "I haven't checked my voicemail since I've been here, and like Bruce said, maybe the satellite were out of alignment when he called too."

"Well how nice for you, Bruce that she was already down here."

"Yes...very."

"Do you travel much with your job?"

"A little."

"Must be hard if you have a family."

"There's no family. Maybe one of these days I'll settle down."

"I see. Like wooing the ladies, do you?"

"You could say that."

The leer he snuck my way sent my appetite plummeting, and it was all I could do to get down a single tuna finger sandwich. What a mess I'd gotten myself into.

Bruce continued to ooze out boyish charm while Mrs. Van Buren politely listened and nodded.

"This place certainly is paradise on the half-shell," he continued on, "I can see why you never leave."

"I leave from time to time."

"Vacations?"

"Don't I wish," she laughed. "Mostly doctor visits in Fort Myers."

Isa put a pitcher of iced tea on the table. "That reminds me Mrs. V that your doctor's appointment that was scheduled for this Tuesday got pushed up to Monday at one o'clock."

"Heavens to Betsy, that means Stephen can't take me, he's got to pick Josh up from the airport. He's flying in from South Africa."

"Don't worry Mrs. V, I can take you," Isa said, filling our glasses with tea.

Bruce raised his eyebrows and mouthed, "Empty house," followed by a wink.

Mrs. Van Buren put down her fork and looked at me and then my plate. "Feeling alright, dear? You've barely touched your food. If you'd like, Isa can make you something else."

"No, no, Mrs. Van Buren. I'm fine. Just still a little jet lagged is all."

She tilted her head, then shrugged it off and turned to Bruce. "So how long have you worked for the paper?"

"Ten months," he said, wiping his shadowed beard with an embroidered daisy napkin. "Prior to taking the job in Atlanta I had a nice offer to be sports editor at a small paper just outside of Birmingham, but I decided to take the lesser position of assistant sports editor in Atlanta. It's a much bigger paper with bigger opportunities and…"

While Bruce went on about himself he managed to slyly squeeze my thigh under the table which caused a jerk of my knee and a jingling of the ice in our tea glasses.

"Oh my, mouse under the table?" Mrs. Van Buren said with a giggle.

I cleared my throat and lasered a stare at Bruce.

"My legs are so darn long it's hard to cross them in confined spaces," he said, readjusting his position.

Mrs. Van Buren waited till he resumed eating. "Settled in now are we?"

"Yes, ma'am, sorry about that."

"So you were saying you liked working for the paper in Atlanta."

"Yep, love it. This little cutie makes my work space much more enjoyable."

"I thought you worked for sports. Your work area is close to the Life section?"

"We're across the hall from each other," he explained. "The walls are plates of glass."

"Can't get through the day without seeing Bruce," I said with a fake smile.

Mrs. Van Buren kept shifting her eyes between us. "Yes, I see. Well, Atlanta certainly has many professional sports teams to write about, lots to keep you busy."

"You're originally from Atlanta, aren't you Mrs. Van Buren?" Bruce asked.

"No, I'm actually from a town called Macon, close to Atlanta. I love both cities, but the big city life is far too much for this old girl. Back during the height of my career, I traveled from here, to Atlanta and New York and back all the time. Keeping busy was good for me after Henry's death."

Bruce patted Mrs. Van Buren's arm and said, "I assume Henry was your husband?"

"You assume correct."

"And never married again?"

"Never..."

"How lonely you must have been after he was gone."

I stared him down. "That's her private business, Bruce."

Mrs. Van Buren held her hand up. "No, that's alright, Julia. I never married again because that was my choice. Choices make us who we are, young man. I never said I was lonely."

People are not always what they appear to be, now are they Bruce?"

"No, ma'am, they're not," he said, looking over at me.

"For example," she began, "one may say they aren't ready to settle down, but perhaps it's because the one with whom they want to settle does not want them."

Bruce shrugged his shoulders and smiled jokingly. "Well I'm sure that once I decide on the right woman, she won't be able to resist my charm."

"A word from the wise?"

"Sure."

"Excessive charm often hides a darker truth." She realigned her scarf again and tilted the plate of sandwiches toward him. "Another sandwich, dear?"

After we finished eating, Mrs. Van Buren offered to take us upstairs and get Bruce an autographed copy of her last published novel. She said to give it to his mother or his girlfriend, if he had one after which he winked at me.

Isa opened the door off the kitchen to the minuscule elevator. It took Bruce by surprise like it had me.

"Elevator? How cool is that. I thought that was a pantry or utility closet or something."

"It's easier for Mrs. V to get around," Isa explained. "I'll send it back down if you'd like to try it out. Julia won't go near it."

"What can I say, I hate small spaces."

"I didn't know that about you," he said.

"There are a lot of things you don't know about me," I said harshly.

Isa stopped helping Mrs. Van Buren onto the elevator, my tone having troubled them.

"He'll take the stairs," I told them.

"If you'll help Mrs. V off upstairs, I'll go ahead and clean up lunch."

"Sure Isa," I said.

Halfway up the steps, out of Isa's sight, Bruce grabbed my hips and spun me toward him.

Eye to eye he whispered, "Don't be mad with me." His hands ran over my back side, and he kissed my chin. "I know I lied to get here, but I couldn't sit still knowing you were on the other side of that bridge. I miss you."

"I can't do this."

"You could sneak me in late tonight and we could do it in the elevator," he grossly joked.

"Grow up! That's not funny. We need to get upstairs." I peeled his hands off my hips and quickly made it to the second floor.

The door had already opened when I got there. Mrs. Van Buren stood with her cane, waiting patiently. "Are you okay, dear? You look a little flush."

"Just winded from the stairs."

After she gave Bruce the copy of her book, he said his goodbyes and I gladly saw him out to his SUV where he tried to steal another kiss.

"Will you stop it with the kissing?"

"I know you're under a lot of stress about this biography, but pushing me away will only add to the tension. You need to release it, and the only way to do that is to come over and let me take care of you tonight. You were hot last Monday after PTA, and I'd be willing to bet I could take you there again tonight."

"Don't call me hot. My boys call their crushes hot. I'm too old for that."

"I can't possibly see how your husband ever passes you up. If you were my wife, I'd treat you right."

"He does treat me right."

"But he doesn't pay a damn bit of attention to you, does he?"

"I never said that."

"That's what you told me and the bottle of merlot we shared last month in the hot tub."

"Just go," I insisted. "And don't count on seeing me later."

His eyes drooped like a hound. "What? After setting all this up for us, our one night together away from everybody? You can't stand me up. I ordered roses and champagne for to-night. I even found a mall near my hotel and picked up some of those chocolate-covered strawberries from the Godiva store that you love."

"You did all that?" I didn't believe him.

"Of course I did. Now you wouldn't want to pass that up."

"I need some time to think," I said, wanting to pacify him with an answer that would shut him up.

"Okay then. Let that pretty head of yours think about it, and call me by eight. And if the mood doesn't strike you until the middle of the night, well that's okay, too. I'll come get you whenever you're ready."

"Aaugh! Goodbye Bruce."

"Kiss on the cheek at least?"

"No."

I slammed his door and waited till the truck was out of sight before returning to the house.

☙❧

When I went back upstairs to the sunroom Mrs. Van Buren sat in the overstuffed chair, the brown leather binder in her lap. I sat on the sofa where I took in a much-needed calming view of the gulf.

"Let's see, where did we leave off from last night?" she asked, turning the pages.

"Margie had just moved in as a boarder and Haley was showing her around upstairs. They were discussing how they might take sewing classes together."

Mrs. Van Buren put her glasses on and continued...

"Sewing is something I could use a little help with," I told Margie.

"Maybe we can take a course together, and I can help you."

"That'd be swell," I said. "At orientation this Friday, I'll see about signing us up."

Margie flung open one of the two black travel trunks her driver had brought in.

"Wanna help me unpack, Haley?"

"Sure," I said, curiously admiring several hat boxes stacked on the unopened trunk"

"Go ahead and take my hats out. You can try one on if you like."

I opened the lavender octagonal box first and pulled out a cream felt dress hat with floppy brim adorned with pink roses. The soft brim settled nicely just below my brow.

"Fits you perfect. Borrow it any time."

"I'm going to sure like having you around."

Margie dug through the first trunk pulling out several skirts made of tweed and wool; then a few silk and cashmere tops; and last, a handful of scarves. At the bottom lay pictures wrapped in some of the scarves. She unraveled the first one and showed me.

"These must be your parents," I guessed, studying the photo of a couple standing in front of a Christmas tree. The older woman looked just like Margie—richly dark hair and eyes, and a contrasting smile, warm and friendly. The gentleman standing beside her looked far older.

"You can put that one on my nightstand if you don't mind."

I walked the photo to the lace-topped nightstand and gently placed it next to a small vase of dried flowers. "And can I assume that these pretty girls along side you in this photo are your sisters?"

"Yep, Mary and Melissa, I'm the youngest. Mary is getting married next June."

"How exciting! You will be a bridesmaid no doubt."

"Yes, ten in all! She's going to New York to pick out the dresses with Mother come January."

"Both of your sisters look as lovely as you. How lucky you are to have them." I placed the photo on the dresser next to the one of her parents.

She stacked the hat boxes on the cushioned window seat and then opened the second trunk. It carried all her undergarments: stockings, garters, and bras the size I wished I could be; toiletries galore, hand cream and a beautiful bottle of Shalimar perfume.

"Wow, the only fragrances I've ever owned are from my Ivory soap and the lavender hand cream Mother's pharmacist mixes for us."

"My father got it for me when he went to Chicago last spring."

"What else have you got in there?"

She pulled out a false bottom revealing her stash of cigarettes and a bottle of brandy.

"If my mother sees this she'll hit the roof!"

"I take it you've never had a ciggy?"

"No, but I did have some champagne at a wedding last year."

"Want to try one?"

"Maybe...we just can't smoke in the house."

Margie pulled me into the bathroom and opened the window over the claw foot tub. She lit the cigarette with a silver Zippo lighter that let out a flame at least an inch high.

"Hang your head out the window when you exhale," she advised.

I coughed a few times, but then enjoyed the lightheadedness it lent after exhaling.

The two of us instantly bonded. Thank God Mother didn't smell anything but Margie's Shalimar when we went down for dinner. The overpowering smell of fried chicken helped saturate the air, too.

Chapter Two

Margie and I woke up early Friday morning so we'd have extra time for putting together just the perfect outfits to wear to orientation. I chose a glen plaid skirt in shades of green and topped it with a yellow blouse with ruffled collar. Margie lent me a yellow wool beret that matched perfectly and picked up the yellow flecks in my eyes.

The royal blue knit dress she wore scooped at her bust line, then flowed fluidly to just below her knees. She softened the look with a floral silk scarf tied in a bow around her neck.

Mother had just brought in the milk from the front porch when we came downstairs.

"Milkman's earlier than usual," she said already dressed for the day. "I've whipped up some scrambled eggs and cheese grits for you girls."

"Thank you Mrs. Anderson, it smells lovely."

"Shall I set the kitchen table, Mother?" I asked as we followed her to the kitchen.

"Already done. Ya'll just relax. Exciting day ahead."

"I don't know if I can eat." I held my stomach.

"What's the matter, dear?"

"Nerves, I suppose."

"You shouldn't be nervous about going to Wesleyan. It's such a familiar place to you."

"I know, but all the professors know I'm your daughter, and they'll be expecting great things from me."

"They'll be expecting you to do your best and that's all."
She set down the wooden spoon she was stirring the cheese
grits with, hugged me around the shoulder and patted my
tummy. "It will all work out just fine, you'll see."

"Do you have a Coca-Cola?" Margie asked. "My mom
always gives me a few sips when my stomach is queasy."

"That's a good idea," Mother said, scraping the scrambled
eggs into a bowl. "There's one in the ice box."

Margie popped the top and handed it to me. "A few sips of
this combined with a few bites of breakfast and you should be
good to go." An encouraging smile followed her words.

After breakfast mother drove us to school in the Chrysler
Imperial my father had bought her when I was eight. An in-
vestment in itself, the thing was a huge steel heap and could
comfortably hold six or seven. At the time Papa bought it, he
was sure they would fill the seats with three or four more children. That was before Mother realized she couldn't conceive
anymore.

Mother normally walked to work since the college was
just a few blocks from our house, said she enjoyed the fresh
air. But the fall winds were unusually blustery, and Margie and
I wanted to stay properly primped for meeting the other girls.
Plus Mother said we could borrow the car after orientation
and go to the drug shop for a soda as long as we returned
by four-thirty to pick her up from work. This was a delight as
Mother rarely let me take the car anywhere without her, and
I'd only had my driver's license for a few months.

The oversized Chrysler came to a crawl once we turned off Forsyth Road and onto campus.

"I'm going to drop ya'll as close to the Quad as I can get. You'll be crossing over that grassy area quite a few times during the school days ahead. When the weather's nice, some of the girls bring along a blanket and study between classes."

"What a great idea," Margie said, grabbing my hand with excitement.

"Ya'll get a move on now. I see several girls already heading from the freshman dorm over to the gym."

"Yes mother," I said, shutting the car door.

"I'm going to park over by the library. The keys will be under the seat. And don't forget to get me at..."

"Four-thirty, Mother, we won't forget."

Arm and arm, Margie and I walked diagonally across the finely manicured Quad the size of a football field, landscaped with young trees, shrubs and annuals. Most of the buildings carried what Papa would have called a Georgia revival style, with two to three floors of red brick, and A-framed roof lines with white columns upholding their southern charm.

This particular campus had only been open a few years. The original downtown campus which opened in 1836 was no longer adequate for the growing student population. With the amount of women attending college on the rise, thank goodness some kind souls donated the land and money to expand. The live oaks that dotted the school grounds were still mere babes with decades of change ahead, a lot like the women who attended Wesleyan.

"There's electricity in the air, Haley! Can't you feel it?"

"All I feel is my stomach still churning."

"Why don't you tell me the names of all the buildings around us. You've got an edge knowing more about this campus than any other freshman. And focusing on something specific will get your mind off of your nerves."

I did like knowing all about the campus before the new students. After taking a cleansing breath, I began. "Mother dropped us off near Tate Hall, that's one of the buildings where classes are held," I pointed behind us. "Further beyond Tate Hall is the library. Porter Gym is straight ahead and we'll attend chapel there along with other activities. And to our left is Taylor Hall which is another academic building. Porter Hall is also to your right which has a nice dining hall and lovely parlor. The President lives on the top floor."

"Oh, so that's why they gave it a façade like the White House, except for the red brick, of course."

"And last are the dormitories, three in all, one for freshman, one for sophomores and another for the juniors and seniors. Come to think of it, why didn't you want to live in the dorm? I'd imagine that would be fun."

"My father said he wanted me to be in a family environment, but I really think he wanted another mother figure to always have a close eye on me, make sure I still ate my vegetables."

"Or keep you away from that brandy," I teased.

"Just for the record, I never have more than a quarter snifter at a time."

Our stroll to the outside of the gym went by far too quick, and soon the buzz of gabbing privileged young ladies rang in my ears.

"What if I don't fit in, Margie?"

"What? Don't be silly, I felt comfortable around you the moment you said hello. You have kind eyes and an honest smile."

"What happens if they find out my mother works here? They might think I get special treatment and then they'll hate me for it. Or worse, they may think I'm below them because she does work here."

"First of all, you can't buy class, and any girl that would think those things about you, no matter how much her family owns, holds absolutely no class of her own, and you wouldn't want to associate with her anyway. And then there are girls from privileged backgrounds like me who've been fortunate enough to have a mother that came from simple means and could teach them about the haves and the have-nots. 'Having more doesn't mean we're better than anybody else,' she'd say in her thick Italian accent. And then she'd remind me, 'Your grandfather was a blacksmith, and he taught me that wealth should not be measured in dollars, but by how much of yourself you pour out for others.'"

"Where in Italy was your mother from?"

"Florence. That's where she met my father. His family used to spend summers there. And though my father comes from blue blood, he's never been one to put himself on a pedestal. My point is that it's the people who offer of themselves, not of their material things, that have class, never putting themselves above another human being. These are the people that you'd want to associate with, right?"

"Right."

"Good, I'm glad we go that cleared up."

"You know, that's the first thing that's made me smile all morning. I'm so glad Mother and I took on a border."

"You can stop your worrying. They're going to love you. Now come on."

As Margie pulled me through the double doors and onto the wood floors of the gym, I couldn't help but notice how the other girls were clustered in two's and three's, most of them shifting from foot to foot, scanning the room with their eyes as if they were looking for someone. The awkwardness of freshman status filled the room. Several girls I said hello to returned my greeting with a genuine "hello" or a "hi there," truly happy to meet me. I don't know what I was so worried about. The dozen or so new girls I met were as sweet as pie. Many of them came from Atlanta and others from surrounding states. We all had one thing in common though—to better ourselves not only as people, but as women. Once I made that connection, I realized we shared a rare sisterhood for our generation, and the knots in my stomach finally began to unravel.

After a surprisingly smooth half day at orientation we drove into town, and I pointed out two of the houses that Papa had designed along the way.

"Your father was an architect with extravagant taste."

"He had some extravagant clients," I said. "All of the buildings and homes he designed here were built before the depression."

"What about the train station ahead. Did he design that, too? It's magnificent!"

"No. That was built before I was born."

"Can we drive a loop around the station before we go to the drug shop? I love watching travelers."

As we got closer to the train station Margie's excited eyes took in the three story, beige stone building that dwarfed everything around us. "Are those statues of eagles perched at the top of the columns?"

"Yes. When I was a little girl, Papa used to tell me they kept an eye on all who came and went from our city, protecting its citizens from evil. He always had a way of making me feel safe."

"Seeing everyone hustling about makes me want to go on a trip."

"You mentioned that your family travels a lot. Where was the last place you visited?"

"Palm Beach."

My heart skipped a beat. "You're kidding?"

"Have you been there, too?"

"No, but I plan to stay at The Breakers on the beach some day. It's the most beautiful place I've ever seen. Did you get to stay there?"

"Don't I wish. We stayed at my uncle's house last summer. It's on the water about a mile down from the resort you refer to. How do you know about The Breakers?"

"It was one of my father's favorite buildings. He gave me a rendering of it before he left us."

"Before he left? I thought your father had passed away."

"He left us when I was eleven, and we haven't seen him since. He sends Mother some money every few months, but that's all."

"I'm so sorry, Haley, I didn't know." She placed a hand on my shoulder.

"That's okay."

"Do you know where he is?"

"The envelopes come postmarked from Utah. That's all we know. Anyway, if you remind me, I'll show you the rendering when we get back to the house if you'd like. It's hidden in my closet."

"Yes, I'd like that."

After circling the train station one last time, we drove back down Cherry Street toward the drug shop. "There's my favorite restaurant right next door," I pointed out. "Maisy's Diner has the best smothered pork chops and fried okra around. If you roll down the window you're sure to smell it. Mother admits they're even better than hers. She said she's going to treat us there tomorrow night for my seventeenth birthday."

"Seventeenth birthday? I thought you were at least eighteen like me. I didn't know your birthday was coming up. I would have gotten you something."

"Don't get me anything. Making a new friend has been a gift in itself."

Margie smiled.

"I think I'll have a Coke float today," I said.

"Feeling better now?"

"Much."

"Have you heard where the boys like to gather? I mean, not that I'm looking, but it's always fun to flirt."

"Maybe we'll see some there," I said, pointing out two dapper young men. They were leaning against a shiny black convertible outside the drug shop.

"Now there's a nice lad from the right side of the tracks, and a good looking Studebaker to go with him."

"Wonder which one of them owns it?"

"My guess would be the one with the wing-tipped shoes; the keys are in his hand." Margie quickly powdered her nose while observing them from the corner of her eye.

I pulled into the angled parking spot two down from theirs so not to look overzealous about their presence. Margie lit a cigarette and propped open her door. "I call Mr. Wing-tipped shoes."

"You can have him. The shorter curly-head one with the blue shirt is kind of cute."

"Shh, they're coming this way."

"Hello ladies," the one with wing-tipped shoes greeted with a debonair twang. "My name is Allen and this is my pal Roger." Allen offered Margie his hand and helped her out of the car, then turned to his buddy. "Go on over and open the door for her friend ya dingbat."

Roger opened my door, but I didn't take his hand when he offered it. "Thank you, but I can manage," I told him.

We all gathered on the sidewalk in front of the car, clustering into an awkward circle.

"I don't believe we got your names," Allen said.

"Sorry, I'm Margie and this is Haley. Sure is a snazzy car you've got over there."

"Like that do ya?" Allen rattled his keys. "I endured a lot of sweat and splinters to earn money for that baby. My dad agreed to help me buy it if I worked in his lumber yard the past two summers. He's the big cheese at the mill where I'm from and says nothing in life should come easy, especially if you're the son of the wealthiest man in town."

"No kidding?" Margie tapped his shoulder. "My daddy's in the lumber business, too. Ever heard of Cutco Mills?"

"Sure have. I wouldn't be surprised if my old man knows yours. Ask if he's ever heard of a Butch Jenson the next time you talk to him."

"Will do. So are you fellas out doing some shopping?"

Allen lit a cigarette with a silver monogrammed lighter. Exhaling, he answered, "Just picking up a few things here and there. Where are ya'll headed?"

"For a soda at the drug shop," Margie answered. "Like to join us?"

I elbowed her side.

"How 'bout we treat," Allen offered.

"It's a deal," Margie quickly accepted, neither one having taken their eyes off of each other.

"So where are you boys from?" I asked.

"We're both from Savannah." Allen slicked his long black bangs back with his fingers. "We've got two more years left of medical school at Mercer and then off to bigger and better things than the lumber mill."

"Medical school, huh?" Margie hooked an arm through Allen's as he escorted her to the drug shop. She looked back at me to do the same with Roger. I shook my head no. Since I was about twelve years old, my hands would sweat and I'd get all tongue-tied in the presence of any boy that gave me the time of day. Ever since Papa left, I decided that no man was ever going to own my heart in its entirety. He could have a little piece of it, but the rest I'd keep to myself. This was advice Mother had pounded into my head from the first day I'd taken a liking to any one boy.

Small talk came easy for Margie who was chattering away in Allen's ear. So I tried striking up a conversation with Roger.

"Ya'll certainly must burn the oil of midnight..." *there I go again*, "I mean the midnight oil, with all the studying that's required for the medical field."

"Yeah, but we can always make time for the girls."

Now that I got a better look at Roger, the distant good looks I'd observed earlier went downhill fast. The first thing I noticed was his lazy eye, which made it real difficult to carry on a conversation as we walked toward the drug shop. But what bothered me the most was the way he smacked his gum. Rolling my eyes when Margie glanced back at me, I thought, *Maybe I was destined to be an old maid.*

The door jingled when we entered, and the guys hung their hats on a wooden post near the door. We sat on red leather stools just in front of the soda fountain.

"Two Coke floats, please," I said to the man dressed in white behind the pale green counter.

"Make that four." Allen threw a few coins next to the register, and we all sat down, girls in the middle. "What else are you girls up to today?"

"We just finished orientation at Wesleyan," I said.

"Ah, yes, Wesleyan," Roger sang out, his lazy eye falling on me. "Beautiful campus there."

Allen tapped his fingers on the back of Margie's stool. "Yes, beautiful campus and beautiful girls, and none could be as pretty as this one," he said to Margie who slightly blushed, then sipped her float. "So are you girls staying at the freshman dorm? We could stop by some time during visiting hours if that's alright. Or, you could always meet us out if that sits better with you."

"Meet us out?" I nervously questioned, then whispered to Margie, "I think they'd have to come to the house first and meet my mother. She doesn't allow me in the company of boys she's never met."

"Blame it on me," she returned and then turned back to Allen. "We're not at the dorms. Haley and her mother took me in as a boarder. We're at two hundred Rivoli Drive. You can't miss it...big powder blue tank out front."

"Okay, that's all the time we have," I said flustered now that Margie had blurted out my address. "Thanks for the floats Allen." I grabbed both of our pocketbooks. "Come on Margie, we've got things to do."

"But wait," Allen stopped Margie. "Is it okay if I see you this weekend?"

"I'd be distraught if you didn't," she replied as we walked out the door.

Once in the car, Margie slammed the door. "Now why did you have to go and cut a good thing short? He was the cat's pajamas."

"Sorry, but I was feeling uncomfortable," I said, fiddling with the car keys. "Dag nabit! The key won't go in!" The boys came out of the drug shop, and Allen tipped his hat at Margie. By the time he'd backed out, my shaking hands still couldn't get the key to go in. "Horsefeathers!" I hit the steering wheel.

Margie leaned over and calmly turned over the ignition. "See there? Magic touch." She patted my shoulder again like she'd done when she found out about Papa leaving. "Is everything alright?"

I took my hat off and scrubbed my hair. "Boys make me uneasy."

Silence lingered while we sat idle.

"You've never been kissed, have you Haley?"

Still didn't say a word, but cracked a smile as I backed out.

"A doll like you and never been kissed? Well, I declare, we're going to have to work on that."

"I never said never. Our neighbor from two doors down, Bobby Baker kissed me on the cheek in the fifth grade, but not the lips."

"But you do want to kiss a boy, right?"

"Of course."

"What's been stopping you?"

"For starters, I haven't found anyone I'd really like to kiss, and also, I'm afraid of falling in love."

"Why on earth would you be afraid of falling in love? My sister Mary said that when you find the right one, loving him will come as easy as breathing."

"What if he leaves me like my father left my mother. She's been brokenhearted going on six years now." Tears fell to the ruffles of my yellow blouse.

Margie got a handkerchief from her purse. "Gosh, I didn't mean to upset you. Here, wipe your eyes and we'll talk about something else."

"Thank you. You've been here only a few days, and I've showed you nothing but a nervous blubbering idiot with an odd way around men. How ridiculous I must seem to you."

"I don't think that at all. You've got to remember, having two older sisters taught me a thing or two at an early age."

"Like what?"

"I used to hide behind the swinging kitchen door that led to the dining room. You could see straight through to the living room where they always brought their dates. Sometimes they wouldn't catch me for a whole ten minutes. Then they'd start necking and my giggle would always give me away."

"Anything else?"

"Usually it was all mushy talk and quick kisses. But this one evening, my parents had gone to a play and wouldn't be back till late. I was around twelve years old and Melissa was watching after me. Mary came home early with her date and she assumed Melissa and I were upstairs reading. What she didn't know is that we were both hiding behind the kitchen door this time. At first they started with the mushy talk, 'Oh, how lovely your eyes are Mary,' and 'kiss me before I faint.' It was a hoot. Then I couldn't believe my eyes. That boy un-buttoned her blouse and kissed her from the lips right down to her bare navel! At that point, I didn't get to see anymore because Melissa covered my eyes and then ran me back up the kitchen staircase."

"Did Melissa go back downstairs?"

"Yes, but she didn't know I had gone around to the front staircase. The view from over the banister was even better than from the kitchen. And by that time, they were so gaga over each other, they wouldn't have noticed me even if I'd done a jig."

"I've only read about this kind of stuff in a few of mother's romance novels I've snuck over the years. Please go on, what else did they do?"

Margie blushed.

"What! Tell me!"

"My own sister reached beneath her date's belt and felt it."

"Felt what?"

"Margie shot me a wide stare."

Ohhh, that what. Did she ever tell you what it felt like?"

"I'll tell you, but you've got to slow down before you kill us both."

"Oops, sorry." I stomped the brakes and swerved in time to avoid hitting the Baker's mailbox. "Now go on..."

"I was about fifteen when I finally got up the courage to ask her about this sort of stuff, and when I did she said it felt like a firm banana without the peel."

"Eew, I know I'll eventually have sex some day, but I'm not so sure I'm looking forward to it."

"You will when the right man comes along."

"Have you ever done any of that stuff your sister did?"

"I've kissed three boys, one of which tried to feel me up, but I caught his hand in the fold of my elbow before he made it there."

"I can't even imagine," I said stunned. "There's always some little thing that bothers me about the boys I've met. Like Roger back there, did you notice his lazy eye?"

"He wasn't all that bad."

"And smacking that gum like a cow chewing cud. Looks like the day for my first real kiss will never come."

"Well, we're gonna have to fix that now aren't we?"

"Mrs. V?" Isa interrupted.

"Yes?"

"Stephen is on his way."

"Thank you." After Isa left she said, "There's a paragraph I wrote that I wanted to share with you before we drive out to the Sanibel lighthouse." She flipped to the end of the binder where it looked like she'd made several entries of short passages. Running her fingers along the blue ink, she found the spot. "Here we go…"

There had only been one man with whom I had laid next, bare. Bare is how it felt, inside and out; the idea of making love being foreign to me. I was only familiar with his art of the actual act. Maybe art is too kind a word for what we did. Art is full of color, my life had remained gray up to this point. So I wondered if I would carry over the same dull color when I lay with the one God had intended for me. Fearing I'd disappoint him, my procrastination only aroused our senses more. Could we possibly let our bodies melt freely together with no inhibitions to quench the fire? These troubled thoughts clouded my urges, and for a moment, I hesitated to lie beside him on the blanket by the sea. Surely God would accept us together. How could He condemn something that felt so right? Some souls are simply tardy in finding each other, an acceptable excuse, I thought. But was it too late for us? The lighthouse would be the first to see.

Before shutting the binder, a single tear meandered down wrinkles of time, dripping to the blue ink with a soft tap. She quickly blotted it dry with the sleeve of her lavender blouse.

Isa appeared at the top of the stairs to let us know Stephen had arrived. She helped Mrs. Van Buren onto the elevator and I met them in the kitchen to help her off. Stephen got us settled in the car, and we were off.

Chapter 6

During the twenty minute ride to the southern tip of Sanibel Island I asked Mrs. Van Buren about trivial things such as her favorite color, movie and book of all time. I was tickled to hear her favorite movie to be *Tootsie*. She said, "It just goes to show you what lengths people will go to in order to be with the one they love."

The lighthouse finally came into view. At least a hundred feet tall, an iron rusted skeletal structure with a central column down the middle.

"Is the light still functional?" I asked.

She and Stephen answered in unison, "Yes."

Stephen continued. "It was first lit in 1884 after a hell-of-a-time in the making."

"How so?"

"All its parts came on a schooner from Jersey City, but it sank just two miles from the site. Amazingly enough, divers were able to find most everything, and they were still able to get 'er built in a matter of months. Soon after that, the keeper's dwelling was built."

From the backseat, I pointed out the narrow front windshield of the old Chrysler. "And that would be the white square building over there with the pyramid-shaped roof."

"They made the roofs aerodynamic so they'd withstand hurricane winds."

Mrs. Van Buren cut in. "Go on any longer and you'll bore her to tears."

"On the contrary, I find this very interesting. Being married to a history buff has rubbed off over the years. So is there still a family that takes care of the lighthouse?"

"No," Stephen answered, "the US Department of the Interior took over and automated the light in the late forties."

Mrs. Van Buren chimed in, "It became like a lover's point when that happened, didn't it Stephen?"

He smiled over his shoulder at her as he shifted the car into park, adding, "You'd hear about high school kids getting caught drinking beer and carrying on up there on that wraparound porch ."

To the south of the lighthouse stood a fishing pier where a handful of locals and tourists tried their best to hook a catch of the day. The pier jutted out about thirty yards and had a covered gazebo area midway down lined with benches. Stephen and I assisted Mrs. Van Buren to one of the four benches where we sat and took in the view. The invigorating March breeze carried gulls and pelicans overhead as I observed round-leaved seagrape hedges lining the lawn in front of the old keeper's cottage, and sea oats tickling the long-legged beams that grounded the lighthouse.

"This is like something you see on a postcard."

"It is on a postcard," Mrs. Van Buren said. "Many artists come down here and paint the sights."

"I see my buddy Marty over there fishing at the end of the pier," Stephen said. "I'll go see what he's catching and let you girls talk."

When he was out of hearing range, I carefully asked, "What you read to me before we left, about the lighthouse, do you mind if I ask if that was about you and Stephen?"

She shifted her body toward me and spoke softly so only I could hear. "The month before Henry's death, Stephen and I did come here. We'd been seeing each other on a friendly basis, nothing more. Stephen's family had a jewelry store."

"Yes, he told me earlier on our boat ride that his family has a diamond mine in South Africa."

"I see. What else did that rascal tell you?"

"Just that his wife died a year ago and his son, Josh, was now seeing to the family business."

"Anything about me?" What few eyelashes she still had batted at me.

"He said you were something special, but that's all I could get out of him. I swear."

"Don't swear, child, it's bad for the spirit." Her smile retreated. "Special, huh…that's what I've had to be, and it's the kind of special that causes you to make so many adjustments and amendments in your life that you don't get to feel the perks that go with being special."

"When did you first meet Stephen?"

A smile crept back onto her face. "I'll never forget the first time I saw him. I was doing a write-up on Jessie's grill. They claimed to have had the best chicken salad in town so I'd gone to verify the claim. I dined alone that day so the seat across from me was vacant, and I felt horrible about it because there was a line of people waiting to get in. My seat was next to the window, and on the other side of the window was…"

"Stephen."

"Ding, ding…you are correct, my dear. Those round green eyes looked at me like we'd known each other for years. We had chemistry through the glass. I don't know what came over me, but I motioned for him to take the seat across from me, and after wedging through the bottlenecked entrance, he introduced himself and sat down. We saw each other almost every day from that one forward."

My eyes kept shifting between her perky face and Stephen's stout stance at the end of the pier.

"I see you found my pink scarf." She reached up and grazed the end of my ponytail.

"Yes, on Stephen's boat." I began untying it.

"You keep it, dear. Pink is becoming in your blonde hair."

"Thank you."

Stephen walked up and politely interrupted. "Are you girls ready to head back?"

"Already?" Mrs. Van Buren said in a childlike whine.

"Isa said you need to take some medication by three-thirty, and if you still want me to take the scenic route home and show Julia some of your favorite spots, I suggest we get going."

"Oh hell's bells, can't the medicine wait?"

"No, ma'am. We're gonna keep you alive and kicking for as long as possible. Right Julia?"

"Yes sir."

"And Marty asked if I could meet him at the driving range by four. Our tee time this morning got rained out."

"Oh, so that's the hurry," she said like the better half of an old married couple.

Back in the car, Stephen turned up his Sinatra CD, and the blue Chrysler crawled down side roads at Mrs. Van Buren's request. The light breeze whooshed through open windows as he sang "Night and Day" in a voice almost as pure as Sinatra's. Flashing his eyes in the rear view mirror, Mrs. Van Buren joined him, and they harmonized the chorus like they'd done it a hundred times.

She tapped the back of his seat. "Stop here. I want Julia to see the Chapel by the Sea."

The car sat idle, sputtering, in front of the small A-framed chapel. Draped in shade, the white clapboard building carried a modest steeple set aglow by filtered rays of sunlight.

"This used to also serve as the island's schoolhouse," Mrs. Van Buren said. "Isa attended class here till she was ten or so." She waved her hand for Stephen to move on.

"She told me about that this morning while we made muffins," I said, imagining how spectacular it must have been to have the beach as a playground for recess. "I didn't realize how long ya'll had known each other."

"Long time. I'd like for you to join Isa and I for church tomorrow. The service is at nine-thirty. With so many snowbirds down here in the winter, they keep the service interdenominational. Do you attend church in Atlanta?"

"I go to the Baptist church there off Peachtree. They have wonderful facilities for the youth group which the twins are active in."

"Twin boys...How did you ever get through the terrible two's?"

"We managed. Mama has lived with us since Daddy died when the boys were little. I couldn't do it without her"

"That's right."

"Oh, I'm sorry. Did I already tell you that?" I didn't recall telling her anything specific about Mama or the boys.

"I think you did, or maybe you relayed it in your column at one time or another."

"I'm afraid tomorrow's column is from my rainy day file," I said. "I'm having them run the one I wrote about how couples need to lock their cell phones in the glove compartment when they go out to dinner. Give the babysitter the restaurant number for a real emergency like the old days. You can't have a romantic dinner with your husband if one of the kids has memorized your cell number and calls to ask, 'Can we have ice cream for dessert instead of gummy worms?'"

Mrs. Van Buren slapped my knee. "You're absolutely right. I don't know how parents get any relief nowadays."

When we got back to the cottage, Stephen pulled up under the carport next to Isa's sea-foam green minivan. The hatch was open and she held a paper sack of groceries.

"Need some help?" I asked as Stephen opened the car door for me.

"That'd be great."

While I helped with the groceries, Stephen walked Mrs. Van Buren in through the back door and then quickly came back to cover the car with a tarp the same shade of light blue as the Chrysler. Stephen's car, a white Range Rover, sat parked under a banyan tree at the edge of the property.

"She likes to keep it covered when it's not in service," he rolled his eyes. "I'll see you ladies later."

I grabbed the last bag and followed Isa in through the laundry room and to the kitchen where the delicious aroma of a slow-cooked pot roast permeated the air. "That smells as good as Mama's."

"Good, we want you to feel right at home here," Mrs. Van Buren said, sitting in the swivel chair under the phone. "I told Stephen to plop me here and go on to meet Marty at the driving range. They were supposed to play a full round this morning, but it rained as you know from your walk earlier."

"At least he got to go fishing," I said.

"Oh, yes, that's when you found my pink scarf. Tell me, Julia, are you sure he didn't share anything else with you other than that I was special and about his wife passing last year?"

"No, ma'am, that's it." I turned to Isa and asked, "Do you need any help with dinner?"

"No thanks. I'm in good shape. It'll be ready in about an hour. I figure that'll give you a few hours after dinner for interview time before Mr. Crawly comes to pick you up. You sure are dedicated to your work."

"Yes, my office hours certainly aren't nine to five." I turned to Mrs. Van Buren and said, "I'll help you to the sunroom while Isa finishes in here. I'd like to freshen up and call home before dinner." I told Isa to call me when dinner was ready so I could help bring everything up.

While Mrs. Van Buren clicked the TV to a cable channel showing "Murder She Wrote," I retreated to my room for a quick shower after which I put on a black crinkled cotton dress with drawstring waist. I thought that if I got forced into seeing Bruce later either by surprise or my own breakdown, a frumpy dress might be a turnoff. After hearing about Mrs. Van Buren and Stephen's encounter under the lighthouse, my hormones had got to flowing again. Sexual addictions sure make us weak, I thought, still craving to be touched.

Before I went out to join Mrs. Van Buren, I sat on the edge of the bed and called home. Mama answered after two rings.

"Hi Mama, it's me."

"Hey sugar. How's every little thing?"

As much as I needed to vent about Bruce, I had to lie and say, "Every little thing is great."

"What color scarf did she wear today?"

"How did you know she wears scarves?"

"I think the last few pictures of her in public had her wearing a scarf tied around her head, right?"

"It was turquoise. Why do you ask?"

"I love hearing little details about people. Meet anyone else?"

"Yes, you remember her nurse that initially called me."

"Oh yes, Isa." She paused. "Anyone else?"

"I met her driver and that's it."

Mama couldn't help but be nosey, it's been her nature as far back as I can remember. The walls would mysteriously grow ears whenever Darrell and I had an argument. She always has a way of knowing what's going on in that house. It made me wonder if someone didn't hide something from her years ago. She hates being left out of any gossip stirring—always in my business. I remember the first serious confrontation I had as a child. Kindergarten was the grade and Rhonda was her name. All I did was pull at her pigtails, ever so gently, and then she slugged me right in the stomach. Peanut butter and jelly sandwich hurled right out of my stomach onto her jumper. The school principal handled it fine, but when Mama caught wind of it, she went straight to Rhonda's house and gave her mother a book on child bullies. Yep, she tends to cross the line sometimes when it comes to looking out for my well-being.

Our conversation continued...

"Is there some other important person that I'm supposed to meet while I'm down here?" I clinched my teeth and squinted while waiting for an answer, praying she'd never overheard me talking to Bruce about anything other than work. She'd never met Bruce, but did once ask why I talked about him so much. I told her it was because he sat so close to me at work and that we'd become good friends. I was pretty sure she'd bought it.

"No," she said, acknowledging my sarcasm, "I just thought you may have met some other famous recluse people that might be hiding on that island. I once heard Jimmy Hoffa had a place there."

"Sure you did, Mother, now let's get back to the real world. Are Darrell and the boys home? I'd like to speak to them."

"They've gone out for pizza. Darrell took the whole team out for a winner's supper."

"Great! So they won their games today?"

"Yep, Ryan scored two and Dylan scored one."

"Fantastic! I hate that I missed it. Tell them all I love 'em and I'll call tomorrow morning. Too much keeping me busy to call back later tonight."

"I'll tell 'em, but they'll be disappointed."

"When was Darrell ever disappointed that he didn't get to talk to me?"

"Julia, are you sure everything's okay between you two? You know you can tell me anything."

"What makes you think something's wrong?"

"I don't know, mother's intuition."

"I know that tone, Mama. Are you not telling me something?"

"Now promise you won't get all worked up when I tell you this. There could be a hundred explanations for the mileage I noticed on Darrell's truck."

"Of course there's mileage on his truck, he just got back from meeting with the Brother's."

Mama did a doubtful sigh.

"Remember how I took you to the airport yesterday in his truck and not your car?"

"Yeah...so."

"Well, once I got back to our neighborhood, the truck made a dinging sound and a light came on indicating that he was due to get maintenance. The odometer read 30,000 miles."

"Okay, and?"

"After he got home from the mountains today I glanced at the mileage again while we were outside getting things ready for the boys' soccer games."

"Why did you go and do that?"

"I was curious after we realized he hadn't taken his Confederate uniform with him."

"Just spit it out, Mama."

"He'd only put sixty miles on the darn thing. It read 30,060, and that's all. He should have at least put two hundred miles on it."

"What time did he leave yesterday?"

"Two o'clock."

"But he has a class at two," I said, my gut beginning to ache. "When did he get back from the mountains today?"

"Around noon. Now for all we know he could have hooked up with one of the Brothers and rode with them so don't get your nose bent out of shape yet. All I'm saying is that I'd like to keep my eyes and ears open for you."

"If you find anything out, promise you'll call right away?"

"Of course I will. I think you two need some time away together. Hey, I've got a great idea?"

"Uh oh, the last time you had a great idea I embarrassed myself trying to seduce my husband."

"Forget about that, will you? You've been wallowing in that for months now. What I was going to suggest is that maybe he should come down there after you're done with the interview. It'd give ya'll time to reconnect. I've got the boys under control. Go to one of those resorts on the water. Heck, ya'll haven't been alone together since you took that vacation to the Bahamas for your ten-year anniversary, and that was years ago!"

"No, no, Mama, no one needs to come down here. I promise I'll plan something after I get back."

"You'd better. Ryan just asked me the other day if you and his Daddy ever did divorce could he and Dylan stay here at the house, or would they have to move."

"He did not ask you that!"

"He did. You don't think they can't sense the rift between you two? Well you're wrong. Now I don't mean to upset you with all this, you've got a lot on your plate right now. But I do think you need to be more aware of what's going on in your own family. You've been distant lately. Now get back to work and call us when you can, and when you talk to Darrell, mums the word about the mileage thing, ya hear? He thinks I'm a busybody as it is."

"Yes ma'am."

Ending the call, I slumped over, face in hands. Never had I felt this low. Why in the hell did I ever think getting involved with Bruce Crawly would solve anything?

Chapter 7

After freshening up, I walked out of my daisy room to find Mrs. Van Buren sitting at her desk, back towards me. The swivel chair squeaked as she leaned back to read a letter, one of many scattered about the roll-top desk. Unaware of my presence, she pivoted around, her profile catching light off the Tiffany desk lamp. No longer did I see an old woman, but rather a face well lived, carrying a Roman nose, narrow chin and cheek bones well defined. There was still a radiance about her. The blue scarf relaxed around humped shoulders, shoulders that years ago held a confident posture. I couldn't help but stop and stare, imagining her as a determined young woman sitting right there at that very desk, decade after decade, despite the pain from her losses, creating timeless love stories. How did she do it for so long while living such a lonely life? Caught up in this vision, an uncontrolled sneeze flew out of my nose.

"Julia, dear, I didn't know you were there," she said startled. "And God bless you."

"Thank you. Was I interrupting?"

"Not at all, I was just looking through the mail."

She pushed the opened letters and envelopes aside and stuck a Post-it note with a phone number scribbled on it to the bottom of the computer monitor next to my business card. I had attached one to her copy of the legal documents she'd signed the day before.

I said, "During my research I found a website about your novels that your agent had listed, but no e-mail address. Do you have one?"

"Too hi-tech for this old broad. I dabble in the e-mail with a private address that I've given to a few old friends, but as for mail from fans, I answer what I can the old-fashioned way. The publishing house in New York sends me about fifty each month. That's all I can handle. I try and answer one or two a day. It's gratifying to know that another generation is enjoying my work."

"I told Isa I'd help her bring up dinner. Can I help you with anything before I go down?"

"No, no," she said quickly. "You go on ahead while I finish up here. I'll make my way over to the table eventually."

About fifteen minutes later, Mrs. Van Buren, Isa and I sat down for our first meal together, just the three of us, the orange glow of dusk softly lighting the balcony for our conversation.

"Your pot roast looks and smells divine," I said inhaling the steam from the mashed potatoes. "There goes my diet."

Isa puffed up. "My mother taught me everything I know about cooking, didn't she Mrs. V?"

"What a fine, fine woman Constanz was, traveled all the way over here with a toddler on her hip after the war, determined to make life better."

Isa's head dropped. "I still miss her terribly."

Mrs. Van Buren squeezed her arm. "I do too. But you've certainly mastered her recipes, and we think of her fondly every time you make one of her dishes, especially that delicious spaetzle and chicken with the creamy mushroom sauce. Isa will have to make that for you sometime."

"I'd love that. Have you been back to your hometown?"

"No, but when I do, Mrs. V has got to come with me and see the castle."

"Which castle is that?"

"My birthplace was in a small town in the Bavarian Alps called Füssen, just a few miles from the Neuschwanstein Castle. It's the one that inspired Walt Disney's design for Cinderella's castle."

"Wait, I think Darrell told me something about this the last time we were at Disney with the twins. Wasn't it King Lod-something that built it?"

"Close, King Ludwig the Second. Some considered him to be mad or insane, and in the history books you'll see him referred to as Mad King Ludwig because he was considered to be a hopeless romantic, obsessed with building the perfect castle rather than focusing on his political duties. He already had two royal palaces, but he wanted to build a fantasy palace filled with frescos and stone monuments representing visions that had come to him during operas he'd seen as a child. It's quite a new castle as far as castles go. It was built in the late eighteen hundreds on a hillside between a lake and a river with the Alps towering above it, quite breathtaking in the pictures I've seen. Mother used to visit there before the war and talked about it often.

The designers set it up with the river above to provide water pressure so they could install running water and flushing toilets throughout. And in those times, being able to flush away what you tinkled was a modern luxury. Unfortunately, Ludwig died before he got to flush. But I've heard he lived in the completed portion for a few months until he was dethroned for being considered insane. Two days later, they found him drowned in a nearby lake. No one knows if he was murdered or if he killed himself. After his death, the castle was opened to the public and became a historical landmark."

"What can I say," Mrs. Van Buren shrugged, "I'm a sap for castles and romantics. You'd better book a flight soon. I'm going downhill fast."

"Nonsense," Isa declared. "Take your medication regularly and keep yourself moving, and I'd say you have another twenty."

"One-hundred and six, oh my, I'll be shriveled to a raison by then."

After we finished eating, Isa excused herself from the table, cleared the dishes and offered us coffee.

"Could you put a spot of Bailey's Irish Cream in mine," Mrs. Van Buren asked, head turned, waiting to see if I also wanted some.

"Sounds yummy."

Isa said motherly like, "You know the doctor said not to mix alcohol with your meds."

"Heavens to Betsy, do I have to get up and pour it myself? It won't kill me."

Isa reluctantly nodded yes, and went to fix the coffees.

We moved over to the padded wicker rockers and watched the sun finish sinking into the gulf.

"How could anyone ever get tired of this?" I said.

"I never do." She pointed a crooked finger out at the blue mass to the silhouette of a snowy egret. "Watch him...see there, he's cracking coquina shells with his beak. What lovely creatures they are. Too bad you have to go help your friend tonight. I wouldn't mind having someone to share a nip of brandy with later. Isa doesn't drink, you know, and she scolds me when I do. But I sneak it sometimes. You look like you could use a brandy yourself. That Mr. Crawly clearly agitated you at lunch today."

"Agitate me? A little I suppose. It was embarrassing that he showed up unannounced."

"Oh, don't be embarrassed. If anyone should be embarrassed it should be him." She pursed her lips. "So he says he needs your help on an article, eh? Just couldn't wait till you were finished here?"

"Bruce is a very determined and efficient reporter." I quickly shrugged it off and picked up my pen and notepad from the end table. "So how long after you'd been married to Henry did you meet Stephen?"

Isa had returned with our spiked coffees when I asked the question, her face shocked by my inquiry.

"It's okay, Isa," Mrs. Van Buren said. "When I said I was going to tell Julia everything, that meant *everything*. Henry and I'd been married for a little over seven years. I suppose I got the seven-year-itch right on time, but it's not as though I was looking for it."

Isa snickered. "Do you need anything else ladies?"

"No thank you. I'll send Julia after anything we might need." She winked at me.

"Just as long as it isn't more Bailey's," she shook her head at me like a mother does when a child wants more candy. "I'll be in the kitchen cleaning up."

"Did Henry know you were unhappy?"

"If he did, he didn't show it."

She stopped rocking and took a long sip of coffee. I did the same and realized that her story was beginning to snowball into something bigger—deeper territory than I'd prepared to explore. Firing off questions about someone's affair took a tactful tongue, and I was hesitant to continue.

"Did Henry ever find out about Stephen?"

A long pause followed by more sips of coffee.

"Does your husband know about Bruce?"

The blood rushed from my face, and I wiped my palms across my lap. "There's nothing to know except that we have a close work relationship."

"I wasn't born yesterday." She continued rocking. "Coworker or not, no man goes to the lengths that Mr. Crawly did in order to find my private home unless he was either driven by love or testosterone. I can't even imagine who he must've paid off to get my address. And don't think I didn't realize why our tea glasses splashed around this afternoon during lunch...the nerve of that man feeling your leg under the table. I knew he fancied you the moment he sat down."

"Bruce has a small crush on me, I guess. That's all it is, a harmless crush."

Mrs. Van Buren reached across the end table and gathered my hand in hers, concerned eyes penetrating mine. "They call them crushes because someone always gets hurt. Be careful is all I'm saying. Being attracted to another man is normal, nothing to feel guilty about there, but if the attraction seeks validation, now that can get you into trouble. You still love your husband right?"

"Yes."

"Don't lose sight of that."

I put my other hand on top of hers. "You're a very observant woman Mrs. Van Buren. I do love my husband, and I appreciate your concern. Faith will show me the way."

"Not always. Never forget who holds the reins."

"God?"

"And you, dear. You are held accountable for every choice you make."

"Yes, I'm aware of that." My head lowered with guilt.

She stared into her empty mug for a moment. "I feel cold. Is it getting cold out here?"

"Actually I'm quite warm, but we can move inside if you'd like."

"Yes, let's do. Then I can continue reading to you. I'm sure more of your questions will get answered tonight. But the one about whether Henry knew about Stephen, that'll be answered later. We still have to get the girls out of Wesleyan College and on with their lives."

I got her situated on the sofa and then noticed that Isa had left the carafe of coffee on the edge of Mrs. Van Buren's desk.

"Refill?"

"Yes please."

"More Bailey's?"

"No thank you, dear." A knotted bowl of fingers caressed the coffee cup. She closed her eyes, took a few sips, then touched the scar with her left hand. The manuscript sat on the coffee table and I handed it to her. The delicate frayed edges tickled my fingertips.

"Chapter three is where I think we left off. You've already heard about Margie's spying experience when she caught her sister Mary getting a handful, correct?"

Her frankness amused me. "Yes."

"Alright then…"

Chapter Three

Our freshman year quickly turned into our sophomore. Mother and I began to consider Margie more like family. I'd proved myself to the professors at Wesleyan, making excellent marks in every subject, and Margie and I decided to join the Alpha Delta Pi sorority and take up soccer football for recreation. Our games were held just outside Porter Gym beside the Quad. It was the only time deemed appropriate by the college for us to run around in knickers. Allen never missed a game, and he and Margie hadn't missed but maybe two Saturday nights together since they'd met outside the drug shop a whole year ago. But as for me, of the three dates I'd had over the last school year only one of them was worth kissing, and he wound up having horrible halitosis.

My curiosity about boys continued to blossom, mostly due to some of the late-night brandy induced conversations Margie and I'd had in the bathroom. I'd sit on the hamper and Margie on the toilet seat, all while puffing out rings of smoke. Needless to say, the brandy helped dampen my shyness to speak freely on the topic. It wasn't that I didn't want a man; it was more about finding one worth having. But this one particular Sunday night in the early spring of our sophomore year, we were gabbing and smoking in our usual spots while Margie did my hair. No brandy on this occasion seeing that it was a school night.

"You've been with Allen for a while now, and I still haven't found anyone I like," I complained.

Margie said, "That's because you're so darn picky. You won't let yourself find anyone…always excuses, he's either too tall or too loud, and of course there was Roger with the lazy eye."

"That's ridiculous. I'm not picky."

Margie rolled her dark eyes at me in the bathroom mirror, then continued pin-curling my hair in spirals around her finger. "Do you think your mother's asleep yet?"

"She went to her room over an hour ago," I said. "Wait…" Her coughs carried down the hallway. "She's still up. Why do you ask?"

"Because Allen will be throwing pennies at my window at any minute now."

"Not again, Margie. It's Sunday night. You can't sneak out on a school night."

"Normally I wouldn't, but I just have to see him tonight. It's very, very important." She stretched a hair net around the mass of bobby pins plastered to my head. "There, you'll be curlier than Shirley tomorrow."

Margie took off her robe and went to her closet where she put on a loose-fitting striped dress. I sat on the bed and watched while she looked in the mirror over the dresser.

"I look pale," she said, frantically pinching her cheeks. "Where's my lipstick? Do you have my cherry-red lipstick?"

Drawers started flying open, their contents tossed to the floor. I'd never seen Margie lose her composure over something so frivolous.

"Stop," I said, putting my hands on her shoulders. "What's the matter with you? One minute you're as calm as a clam, pin-curling my hair, and the next you're flying off the handle. Is it your lady time?"

She dropped to the floor, drawing her knees to her chest and sobbed. "That's just it Haley my lady time hasn't come yet."

Then it occurred to me. "I thought you said you and Allen had only necked."

Beet-red eyes flashed at me with shame. "We couldn't help ourselves. It just happened. But I never thought that one time would get me pregnant."

"Now don't jump to any conclusions. You might just be late."

"I'm never late."

I helped her up. "Come sit on the bed, and I'll get you a cool rag."

As I turned the spigot on and cold water flowed through the wash rag, Margie began wailing. I quickly wrung it out and rushed back to her side.

"Here, wipe your eyes and take some deep breaths, we can't have Mother hear that crying."

Once she caught her breath she mumbled the word *shame* over and over.

"What about shame?"

"Shame on me for being so naïve. He'd said to me, 'You can't get pregnant if I pull out.' I should have known better but I couldn't control the urges I had. They were more powerful than anything I'd ever felt."

"Do you regret it?"

No immediate answer. "Not really, I do love him. I mostly regret the shame I'm going to put on my parents, my mother especially. She was so proud that all three of her girls went to college, though we all picked different schools. And now I won't be able to finish." Her hands flew back up to her eyes.

"You could still finish Wesleyan. What if I help keep the baby... or mother, or you could hire a nanny. There are still so many people out of work and I'm sure that..."

"Stop Haley, it's no use. A mother should be at home with her husband and child. You're a dear to offer though."

"So what are you going to do?"

"I don't know yet, I have to discuss it with Allen tonight. He still has no idea."

"For what it's worth, you'll make a wonderful mother."

Half a smile rose on her wet face followed by pennies tapping the window.

"That's him." She quickly wiped her eyes and walked to the window. "Try not to worry for me. I'll be back in an hour or so."

"I'll say a prayer for you." I hugged her tight before she opened the window.

"Don't wait up."

"Oh please, I'll be on pins and needles till you get home." I watched as she scooted from the foot of the dormer down to the edge of the roof where jasmine tangled around a lattuce. "Be careful climbing!" I loudly whispered.

Three hours later Margie entered my room, the moonlight that shone through the window revealed swollen eyes still glazed with tears.

"I'm not feeling so hot."

"Well I guess not." I sat up and patted next to me. "Come and sit. What did Allen say?"

An unexpected smile stretched from ear to ear.

"He said he wanted to marry me even if I weren't pregnant, that I was the light of his world and that," more tears, "he fell in love with me the day we met outside the drug shop. He told me he'd take care of me forever and that we could have a whole dozen babies if I wanted and..."

"Whoa, slow down, one baby at a time. What about all that shame you were feeling earlier?"

"Oh it's still there, but I can't quite explain it. Allen makes me feel like I can conquer any challenge ahead. This feeling of being in love is empowering!"

We hugged, swaying back and forth, both of us crying tears of joy and tears of the unknown, and for me, a few hopeless tears for the possibility that I might never find what she and Allen had. For the first time in my life, the desire to fall in love entered the empty place in my heart. Maybe I had been too picky.

The following Saturday Mother, Margie and I lingered in the kitchen eagerly awaiting Allen's return from his parents' home in Savannah. He'd gone to explain the situation to them first before he and Margie set off to Atlanta to tell her parents and ask permission to marry.

"He should be here by now." Margie paced circles around the kitchen table, peering out the back door with every lap. "Mrs. Anderson, I think I'm going to be sick."

"Now, now, dear, stop your pacing and sit down. A woman in your condition has to pamper herself."

"But Mother, she hasn't even begun to show."

"Doesn't matter. One of the worst times of pregnancy is in the beginning when you're feeling queasy. I upchucked every day for the first four months with you. You've got to take care of yourself from the get-go. How 'bout I get you a Coke?"

"Yes, that might help."

Margie sat beside me at the kitchen table and placed her head on my shoulder.

"He'll be here soon," I assured her.

As Mother rummaged through a drawer for the bottle opener, she went into another one of the coughing fits she'd been having lately.

"You okay?" I asked

She held a finger up at me and coughed three more deep vibrating times. After a sip of water from the spigot, she quieted down and popped the lid off the Coke. Sitting on the other side of Margie, she gave her a sympathetic squeeze around the shoulders.

"I was eighteen when I had Haley, just a year younger than you. Now surely I don't condone your situation, but if you love each other like you explained to me last week when you and Haley first came to me about this situation, then nothing should stand in the way of your happiness together." She kissed the top of Margie's head. "But do expect your parents to be disappointed at first, and rightfully so. After the initial shock wears off, I'm sure your mother will be making speedy plans for you to wed before you begin to show."

"I hope you're right."

A knock finally came at the back door, and Allen joined us in the kitchen.

Margie stood up, hands pressed to her cheeks. "How did your parents take it?"

"Not good, but better than I expected. Dad likes the idea of him and your father both being in the lumber business. Said something about buying him out." He winked. "No, really he and my mother were relieved to hear it was you."

Margie's nose twitched. "As opposed to whom?"

"You know what I mean, as opposed to any other girl that I've ever brought home. She just knows that your mother will follow proper protocol for all the pre-wedding parties that are always held for the high-society hoopla. I know that sounds shallow, but that kind of stuff is important to her. You know my parents came to adore you after you spent some time during the Christmas holiday at our house."

"They did? Really?"

"Yes. Why my dad has already called about an empty lot in that nice area called Buckhead near where your parents have a home. He said that between him and your father, they'll have access to the materials to build one of the finest houses in the area."

"Atlanta…build a house…near my parents? They don't even know I'm pregnant yet. This is too much at one time." Margie sat back down.

"That's where I want to practice medicine after I graduate." Allen cradled her head in his hands. "Don't you want to be near your family? We can do this. It will all work out, I promise."

Mother began coughing again so badly she had to leave the room.

Allen asked me, "How long has she had that cough?"

"Just this winter, I'm sure it's just a nasty ole cold."

"Make sure she sees her doctor if she's still coughing in a few weeks," he advised.

"She hates going to the doctor. And it costs money, but I'll see what I can do."

Allen helped Margie into her coat, and I walked them out to his car.

"If all goes well I'll be back late tonight," she said. "If I don't come back at all just know that my father probably strapped me to one of his lumber trucks and drove me out of the state of Georgia."

"At least you still have your sense of humor," I laughed, then gave her a farewell hug.

Mrs. Van Buren took down her glasses and smacked her lips. "Julia, after all this talk about brandy I think I need me a little glass. It's downstairs in the living room on the bar. The good stuff's in the crystal decanter. Get yourself one, too, but don't let Isa catch you."

"I'll try my best." I hesitated before going downstairs. "You know, I think I'll call Bruce and tell him I can't help him tonight."

"Good choice," she nodded firmly.

Isa was still cleaning up in the kitchen when I passed. "Just going to make a quick phone call in the living room."

A set of short etched crystal glasses sat clustered around the decanter. I poured her a jigger's worth and myself a little more. After setting them on a narrow sofa table behind the pink velvet loveseat, I flipped open my cell phone and dialed Bruce's number.

"Bruce, it's me, Julia."

"Changed your mind, huh? I figured you'd come around after telling you about the champagne, the chocolate covered strawberries and all that I'd prepared for you tonight."

"No I didn't change my mind. I can't see you tonight or any other night, for that matter. My work here is far too important to even take a second away."

"So I get the brush-off, huh? Getting too high and mighty now that you're gonna have a top-name interview under your belt?"

"No, it's not like that at all. It's this whole adultery, guilt weighing on my conscience thing. I can't do it anymore. It's ripping me to shreds. It's over, Bruce. I would rather have talked about this in person when we got back to Atlanta, but you've pushed me too far. I think it's best if I just shut you out of my mind, especially while I'm here. Getting involved with you was a big mistake."

A long sigh blew over his lips. I heard a cigarette lighter click, followed by strong puffs of nicotine. Very calmly, he said. "A mistake, huh? Something like you slapping me across the face this morning, now that was a mistake."

"I told you I was sorry about that."

"Apology accepted," more puffing noises, "but turning down a guy who has bent over backwards just to please you... now there might be a heftier price to pay for that mistake."

My pulse raced. I tried letting him down in less offensive words. "It would be a bad choice at this point to continue seeing each other."

"Why?"

"This can't ever go anywhere, surely you see that. I've got two kids and a marriage that I might still be able to salvage if you'd just let me go."

"It's not that easy to let something go that I know needs my attention. Now I'll call you tomorrow when you're in a better mood. Hopefully you'll have changed your tune by then and realize that you need me, cause I surely need you, darlin'."

"Yeah, right," I chuckled, trying to figure out another way to get my point across. "I'm sure there are hundreds of girls more appropriate for you out there. But me? You don't need me."

"I'll decide who I do and don't need." An unfamiliar uneasiness surged through his words. "Take my mother, for instance. I haven't needed her since she told me to get lost when I was a kid at one of her damn coke parties in the seventies, and I don't mean Coca-Cola."

"You never told me your mother had a drug problem." At that moment it occurred to me that I knew nothing about his past other then that he'd played baseball for the University of Miami and worked for *The Herald* for a year or two.

"It's not something you needed to know. But here's something you do need to know, no girl walks away from me...I do the walking. I'm not giving up simply because you're too busy or because you think that jackass of a husband deserves you."

"I know he's not perfect, but who the hell is? I know I'm not. When you and I were together that first time, as wrong as it was, I admit it...I couldn't wait to see you again. Darrell didn't want me, or so I thought, but you did. When we think we've failed at something what do we do?"

"Oh please, do tell me."

"We feed the failure with something that'll make us feel better. Addictions aren't always drug-related, and that's what you were to me...a quick fix to make me feel better rather than dealing with the real problem at hand."

"Being addicted to sex with me doesn't sound so bad," he said irritated.

Silence lingered for several seconds.

"Are you still there..."

I unclenched my jaw. "No one was ever meant to get hurt."

"I'm hurtin' all over right now, darlin'. You found me attractive, I found you attractive, no strings attached. What's not to like? I'm not ready to give you up."

"Go pick up some random girl at a bar tonight if you're that hard up, but you can't have me. It's time I reconnect with my husband, no one else. So with that said I'm going to say goodbye."

"You hang up that phone and you'll regret it."

"This'll be the one thing I've done lately that I won't regret."

I flipped my phone shut and reached for the brandies. Mr. Crawly had officially begun to make my skin crawl.

"Isa! You startled me." Her towering frame stood in the doorway that led to the kitchen.

"Brandy for two?"

"How long have you been standing there?"

"Not long." She took one of the glasses and poured half of the amount back into the canister. "Tell Mrs. V she can have this much."

"I'll tell her." To my relief, her issues with the brandy seemed to be her only concern, and I took the glass from her hand and smiled like everything was fine.

Chapter 8

*W*hen I returned upstairs with the brandy Mrs. Van Buren sat snuggly with a chenille blanket draped across her lap, slippered feet propped on the coffee table, wiggling them to a familiar tune...

"Kookaburra sits in the old gum tree..."

I sang back, "Merry, merry king of the bush is he."

She continued... "Laugh Kookaburra, laugh Kookaburra, gay your life must be."

"My Grandma Peg used to sing me that when I was little."

We shared a smile.

"Here's your brandy."

She swirled around the wee bit in the glass. "I see you almost got past the Gestapo. Did she have you pour some out, or did you sip it on the way up?"

"She caught me red-handed and poured it back in the decanter herself." Sipping mine, I said, "I see you're nice and comfy. Was she up here while I was on the phone?"

"Briefly, just to bring my favorite fuzzy slippers. I hope Bruce didn't get his nose bent out of shape because you wouldn't help him tonight."

"No, he's fine with it," I fibbed.

"Good. I'll enjoy my mere sip, and then we'll continue reading."

I sank into the overstuffed chair, hoping Isa hadn't reported anything she may have overheard. Putting focus back to her story, I said, "Sure hope Margie's parents aren't too hard on her about the pregnancy."

Glasses rose back over her green eyes. "We shall see..."

———————————————

Eleven o'clock Saturday night the white-walls of Allen's Studebaker squeaked to a halt in our driveway. Mother and I had waited up, both of us reading by a tarnished candelabra in the living room.

When I turned the knob, the front door flew open with a thud, the smell of rain whirling inside causing our candles to wink. I watched as Margie and Allen raced through a wall of rain from the car to the front porch.

"Terrible spring storm out there," Allen said, pouring off water from the brim of his hat.

Mother rose to her feet and said between coughs, "Thank God ya'll made it. We lost power over an hour ago and have been worried sick. Poor girl, your coat is soaked."

Margie peeled off the coat and handed it to Mother. "We're fine. Allen drove like a turtle, thought we'd never get here."

"I have a family to protect now," he boasted.

"I'll get some towels." I hurried to the linen closet upstairs and returned with a stack of four. "So I see your father didn't drive you across the Georgia state line. That must mean something good, yes?"

Allen wrapped a towel over Margie's head and shoulders before putting one over his own. "And he didn't come after me with a shot gun either, right sweetie?"

"That's right," Margie said, scrubbing her hair with the towel.

"What's that I see twinkling on your wedding finger?" Mother asked.

She posed her hand. "My future husband picked it up from the town jeweler before he came this morning. Isn't it stunning?"

Mother and I took turns delicately touching the brilliant stone set in etched platinum.

I nodded. "So that's why you ran late getting her this morning. What did your mother think about all this?"

Allen spoke before Margie could answer. "Ha! She certainly stopped my pulse today." He beat a fist to his chest. "I knew those dark Italian eyes meant business when she put a red-painted fingernail in my face and said, 'You fail to take care of my baby girl and you will have me to deal with.'"

"Nice impression sweetie-pie, but that's just her way of saying she loves you. She's fine with it and actually excited about being a grandmother since my sister Mary hasn't had a baby yet."

Mother cleared her throat. "So I presume wedding plans are underway?"

"Father is going to talk to our pastor after church tomorrow about a date next month."

"Next month? Golly, that doesn't give you much time to shop for a dress," I said.

Margie's cool damp hands grabbed mine. "That's why I need you to go shopping with me in Atlanta next week. That is, if it's okay with you, Mrs. Anderson, if she spends next weekend at my parents' house."

"Absolutely," Mother said, wedging between the couple, an arm around each of their backs. "This is cause for a toast! Follow me to the kitchen." After coughing half the way there, she reached to the back of a cupboard to the right of the sink and pulled out a bottle of French cognac. "Your father left this behind. I figure it's supposed to be old so it should still be good. It's all I have to toast with."

"May I?" Allen took the bottle and read the label, "Moyet. Why that's a fine spirit, and a little brandy will be good for that cough of yours, too," he said noticing her holding her sides while coughing again.

"Now normally I don't drink, and if you girls feel uncomfortable tasting this I'll pull out a few Cokes."

Margie's eyes caught mine. We bit our lips not to laugh. "No Mother, the brandy will be fine."

"Just a sip for me," Margie said, patting her tummy.

After Allen put a spot in each glass, I raised mine and toasted, "To falling in love."

"And to the birth of a healthy babe," mother added.

"Here, here..."

Chapter Four

The weekend before Allen and Margie's wedding, Mother's illness took a turn downhill. She couldn't get through a sentence without coughing and her appetite didn't amount to that of a bird, yet she still refused to see a doctor. The financial strain combined with fearing the unknown played key roles in her refusal, and I needed to come up with a solution and fast to get her healthy again.

Allen planned to come by that Saturday to help Margie move a few of her things to the small house he'd rented near Mercer's campus where they'd soon make their temporary nest. Considering he was a week away from getting married, and six weeks shy of earning a medical degree, his wits stayed intact. Not even the residency lined up at the newly renamed Emory Crawford Long Hospital in Atlanta nudged his confidence toward arrogance of any kind. Dr. Crawford Long had been the first Georgia physician to use ether anesthesia during surgery back in 1842, and Emory Hospital honored his name by fastening it to their establishment just prior to Allen's residency. The hospital only took graduates at the top of their class.

When Margie telephoned him from the kitchen to confirm a time for him to come help, I quietly interrupted, gesturing the spoon I'd been stirring Mother's chicken broth with like a telephone and mouthing, "I need to talk to him, too."

"Just a minute, Haley wants to speak with you."

"Hello Allen, I wanted you to know that she still refuses to see a doctor and insists that it's just the flu. She's coughing nonstop and has lost her appetite. Can you bring your bag when you come later? Maybe she'll let you examine her."

"She's a stubborn one, eh? I'll cancel tennis and be right over."

Ten minutes later, Allen's knuckles rattled the back door. He came in the kitchen still clad in his tennis clothes—white pants and a cream cotton sweater.

"Shh, come in and set your bag on the table for a minute while I finish preparing Mother's tray. She has no idea I asked you to come. Margie's upstairs still filling up one of her trunks. We're so sad to see her go, but it's for the best. I sat Mother in the chair and ottoman in the study. It's the only spot in the house with a window that catches the morning sun. She's warm to the touch, but says she feels cold. I thought some sunshine might do her some good."

"Has she been sick to her stomach?"

"A few times, but not more than once or twice a day."

"And when did that start?"

"Three days ago."

"Any sign of blood in her vomit?"

"I only saw the vomit yesterday, but nothing red."

"Good. When did you last take her temperature?"

Before I could answer, Mother's meek voice traveled from the study, "Who's there? I hear a man's voice."

Allen grabbed his bag. "It's just me, Allen."

I followed him through the living room, carrying the tray of broth and crackers I'd prepared. We could both see her through the half-open, beveled-glass door to the study. The sunlight bent through slightly opened blinds, casting thick shadowed stripes over Mother's pale face. We entered together, and I placed the tray on Papa's old desk.

"You're here early," she said, eyeing his black bag. "Thought you were helping Margie around lunchtime."

"I wanted to come early and check on you first, Mrs. Anderson. Haley says you've been quite under the weather." Mother burrowed her brow at me. "What's that for?" Her pointer finger poked through a hole in the afghan that covered her, pointing at the bag.

"I'd like to take a look at you if that's alright," he said calmly. "I promise, I don't bite, and everything in my bag is brand new." He pulled out a shiny new stethoscope. "My father gave me some tools of the trade as an early graduation gift. And the best part is I'm not at liberty to charge you yet."

The ends of Mother's mouth turned upward for the first time in days. "Alright, but I'm not moving from this chair."

"Yes, ma'am."

After twenty minutes worth of listening through his stethoscope, rubbing areas on her throat and abdomen, and peeking in her nose, ears and mouth, a diagnosis came to light.

"Now I'm not a certified doctor yet, but what I have learned is fresh in my mind. Your symptoms point toward pneumonia and here's what you've got to promise me to do for the next week to two weeks, or however long it takes to get you better."

She nodded her head in agreement.

"Drink as much clear fluid as you're able to get down," he began; then took the mug of broth from the tray, placing it in her hands. "Don't lift a finger, and when resting, try and keep your upper torso elevated. Now I'm going to run to the pharmacy and get some vitamin C, cough syrup and everything you'll need for Haley to coat your chest with a mustard plaster three times per day; it's good for the respiratory system and will help calm the cough."

I wrinkled my nose when he looked at me. "I've never done anything like that before."

"Not to worry. I'll write down detailed instructions for you, okay?"

"Can I see you a minute out in the living room."

He held a finger up at Mother. "Be right back."

I shut the door to the study and asked Allen to wait a second while I ran upstairs and got Margie. Once the two of them stood in front of me, with great disappointment, I said, "You know with mother in this condition, I'm afraid I'm not going to be able to be in your wedding. I'm worried she won't be better by next Saturday."

Margie put an arm around me. "You should know we understand, Haley. Your mother's health is more important. As much as we'll miss your being there, you're doing the right thing."

The study door squeaked open.

"You can't miss the wedding, Haley." Mother stood there, afghan dangling behind her like a cape. "I'll call your Godmother Sylvie. I know she'll come up if she can. She's always saying she wants an excuse to get near Atlanta so she can shop for more hats."

"Don't be silly, Mother." I guided her back to the chair and sat on the arm. "I'm staying with you."

Margie sat on the edge of the ottoman, across from Mother. "Haley wants to be here and we understand."

"Well, let me at least call Sylvie," Mother said stubbornly. "You shouldn't have to miss that wedding, you hear?"

As much as I tried to talk her out of it, Mother got her way and Sylvie arrived the following Thursday on the six o'clock train. She and Mother had been childhood friends, clinging to each other like a couple of koalas in a photo I'd seen of them at a family picnic, both gripping a daisy in their teeth. Mother turned to her in times of crisis, especially after Papa had left. My grandparents died in a train accident before I was born and Mother was an only child so that left Sylvie.

Terminal station tapped busy with spring travelers, but I knew spotting Sylvie wouldn't be difficult. She had the height of a giraffe with a long neck to go with it, and the hats she wore always had bright feathers adorned to them like a peacock. I always loved her playful sense of fashion and remember wearing those hats when visiting her home in Fort Myers, Florida, shortly after Papa left us. Simply paradise down there where she and my Godfather Ron's home sat nestled along the banks of the Caloosahatchee River.

"Sylvie," I waved after spotting a royal blue floppy brim shadowing her wire-rimmed glasses.

She rushed to me with open arms. "How is she? Is she eating solids yet? Has her fever gone down?"

"She's doing a little better, but still has the fever. I can't thank you enough for coming."

"Let's get back to your house so you can get me settled with instructions, and then you need to get on the road. The bridesmaid luncheon is tomorrow and your mother said she didn't want you to miss a thing. Now don't dawdle, and carry this smaller bag for me, please ma'am."

When we got back to the house, mother had fallen asleep propped up in bed, her face not looking as gaunt as it had a few days before. I sat on the bed and held her hand.

"Thank you mother," I whispered.

Her eyes slit open. "For what?"

"For letting me go. You know if you want me to stay, I can still cancel everything and..."

Her hand squeezed mine and a light shushing sounded from her lips. "Then who would come home Sunday and report back to me about the big event? You're going and that's final," she insisted, looking over my shoulder at Sylvie. "Thanks for coming on such short notice."

Sylvie sat on the other side of the bed and brushed Mother's matted hair from her eyes. "You and me are like family, Joyce. You should have called sooner."

"I didn't know it'd get this bad...thought it was just an ole flu bug."

"You're going to get better and better and don't think anything less, understand?" Sylvie's eyes darted over to me. "Now Haley, you'd better get moving so you don't get to Margie's too late. We'll go over everything I need to know about Joyce's medications down in the kitchen while I make tea, and then off with you." Her fiery silver-streaked red ringlets bounced with command.

Extravagance touched every detail of Margie and Allen's wedding, from the quartet of strings greeting guests inside the stained-glass sanctuary to the yellow and white roses perched about the altar—the dark days of the Depression were slowly fading away. Even the music took a swig of optimism. "Happy Days Are Here Again" sang through radios from coast to coast, including the small one we played in the church's library where we bridesmaids helped Margie get ready for her sashay down the aisle. All plans ran smoothly until about a quarter to five when the bride-to-be turned as white as her dress.

"I never should've eaten Mama's meatballs for lunch," Margie groaned, holding her stomach in front of the restroom mirror.

Lucky for Margie, the church library, where all brides waited with their bridesmaids, had a private bathroom. The four of us—Margie, me and her two sisters, Mary and Melissa, clustered in front of the gold-framed mirror, checking our lipstick and adjusting our head garlands made from white sweetheart roses and baby's breath. None of us thought to take Margie's bellyache serious since she complained often of hormonal-induced nausea, usually pulling through without tossing her cookies. But this time was different.

"I think I'm going to be sick." She knelt down in front of the commode, the dress bustling around her like marshmallow fluff. Looking up at me, she said, "Why can't morning sickness be just in the morning?"

"You don't look so good," I said, watching the color exit her face.

"She looks fine," Melissa said, elbowing me in the side.

"No, Haley's right," Mary said, holding Margie's veil. "Maybe we should wait and put this on at the last minute... just in case."

"In case what?" Melissa asked.

"In case she gets sick," I said. "You don't want spaghetti and meatballs getting caught up in her veil? It'll catch it like a fishing net and dribble all over that beautiful dress."

The silk beaded gown with Juliet sleeves that I'd helped pick out had a shimmery overskirt to hide any sign of a pooch. Our dresses followed a similar pattern, but without the beading and overskirt, and in a warm hue of gold.

Mrs. Harris, Margie's mother, poked her head in the bathroom door.

"I had to hire two seamstresses to help get those dresses looking proper in a month's time, and my baby girl better not get sick on any of them, especially her own. Now clear out of here, all of you, and let me unzip her."

"I want Haley to stay, Mama," Margie insisted.

Mrs. Harris held up a white-gloved palm and added, "Everyone except Haley." She knelt next to her daughter and signaled for me to unzip the dress. "Now if you're going to be sick, do it now Margaret. Don't embarrass the family walking down the aisle."

Margie continued to moan with her head pressed to the rim of the toilet seat. "Leave my dress alone," she barked. "I don't want anyone touching me."

Her mother and I mirrored a shrug at one another. Then I got an idea. "There's a small tablecloth on the teacart out in the hallway," I motioned out the bathroom door. "I can drape it around her like a bib."

"Good idea. Go quickly," she waved.

Mary helped me clear off the silver tea set, and then I yanked it off like a magician, making it back to the bathroom just before the first heave. Mrs. Harris held her hair back while I wedged the tablecloth between the dress and the commode and then tied it around her neck. Within seconds, we all got to see Margie's lunch a second time.

"Feel better?" Mrs. Harris asked.

"One more time," she said, her last word in another heave.

We all winced at the sound.

"That's got to be it," Mrs. Harris said, flushing the toilet.

I plugged my nose. "Can I go now?"

"Yes," Margie whispered, and then blotted her mouth with a piece of toilet paper. "Would someone please find me some peppermints?"

After finding a mint in the bottom of Melissa's purse, I helped touch up Margie's makeup. Mary pinned on the veil at exactly two minutes past five o'clock.

"Like an angel," her mother sang. "Now hurry and line up girls. I've got to run. I heard they just walked Allen's mother down the aisle so I'm next."

Mary quickly handed out bouquets of tightly bound roses, and I pulled Margie aside for a quick moment. "Thanks again for the gift yesterday at the bridesmaid luncheon."

"Your welcome. The pearl pendants look lovely on all of you."

"No, I meant the small bottle of Shalimar you snuck in my purse."

"Since my bottle had to move to another vanity I felt you needed one of your own."

A bride's glow returned to Margie's olive skin, and my eyes glazed with admiration. "You've been like a sister, always encouraging the timid girl in me to be strong. For that I'm grateful."

"You've made a potentially shameful experience anything but...and for that, I'm grateful." We shared a gentle hug, making sure not to crimp our flowers. "I only wish your mother could be here."

"So does she."

Margie and Allen didn't take their honeymoon until a few weeks after his graduation. And though Allen had attended classes for those five weeks after the wedding, Margie reluctantly dropped out and assumed her role as wife and mother-to-be, taking care of their temporary small home near the Mercer campus

June began with Mother back on her feet again. I helped her make up the work she'd missed processing paperwork for future enrollees at Wesleyan. Losing my live-in soul sister proved to be a harsher adjustment than I'd expected and keeping busy at the college kept my mind off of Margie's absence. She and Allen were not due back from their honeymoon on Jekyll Island, a small resort island off Georgia's coast, for a whole month.

By mid-June she'd sent me a postcard picturing the elaborate Jekyll Island Club, a castle-like structure, four to five stories high. It reminded me again of how much I longed to take a trip some day to The Breakers Resort in Palm Beach—perhaps with my future love, if I could ever find one.

The third of July, Mother and I tried keeping cool in the kitchen, sipping lemonade while preparing potato salad for a Fourth of July picnic given by the Baker family up the street—those are the folks whose mailbox I almost hit when Margie told me about the male genitalia for the first time.

Their honeymoon had supposedly ended the last day of June, and Margie promised to call when they returned to Atlanta.

"Two days late for a simple phone call," I complained to Mother while chopping celery stalks. "She never breaks a promise."

"She'll call soon," Mother said, dicing red potatoes. "I'm sure she had plenty to do when she returned since they'd just moved all those boxes from the small Mercer house into her parent's guest house days before leaving for Jekyll Island. It's a shame she had to set up house twice. A pregnant woman having to go through all that combined with the stress that comes with building a brand new home has every right to be exhausted. Did she tell you when the house in Buckhead would be completed?"

"Next year, I think. Poor thing has to be in that guest house beside her parents with no privacy. Why I'd go crazy if I had..." I continued chopping right to the end of my finger. "God bless America!"

"Gracious child, what else is eating you?"

Blood from my index finger dripped to the chopping block. Mother grabbed my hand and ran it under the faucet like she'd done when I was a child.

"You need a bandage." She wrapped part of the kitchen towel around my finger. "Hold this tight while I get one from the pantry."

The sting in my finger complimented my mood, not sure if the latter came from a feeling of anger or sadness about Margie's absence or about my own fears of never finding a man to love.

"Why so glum, Haley...it's just a cut finger." Mother took the towel off and applied a dab of iodine with a cotton ball. "Remember when you cut your finger with the scissors making Papa a Valentine? You must have been eight or nine."

"Yes, I remember," though I didn't want to. "I thought it'd never stop bleeding."

"But it did." She applied pressure to the cut after securing the bandage and put a hand on my shoulder. "Wounds do heal, you know. A scar may remain, but life has to go on."

The noonday sun shining through the kitchen window brought out the gray in her hair, but other than the gray, Mother's look had stayed almost the same as the day Papa had left—a neat bun spun on the back of her small head, transparent hazel eyes, a favorite feature that I'd inherited, and always floral dotted dresses.

"Why did he leave? And please answer me woman to woman, not mother to child."

She sighed as she looked at my finger. "Sometimes there is more love on one side of the scale. I'm afraid he just didn't love me anymore. I told myself for years that it was because of the miscarriages...you know how he wanted a big family. But I knew deep inside that his love for me had run dry."

"For me, too?"

Mother wrapped me in her arms. "No, never for you."

"Then why doesn't he try to come and see me. A card at birthdays and Christmas, along with the money he's sent over the years isn't enough if you love someone."

"It's me he's afraid of seeing. Maybe when you're off on your own he'll come around. But you can't let what happened to me make you afraid of dating. You'll be twenty before we know it and at an age when most have found their mate. Just remember not to fall too hard so you won't get hurt like I did."

I shook my head in agreement.

"That's my angel. You know why I named you Haley, don't you?"

I remembered, but knew how she loved to tell the story. "No, why did you name me Haley?"

She sandwiched my hand between her cool fingers. "The day you were born, in our old apartment before your papa had built this house, the morning sun had just risen, and it reached brightly through the window as the midwife held you up. Rings of light circled around your little head, and I said, 'Why she's an angel from God, halo and all,' and that's how I decided on Haley."

"That's a nice story Mother, but I'm still upset about Margie."

"Why don't you go pick me some fresh parsley from the herb garden off the side of the house? It'll make for nice garnish for our potato salad and give you a chance to unwind."

I walked out the back door, letting the screen slam behind me. "Destined to be an old maid, I guess," I said under my breath.

The parsley growing against the backdrop of red bricks wilted like my mood. Picking enough to satisfy Mother, I moped across the fresh-cut lawn up to the front porch where I checked the mailbox, hopeful that maybe Margie had sent another postcard. As I opened the lid, a car pulled in our driveway. To my surprise, Margie sat perched behind the wheel of a brand new white Buick almost as big as Mother's blue Chrysler.

"Margie!" I waved, fisting a bouquet of parsley. "Is that yours?" I asked, approaching the car. Oddly, she didn't share my enthusiasm. The red hat she wore tilted more than usual over puffy eyes that matched. "My goodness, what's the matter?"

She got out of the car and extended her arms. "It's the baby, Haley. I lost the baby." Her head fell to my shoulder and sobs moaned from her chest in a painful rhythm. "I just couldn't tell you over the phone."

"I understand. Let's get you in the house." I kept my arm firm around her waist and guided her to the back door. Mother saw us coming through the kitchen window and swung open the screen door.

"Dear God child, what happened?"

"She lost the baby."

"You poor dear. Quick Haley, sit her here." Mother pulled a chair from the kitchen table and then sat beside her, handing her a box of tissues. "When did this happen?"

"Five days ago," she answered, catching her breath, "while we were still at the hotel on Jekyll Island. Thank goodness my husband is a doctor because you can only get to the mainland by ferry. The cramping was unbearable."

"I remember well, and I hate that you had to go through it," Mother said. "After my second miscarriage, Pastor Davis came by the house to pray with me and Haley's father. He said, 'Maybe God needed another babe for his army of angels.' That idea stayed with me and got me through the worst of it. But I understand the loss you feel."

I knelt down, eye to eye with Margie. "You can try again when you're ready."

"I wanted this baby so badly, everything's in order...the marriage, a new house underway, but no baby to go with it. I couldn't go back to school even if I tried. I've already been obligated to the social scene of Buckhead, expected to be involved in so many clubs and social functions that there'd be no time for studying. I'm Allen's wife now, that's all."

"Those are the hormones talking through those tears," Mother said, taking her hand. "You'll tap out soon and when you do, life will begin to look bright again. Believe me, I know."

"You're still happy about marrying Allen aren't you?" I asked

Her other hand dropped away from her eyes, "Without a doubt."

"Think about that," I said, removing her red hat and stroking her disheveled hair. "You have a natural instinct for nurturing others, surely that will be given to a baby of your own someday soon."

She sniffled again. "That's sweet, Haley. You always know what to say when I'm in a state." A long sigh followed by one last blow of the nose. "Look at me, I'm a mess. Let me freshen up, and then I want to help with whatever it is ya'll are fixing over there."

"That's our girl," Mother said. "Keeping busy will be good for you right now."

Margie pointed at the large red bowl on the counter. "What is that anyway?"

"Potato salad," Mother answered.

"For tomorrow?"

"Yes," I said. "Would you like to join us? It's over at the Bakers' house."

"Can't, we're already obligated to see fireworks at the country club with Allen's parents. They're coming up from Savannah today and are staying in the main house with my parents. I hope they all get along okay."

"I'm sure they will," Mother said, "with both your fathers sharing the same business interests and all. Can you stay long?"

"For half the day. If you're almost finished with the potato salad, I'd really like to bake something if that's alright with you. It'll clear my head. I've got a new red-velvet cake recipe that I want to try out and you can take it with you tomorrow. Tell them it's a little red for the red, white and blue from their old neighbor Margie."

"Only if we get to drive to the market for the ingredients in that snazzy new car of yours," I said, feeling better, too. My self-inflicted pity seemed to vanish now that Margie needed me.

"Maybe I'll even let you take the wheel."

"That'd be swell, let's go!"

"Excuse me, Mrs. Van Buren..."

"Yes, dear?"

"Were you expecting anyone?"

"No..."

We both watched headlights creep up the driveway.

"Are you sure Mr. Crawly knew not to come for you this evening?"

"Pretty sure..."

As we heard a car door shut out in the darkness, a bitter taste washed over my tongue.

Chapter 9

Minutes went by. No knock at the front door, no ringing of the doorbell.

"Surely Isa hears that someone's here," Mrs. Van Buren said. "She's got the ears of a canine."

"Want me to go check?" I asked, my heart beating double-time.

"No, no, I'm sure she'll take care of it." Distorted hands formed a callout around her heart-shaped mouth. "Isa!" She tilted her ear toward the staircase, waiting for an answer.

"Knock, knock," a man's voice echoed up the staircase.

"Heavens to Betsy! Don't you know I don't like it when you come through the back door unannounced?"

Sheer relief washed over me when I saw Stephen's face.

"Hope I'm not intruding," he said, "but I saw the light on and figured it'd be okay to come by and say hello, make sure the fish fry is still on for tomorrow night at my place."

"Coming by just to say hello, are you?" Mrs. Van Buren took down her glasses and placed a hand on her hip, "you ole' fool, you're checking up on me, aren't you?"

"Guilty as charged." He sat down next to her and tapped her knee. "Did you take your medicine?"

"Yes sir, with a swig of brandy. Want some?"

He shook his head and rolled his eyes. "I had my quota for the night with a stiff scotch Marty fixed after our nine holes this afternoon. We played cards at his condo from five till..." he looked at his watch, "my God, is it already nine-thirty? Shouldn't you be getting to bed young lady."

"Hogwash, we just got cooking, didn't we Julia?"

"Yes ma'am. Mrs. Van Buren was reading more of her book."

He held up a hand. "Say no more, I'll be out of your hair in a jiff. She's never read any of it to me, but I have a pretty good idea what the gist of the story entails."

The couple exchanged a giddy glance. "On my way up, I noticed a loose board where the stairs meet the kitchen. Want me to fix that?"

"You'll throw your back out."

"Says you." He leaned over and kissed her good cheek. "I'll secure it in the next day or two. Remember, I'll be at the first assembly of golf in the morning so it'll just be you ladies at church tomorrow. No need to get up, Julia. I showed myself in, and I can show myself out. By the way, after I let myself in the back door, Isa was nowhere to be found, but I heard snoring coming from the living room. She's slouched down in the loveseat with an issue of *Woman's Day* lying across her chest. Want me to wake her?"

"Let her rest," Mrs. Van Buren said. "She's been on her feet most of the day."

"Alrighty then, till tomorrow." He tipped his white golf cap.

"Goodnight dear," she waved as he descended down the stairs.

"Mind if I ask something personal about you and Stephen?"

"Depends on what it is."

"Why doesn't he live here with you?"

"Hmm," she twisted her lips, "we're both set in our ways, I suppose. Having him just around the bend is comforting enough, and not having to answer to nosey neighbors is a plus." She fiddled with the empty brandy glass for a moment. "Mind if I ask *you* something personal?"

"Me? Alright, I guess."

"Did you really plan to help Mr. Crawly with an article tonight?"

When I looked up, our eyes locked and I couldn't lie to her. "No ma'am." I turned and put my notepad and pen on the coffee table, and then leaned back, placing a throw pillow in my lap. I twirled the green tassels on its corners.

"And your original plans with him were to what…have a social visit of sorts?"

The lump in my throat swelled, and I could feel a dull pain creeping up my face. "If I tell you something else personal, will you promise not to let it affect our business relationship?"

"I won't know if I can promise till you tell me what it is, but if there's something you need to get off your chest, it won't go past this room."

A cleansing breath passed through my lungs. "A short time ago, Bruce was more than just my colleague."

"Really... and?"

"That doesn't surprise you?"

"Let's just say I had a healthy hunch; and I wouldn't be honest without getting something off of my chest."

I shot her a puzzled look. "Like what?"

"While you were in the shower, I called the paper in Atlanta. I can never be too careful about an unannounced reporter coming by the house."

"You were able to get a hold of someone after hours on a Saturday?"

"You know how most businesses have similar extension numbers in numeric order...like 215, 216 and so on?"

"Yes."

"The business card you gave me has your extension as 3181, so I dialed 3182 and 3183 and kept going until someone finally answered at 3189. I figured I was bound to get a hold of some reporter there on a Saturday. After all, the news never stops."

"Who did you talk to?"

"Don't fret, dear, I spoke with a gal who writes for the Saturday real estate section. I didn't give away my identity or yours and instead told her a little white lie saying that I was calling on behalf of the seniors for softball association, and that I needed to speak with a Mr. Bruce Crawly. When she said he wasn't available, I said, 'He's on assignment?' and she said, 'no, I believe he took a few days off.'"

"So he lied to me."

"It does look like he came down here for other reasons."

Nervous fingers rubbed throbbing temples, and the lump in my throat grew larger. "Please don't let this change your mind about the interview. I never meant to bring my personal life down with me. In fact, I vowed to get my life back on track with this trip leading the way." The black dress I wore became dotted with tears, and as I began to wipe my eyes on the sleeves, Mrs. Van Buren handed me her turquoise scarf.

"Go ahead and blow, that's what washing machines are for. Do you want to talk about it? Isa says I'm a great listener."

"I'm so ashamed. Here I am the do-gooder, advice giver of a column that exemplifies keeping the family together along with…"

"Along with what…being human? We all do things we're not proud of, Julia, but they usually make us stronger once we overcome the regret."

An intense stare followed.

She asked again. "So do you want to talk about it or not?"

"Where do I even start?"

"At the beginning."

Surprisingly, every guilt-stricken detail came off my tongue, and she listened intently, with real compassion.

"Do you feel like you need to tell your husband?"

"I don't know. Bruce has me worried though, like if I don't keep seeing him he's going to do something about it. I just don't know what that something is. Telling Darrell would be the hardest thing I've ever done. But if he's going to find out about this, I'd rather it be from me."

"Do you feel threatened by Mr. Crawly?"

"No, just uneasy."

"Yes, he makes me a bit uneasy, too. That's why I hope you don't mind that I ran a search on him earlier this evening."

"A search? What kind of search?"

"I may have said I was old-fashioned when it came to correspondence via computers, but it doesn't mean I don't know how to use one." Supporting herself with the cane and the arm of the sofa, she slowly rose up and held out her hand. "Come with me. I did some snooping of my own. I'm not usually one to nose around in other people's affairs, quite literally, but the moment Mr. Crawly walked in this house, I smelled a skunk." She pointed her cane at the computer. "Let's fire her up. There's something I found that you might be interested in. I may not be able to raft over the waves anymore, but I can certainly surf the net."

"When did you have time to do this search?"

"Plenty of time while you were downstairs helping Isa get dinner ready. Now pull up that side chair against the wall, and I'll show you what I found."

Light from the computer bounced off her wrinkled face as it loaded. "Here," she tapped the glass, "read this."

"An article from the *Miami Hurricane*? Isn't that the University's paper?"

"Yes."

The article had a team headshot of a younger Bruce with a goatee, wearing a baseball cap.

(CAMPUS REPORT) - Outfielder Bruce Crawly is suspended for the second time from Hurricane base-

ball after testing positive for cocaine during one of the athletic department's random drug tests.

Professional contracts that were in the works for this senior hopeful and Jacksonville native are now on hold until further notice.

Head coach Bob Green said, "He'd come a long way since this happened the first time his freshman year. We're all very disappointed that such a charismatic team-player struck out."

His father, Boca Raton real estate tycoon Luke Crawly, refused to comment on the matter. We did reach his mother, former sixties fashion model Blair Crawly, who commented from the Jacksonville Rehabilitation Center for the Chemically Dependant (JRCCD) saying, "I knew he'd never make it to the pros."

"As for Luke Crawly, I'd heard of him before, and recently, too. My curiosity got the best of me, and I did a search on him as well. The first thing I came across was a wedding announcement in the Society section of the *Boca Raton News* that ran in November of 1997, picturing him and his young bride, probably Bruce's age."

"Hmm, traded in the older model for a newer one; that would've been about the same time Bruce got kicked off the baseball team."

"Well let's look back at the university article and see if it gives us a specific date."

"There," I pointed. "March 3, 1998."

"Kids turning to drugs after a divorce can unfortunately go hand in hand. And maybe that's what sent his mother off the deep end and to a rehab center during that period of time. Who knows?"

I shifted the chair closer to Mrs. Van Buren. "But I don't get why he plays the struggling-reporter card? His mother must still get a chunky alimony topped with her past modeling earnings, and his dad is obviously loaded."

"Maybe his mom blows her wad on drugs or whatever makes her feel better for being, as you said, traded in. I don't recall her name from fashion magazines years ago so she must have strictly done runway shows or catalog work. Back then, models didn't nearly make what the supermodels bring in today. And perhaps his dad cut him off for some reason."

After keying in some words, another article came up. "This is the one I wanted you to see. It's dated a month ago from the Miami *Harold*."

> *MIAMI — Federal law enforcement agents made a sweep of arrests in Miami, Boca Raton and Atlanta after an eight-month investigation into one of the South's most sought-after drug rings.*
>
> *Forty-five men and women were arrested yesterday, several of which were distinguished members of their communities...*

"Oh yeah, I remember this story buzzing about the office, but I've been so busy with my column and the twins, I barely get a chance to see the evening news anymore let alone read the whole paper."

"Go on to the part about Luke Crawly," she said, handing me the mouse so I could scroll down the article.

> *After a warrant had been issued, Luke Crawly, vice-president and co-founder of DBI Communities, Boca Raton's premier builder of luxury high-rise golf communities, was arrested at his penthouse located at 7400 North Ocean Boulevard, for possession of one kilogram of cocaine. Though only a small amount of cocaine was found on the premises, Crawly is thought to be the ringleader of the operation which is said to have been active for at least six years, putting hundreds of pounds of cocaine on the streets worth millions.*
>
> *If convicted of possession with intent to distribute, Crawly could face a minimum of ten years in federal prison.*

"And the latest article I found on his dad ran just days after this one and stated that he'd posted one-million dollars bail and is awaiting trial."

"And I'll just bet he's still got some unfinished business to do."

Mrs. Van Buren added, "Business that his son may be helping him with. I would have to guess that if this man has dozens of empty condo units, what better place to hide inventory. But with all the red tape the feds would have to go through to get warrants for each of those properties, my guess is it could be weeks, maybe months before they'd all be searched." Mrs. Van Buren shook her head. "If Luke Crawly is as powerful as the media portrays him to be, there's no telling what connections he has."

"I have a feeling that Bruce is going to see more than just friends on the east coast."

"What do you mean? Did he say he was going to Boca Raton?"

"No, but he did say he planned to visit college friends in Miami which is just a few miles south of Boca. You were right when you said you smelled a skunk."

"That's enough Nancy Drew for one night," she said, shutting down the computer. "We'd better get to sleep if we're going to make it to church on time in the morning. We'll get back to my manuscript after the service."

I helped her to the elevator. "Meet you downstairs."

While I walked down the stairs, the seriousness of the situation set in. Could Bruce really be involved in something so serious? He'd come to work for the paper out of nowhere six months ago. That would have been soon after the feds had begun their investigation. Maybe he was somehow involved before moving to Atlanta, or even worse, maybe he was the distributor in Atlanta. But how could he have kept all this camouflaged from the feds? The elevator opened. "I was thinking while you were in there and…"

"Maybe Bruce has come down here strictly to move product for his dad?"

"Surely if he's under suspicion, agents have got to be watching him closely." My mouth dropped open.

"What is it, dear?"

"You don't think any of their surveillance equipment could've picked up me and Bruce's interactions or conversations do you?"

"Let's tackle one mountain at a time. Shut your mind off so you can get some sleep. You'll drive yourself crazy thinking up every scenario possible. Right now you should be thinking about patching things up with your husband." She looked at the floor and shook her head. "Maybe I shouldn't have showed you what I found."

"No, I'm glad you did." I stuck my head around the corner to look in living room. "Looks like Isa is still sleeping. Want me to wake her?"

"Yes please, gently though. She startles easily. Why don't you call your husband before bed? It'll make you feel better."

"But it's late."

"Trust me when I say he won't care."

"You're right, goodnight."

After giving Isa a soft nudge of the shoulder, I headed upstairs.

I plopped down on the bed with my cell phone in hand, hesitant to dial, and watched the ceiling fan spin, ticking with every slow turn. Fear began to settle within me, a fear of the unknown about Bruce, and a fear as to whether Darrell was having an affair of his own. How was I supposed to even begin to tell him about my affair? Quickly, I dialed. His voice cracked when he answered.

"Did I wake you?"

"That's okay, Jules, I was barely asleep."

"You haven't called me Jules in a while."

"Yeah, well I miss you."

"How was pizza with the soccer team, crazy?"

"I wouldn't say crazy, but very excited that they won."

"Wish I could've been there."

"Me too."

I paused and pictured him in our bed, sitting up on his elbow, sandy brown hair in a tousle.

"Your mom mentioned something about me coming down there when you're finished with the interview, said she'd take care of the twins. What do you think about that?"

"She did, huh? Did she say anything else?"

"No. Should she have...Julia, are you still there?"

"Sorry, I was thinking."

"About what?"

"About how we do need some time together. Do you know we haven't made love in almost four months? We've got to start making time for each other."

"I know. God, Julia. Our lives have been slammed with minute-by-minute schedules. That's why I want to come down there...no cell phones, no e-mails, no carpools, no classes. We still have two rain checks to make up...one from the night before you left, and the other from the night when I had to get midterms graded. It was hard as hell blocking you out of my mind that night. After you slammed the office door and stormed off to bed, I couldn't focus on anything except how good you looked in that red... what was that, a thong?"

"Oh my God, a compliment?"

"Cut the sarcasm, you know I still think you're sexy. But you've got to understand the struggle I go through on a daily basis, making sure I can be a good provider and father and husband."

"You are a wonderful husband, Darrell, but I need you as a lover, too. I miss that part of our lives. It's the one thing that separates our relationship from all others. And I don't just mean the sex, it's the caressing and the hugging and even the fun-loving flirtations that used to go on between us. I've got to have that intimacy with you—it's part of what breathes life into our marriage; and life into me."

He said nothing long enough to make me worry. "Darrell?"

"You can count on me being there by Wednesday," he said to my surprise. "I'll make the arrangements and call you before I come."

"But the college will never let you have that many days off with such short notice."

"They'll live. Any ideas on where we'll stay?"

"It doesn't matter. We just need to fix what's broken."

Chapter 10

Early Sunday morning the squawk of a seagull perched at the half-open window served as my wake-up. His gray and white tail feathers brushed back and forth against the screen, making a zipping sound until my body rose. We both froze, his round black eyes observing me, sizing me up. His head tilted, another squawk shrilled out, and then he flew away.

My dry mouth headed to the bathroom where the water gave off a slight sulfur odor. As I cupped my hands under the faucet and brought a sip to my lips, Darrell's face came to mind—long and narrow, clean shaven, wavy long bangs pushed over his right brow. I missed his warm amber gaze. The cool water refreshed me, but the reflection in the mirror was anything but fresh. Tired dishonest eyes stared back. Splashing my cheeks, eyes and nose, I tried to rub off the shame. The confession that lied ahead deemed certain to burst the bubble of our happily married world as well as my picture-perfect life. The time had come to tell him.

After hanging up with Darrell the night before, I'd fallen right to sleep in the black drawstring dress. A curled-up impression, a letter "C", lay embossed atop the yellow bedspread...confessions. I never slept without covers; I never slept fully clothed; I never thought I'd cheat on my husband. The real me still hid somewhere beneath my skin and finding her became my quest. That particular morning marked the beginning to the end of the worst part of me.

Out in the sunroom the sliding glass doors had already been opened, and on top of the coffee table Isa had left a wicker tray with a cup of fruit, a few sticky buns and a carafe of coffee. A note wedged under the mug read:

> *Mrs. V had a rough night so I'll be a while*
> *getting her ready for church. Help yourself and enjoy*
> *the peace outside this sunny morning. We'll be leav-*
> *ing at 9:15.*
>
> *Isa*

With pleasure, I did as told and took in the crisp morning air while rocking and sipping hazelnut coffee. The invigorating breeze woke up my senses and kept my thinking sharp. *Tell Darrell everything, suck up the consequences like a big girl, hope we can mend what's torn, and move on.* Yes, it was a good plan, and his arrival Wednesday couldn't come soon enough.

By the time the mug ran dry, the sun had risen high enough over the cottage to break free over the gulf, rays dancing across peaks of gentle waves that sparkled like a million diamonds. I wanted to reach out and scoop up some of that magnificent sparkle and pour it back into my marriage. But that would have been too easy.

During the short ride to church, the three of us chatted about two otters we saw splashing about in the surf.

"What a rare sight to see them in the gulf," Mrs. Van Buren said. "They usually stay on the sound-side of the island. I wonder if they're a couple. Some mate for life, you know."

"How simple," I said.

"What's that?"

"Animals instinctively knowing which mate compliments them best. They look similar to the furry river otters the boys and I saw while camping along the Chattanooga last summer. Cute, aren't they?"

"Indeed."

Minutes later the crushed-shell driveway to the Chapel by the Sea came into view. White dust kicked up behind the minivan while it jogged the small distance to the parking lot, cars already filling the spaces closest to the chapel entrance.

"Pastor George might have standing room only today," Mrs. Van Buren said, waving to a purple-haired woman getting out of a green Mercedes. "That's Dottie Hart...figures she'd take the last handicapped space. Our snowbird friends usually stay until Easter and as much as I love them, boy I can't wait until they head north so the island thins out again." She leaned up and tapped Isa's shoulder. "You might want to drop us up front, then go park by the cemetery over there." She pointed behind and to our left where a few weathered headstones stood partially hidden by seagrape shrubs.

Isa pulled up to the front door where two ushers with gardenia-pinned lapels greeted folks.

"I'll help with the wheelchair," I said, sliding open the minivan door.

Isa pushed a button on the dash, and the hatch slowly popped open. "Are you sure you can get that thing opened by yourself?" She looked back at me while I struggled to slide the thing to the ground.

"My Grandpa Ashton used a chair after he broke his fibula playing tennis, and I used to help out when he'd come for Sunday supper, he refused to sit at the dinner table in it." With a grunt, I pulled the arms outward until it snapped into position. "There, good to go."

Isa got out and rolled it to Mrs. Van Buren. "Steady now," she advised, hovering over her every move. "Don't be in a hurry. You know when the arthritis acts up in your hips you really must take it easy, moving one inch at a time. Too much too soon and you'll pull something or lose your balance and fall. We certainly don't need a fall..."

"Yes, yes, Isa, I know. Why on earth did I have to sleep on my side all night long?"

"You'll be out of the wheelchair by dinner if you quit trying to do everything yourself. Sometimes you need to let me do for you and now is one of those times. We've already been through this once this morning."

After Mrs. Van Buren settled in, she noted, "Ooh, I forgot my purse."

"You look very put together this morning," I said, handing her the red clutch bag that matched her scarf and houndstooth dress.

"Why thank you, dear. It takes some extra effort, but I always like to look presentable for church."

Isa brushed some lint off Mrs. Van Buren's shoulder and straightened her pearls.

"Enough, Isa. Now if you don't hurry and go park the van I'm going to get up and walk into that church by myself."

Isa and I exchanged a sympathetic look, and after she drove off, Mrs. Van Buren said, "She knows I love her."

"I didn't notice the cemetery when Stephen drove us by yesterday. I thought the white lattice fencing separated the chapel from another property."

"You'd miss it if you didn't know where to look. It's the only one on the island."

A stone's throw beyond the fence a bench rested in the center of the cemetery, and a wooden cross the height of a man stood just beyond that, leaning toward us. Hundreds of storms off the gulf must have pushed it so, but it still stood strong, determined to keep peace for those sleeping.

"Any original settlers buried there?"

"The oldest are from the late eighteen-hundreds...mostly fruit farmers and fishermen. Before it became a cemetery, a man named Binder owned part of the land. And in 1900, a woman named Ann Brainard bought it from him, but died a year later of tetanus. Ms. Brainard's parents buried her there and later bought the area surrounding her grave donating it to the islanders to forever be used as a cemetery where only locals could be buried. There are just under a hundred graves there now; the last burial a few years ago. Take me over after the service and we'll take a look around."

When Isa joined us, an usher handed her a church bulletin, then hesitated.

"So the rumors must be true," said one usher whose hair had receded to two small silver patches above his ears. "This must be your lovely niece, and I can certainly see some family resemblance in those bright green eyes you both have."

"Yes, thanks Charles," Mrs. Van Buren casually accepted as the two ushers helped Isa get the wheelchair up the single step to the entrance.

"And your name, ma'am?" he asked, moving his grip from the chair toward my hand for a shake.

"Julia Pa..."

"That's all for now, Charles," Mrs. Van Buren said, "must get in so I can get my seat up front. We can chitchat some other time." She motioned her hand forward so Isa would push her inside.

Trailing in behind them, I stopped at the entrance for a few seconds. The tranquil hues of white and robin's-egg blue instantly calmed my spirit. *A small slice of Heaven on Earth*, I thought...*quiet, peaceful*. Once Isa got Mrs. Van Buren situated we filed in beside her, sitting front and center under the pulpit.

Arched windows on both sides of the lily-lined altar moved sunlight across the congregation while a single ceiling fan swirled overhead. When I looked over my shoulder and observed the cozy group of locals and snowbirds, glowing faces smiled and nodded politely, curious eyes shifting between me and Mrs. Van Buren.

After reciting a series of Psalms and prayers, Pastor George approached the pulpit, his robe as white as his hair. Comforting nonjudgmental eyes met mine first, a welcoming glance for an achy soul. He then lifted them to the rest of the congregation before perching his bifocals upon his nose.

"Today, let us explore the sinful nature," he began, gripping the sides of the pulpit, "something we as human beings cannot avoid. Open with me to Galatians chapter five, verse seventeen...'For the desires of the flesh are against the Spirit, and the desires of the Spirit are against the flesh; for these are opposed to each other, to prevent you from doing what you would.'" The bass of his raspy lecture resonated off the four white walls, penetrating my conscience. He continued, "We've all felt this conflict, haven't we?"

The congregation mumbled in agreement.

"It is when we don't feel that conflict that something is out of sync with our faith."

As he went on, a personal sermon continued in my thoughts about how conflict certainly existed within me. But God and prayer and faith combined wouldn't lighten the remorse. Only forgiveness, both my own and Darrell's could do that, and even then, a faint memory of Bruce would remain swept under the rug in my mind, hidden from everyone but me.

Since I was old enough to reason, I truly believed that God punished me in his own mysterious way for my wrongdoings. Like that time I stole a piece of red candy from a Pak-A-Sak. Laced with hot cinnamon, it set my mouth on fire for at least an hour—small punishment for a small crime. This time an hour's worth of burned-up taste buds wouldn't suffice, Bruce being a much bigger and hotter piece of candy. Letting God down scared me, and I feared He'd retaliate as a form of discipline.

The conclusion to the sermon shed a hint of light on an answer. Pastor George read something from the Book of Peter saying that God said we should suffer for *a little while* for our sins if we are truly sorry. Remorse certainly ran through my veins, though a little while in God's time might be a lifetime on my clock—I hoped not.

For some inexplicable reason, until my feet landed on Captiva Island, the affair hadn't seemed so bad—a replenishment of self-worth if you will. But on that particular Sunday, the message about desires conflicting with the spirit made me realize that it was my own spirit that needed replenishing, not my fleshy desire. Bruce had been a substitute for something much bigger that needed filling. I'm sure Galatians, chapter five, verse seventeen had flowed through my ears at one time or another, but this time my thirsty soul lapped it up.

After the service we strolled toward the cemetery, Isa stopping every few feet to realign the wheelchair in the white shells. When we reached the lattice gate, she pulled the keys from her purse.

"If you don't mind, I'll wait in the van. Graveyards give me the heebie jeebies."

"Yes, go on. Silly girl," Mrs. Van Buren said, waving over her shoulder. "She's very superstitious like her mother was. Every time she spills salt she throws some over her left shoulder, and she knocks on wood and avoids the number thirteen...the list goes on. If you would, be a dear and park me over by the little wooden bench so we can sit a spell."

The wheels took a bumpy ride over a highway of roots through the cemetery until safely landing beside the bench. Arms of a banyan tree dangled down like ropes from a Tarzan movie, some tickling my back. After sitting, my eyes settled on the three headstones before us, the two smaller ones catching my attention first.

"Twins?"

Mrs. Van Buren pulled up her glasses and squinted. "Born April of 1898 and died May of the same year."

"Their mother must've been heartbroken," I gasped.

"And their father, too. To lose a child is like losing part of you. You're always searching for a way to get them back, especially those mothers who have to give up their babies. The hurt never ends."

Pointing to the bigger headstone, I said, "The parents?"

"Yes," she confirmed. "Both lived a full life for those days, the husband made it to seventy-three and his wife, sixty-seven."

"That's what I want," I said, pointing to the couple's headstone.

"You want yours made of granite?"

"No." I knelt down, the headstones three feet away from us, and ran my fingers across the chiseled letters. "She died just twenty days after he did. Think of how much she must've loved him. To die of a broken heart. I want to love like that again."

"You will, Julia." She took down her glasses and placed a hand on my shoulder. Filtered sun set her green eyes aglow, offering a tenderness as familiar as my own mother's. "You want to know what I think?"

"What?"

"Your love for your husband has been overlooked, but not lost. I've seen friends over the years give up too easily. The courts make divorce so simple now, like getting a driver's license, it's just another state-issued document. I think couples forget that keeping a healthy marriage takes effort from both sides. Give eighty percent and only expect twenty back, those are the relationships that last. Passion and love ride together on a rollercoaster, occasionally peaking together from time to time. It's when the love dies that a relationship grows hopeless. You can always rekindle the passion. Hang on to that love you have for Darrell. Nourish it, and I promise you'll see some passion come back as long as he works at it, too."

"I do love him, but the zest in our love-life is almost non-existent."

"Ah, you said almost…there's hope for you yet. Nourish it, dear…eighty, twenty."

"What about what Pastor George said this morning, about suffering for a little while for our sins. Do you feel like you've had to suffer for your affair with Stephen?"

"Good Lord yes, for decades. But over the years, the suffering has slowly dwindled to a tolerable ache."

I patted her knobby hand still resting on my shoulder. "How long is a little while for me? I hope not decades."

She fiddled with her pearls and laughed. "What happened to me doesn't come close to this mere hiccup in your life. You have the means to get back on track. Henry died and the circumstances were far different. Now let's get moving back toward the parking lot. Isa's waiting."

As I opened the gate and pushed her through, she added one more comment that made me worry…

"You didn't take a life."

Once to Mrs. Van Buren's driveway, a silver SUV sat parked near the front steps, and Bruce rocked in one of the four chairs up on the front porch, casually puffing a cigarette, a potted plant of some sort resting beside his alligator boots.

Mrs. Van Buren tapped my shoulder. "Pardon the expression, but you picked a ballsy one, dear; uninvited twice in twenty-four hours."

"Yes, quite ballsy" I said, trying like hell not to hyperventilate.

"It's okay, Julia," Isa said, eyeing me in the rear view mirror. "Mrs. Van Buren briefed me of the situation while I got her ready this morning."

"I tell Isa everything," Mrs. Van Buren told me. "Don't worry, dear, she can keep a secret."

"Do you want me to go on around to the carport or stop up front?" Isa asked.

Mrs. Van Buren then looked at me. "What would you like to do?"

"Just drop me by the front steps," I said. "For whatever reason he's here, I'll get rid of him quickly. Should I ask him to move his truck so you can get by?"

The driveway curved around the front of the cottage before jutting back where the carport connected to the house.

"No," Isa said, "there's enough room to get around him. I'll just get a wheel or two in the grass is all."

"Isa and I will sit here for a minute first to make sure everything's alright. I'll roll my window down so I can say hello to the scoundrel."

When I opened the door to get out, Mrs. Van Buren grabbed my shoulder.

"One more thing," she whispered.

"Yes?"

"Keep your composure in line, and don't mention anything about the articles I showed you."

"Yes ma'am."

Clinching sweaty fists, I walked toward the steps, his eyes penetrating my body.

"What brings you all the way out here again, and why didn't you call first?" I asked with half a smile, nervously tucking a loose piece of hair behind my ear.

He stopped rocking and stubbed out the cigarette on the sole of his shiny boot, then stood up and flicked it in the bushes.

"Peace offering," he said, extending the foil wrapped plant, "and your phone must be dead or turned off 'cause I got your voicemail. I figured it being Sunday morning and all that you'd probably gone to church, so I decided to wait a short bit. Feeling anointed now are you?"

Two pink sweetheart roses barely clung to life on two of the delicate stems of the plant.

"A rosebush? Are you serious?"

"It's not for you, darlin', it's for the old lady," he whispered, waving to Mrs. Van Buren who glared at him from the backseat of the minivan.

"Good morning, Mr. Crawly," she sang out the window.

"Thought I'd bring you a bush for your rose garden." He walked closer to the minivan, and I stayed at the foot of the steps.

"Why thank you," she smiled. "Just set it on the bottom step next to Julia, and Isa will plant it for me later."

"I wanted to offer this along with my personal apology for stopping by unexpected yesterday."

"Do you have a second bush for today?" she asked with more seriousness than sarcasm.

"Well, no, but I'll be out of your hair in no time. I just wanted to go over something with Julia before I head to Miami today."

Mrs. Van Buren's concerned eyes shifted to mine. "Ooh, Miami," she said artificially intrigued. "What part?"

"What part? Um, South Beach. I've got some old friends I'm going to visit from college. But I'll be back later, still got that spring training article to do with the Red Sox." He looked back at me and winked. "Isn't that right Julia?"

I nodded.

"Yes, about this article," Mrs. Van Buren began, "I'm afraid I've told Julia that I need her undivided attention these next few days."

"Can't even spare a little time without her?"

"Afraid not, I could fall over dead tomorrow and then there'd be no biography." She looked at me as cool as a Georgia mountain breeze and added, "Don't be long, dear. Isa's going to take me in through the back door. Good day, Mr. Crawly."

Shells crackled as the minivan drove around Bruce's SUV. He walked over toward me, knelt down, and placed the plant on the step next to my feet.

My arms were crossed and as he rose up, he tugged on my elbows.

"Why all closed up? Let me hold those pretty hands."

Reluctantly, I let them loose. "What are you doing here?"

"Such soft, delicate hands," he ignored, stroking my palms with his thumbs. "I always liked that I could wrap my hands around yours and make them disappear."

My pulse began pounding. I sharply repeated, "Why are you here?"

He applied more pressure.

"Relax, precious. I just came to say goodbye." He gave me the best sultry look he could conjure up before adding, "Goodbye for the time being, that is."

"You'd better get going so you can get back early and be fresh for those interviews."

"I think we both know that there are no interviews," he said casually.

"What do you mean?"

"You're the reason I'm here. But I thought if you knew I came just for you, you might think it too forward, so I told a little white lie?"

Something told me that his little white lie was fabricated too. If his father was in trouble and still had drugs to move, who better to do it than his own son. The idea that perhaps I'd been a smokescreen to cover up the real reason he'd come to South Florida seemed logical, and my discarding him might clear the smoke.

When I tried to take a step back, the large hand that used to caress my every curve gripped my forearm with a bite.

"Uh, uh, uh…remember, break-ups happen because I do the walkin'. I'll be back tonight after doing some business, and while I'm gone, you need to think twice about breaking this off."

Business? Yes, he said business. Don't look alarmed. Stay on topic…

"Why would you want to be with someone who doesn't want to be with you?"

"It's not about what you want." He released my arm, pulled his sunglasses from his shirt pocket and wiped the front of the lenses on his jeans. He bit the stem and spoke through his teeth. "You wouldn't want Darrell to somehow find out about us, now would ya? I'm still not through with you, darlin'"

After he drove off, I leaped up the steps and entered the cottage. The wind slammed the stained-glass door shut, rattling crystal on the bar. Isa stood in the foyer beside the wheelchair, both she and Mrs. Van Buren wide-eyed with worry.

"No need to rehash it, dear," Mrs. Van Buren said. "The foyer window is open. Did you hear him say he had business in Miami? I don't think he realized it slipped out."

"I heard it alright."

"For your own safety, don't even speak to that man again," she advised.

Isa added, "There's no telling what he's capable of."

"Yes, I'm well aware. But he hinted that he'd call tonight. Do you think he's using me as a decoy in case he's being watched?"

"It's certainly a possibility," Mrs. Van Buren cautioned. "If he does call again, don't answer it. Maybe we'll be lucky, and he'll give up and leave you be. The nerve of that Crawly man," she said, rising to her feet. "How dare he come here again?"

"Mrs. V, your hip," Isa said, trying to get her back in the chair.

"My adrenaline's flowing now," she said, taking baby steps over to the pink velvet loveseat.

I sat beside her and dropped my face in my hands. She asked Isa to pour us both a brandy.

"But it's too early for that," Isa argued.

"Please, it's for Julia's nerves...and mine."

I signaled to Isa with my thumb and finger to fill mine two inches.

They sat by me, one on each side, like mother hens. I took a sip of the brandy followed by a gulp that burned my throat.

"We all make mistakes for one reason or another," Mrs. Van Buren assured me. "But this one reeks of danger. You're a clever girl, and I'm certain you didn't premeditate having the affair, none of us ever do, especially with such a shady character."

Each had an arm around me, Mrs. Van Buren's holding me closest, the familiar scent of Shalimar haloing around her.

"What say we try and get back to work? We're almost to chapter five in my book. Haley will be meeting her husband soon. Isa will fix us a light lunch and some strong iced tea. We want to keep our appetites for the fish fry at Stephen's tonight. He makes the tastiest cheesy corn muffins."

"Yes, of course. I need to put these worries on the back-burner and get back to the job that brought me here. I can't wait to hear how Haley meets her husband."

Chapter 11

After a light lunch of sliced mangos and crab salad, Mrs. Van Buren suggested we change out of our church clothes and meet back on the balcony before resuming what I began to call *Helen's Journey to Captiva*.

Twenty minutes later the elevator came up, and Isa helped Mrs. Van Buren get seated in the rocker to my right.

"Love the outfit," she said tapping the collar of my striped linen blouse. "Bright pastels are my favorite, you know."

"Thank you. I couldn't wait to get out of that drab black dress and into the cheeriest thing I'd brought."

"Well it suits you nicely." She looked to Isa. "Would you mind getting us that leather binder on my desk before going downstairs? We won't get very far without it."

After handing over the binder, Isa raised a green canvas umbrella anchored in the end table between us. "Won't be tolerating any sunburns today. The air may feel nice but those rays are intense."

Mrs. Van Buren unzipped the jacket to her purple warm-up suit, set her glasses to the tip of her nose, but then hesitated. "Phone's ringing..." She nodded for Isa to answer it.

A minute later, Isa came back out to the balcony. "Julia, it's your husband."

Instantly troubled, I explained to Mrs. Van Buren, "Your number was meant for emergencies only."

"Maybe your cell phone is still turned off from church earlier."

I snapped my fingers. "That's right, it's probably nothing."

She watched me walk the few steps back into the sunroom and pick up the receiver to the black rotary phone on her desk.

"What's going on Darrell, are the boys in trouble? Is Mama alright?"

"Yes, they're all fine." He sounded oddly distraught, and after a long pause he said, "I'm coming to see you?"

"Yes, I know...Wednesday, right?" I shrugged at Mrs. Van Buren who had angled her rocker so to keep an eye on me.

"No, right now. I'm on I-75 just south of Gainesville, Florida."

"I don't understand."

"After we talked last night, I couldn't sleep. As a matter of fact, I haven't been sleeping well for a long time."

"You're coming here now? What about the kids and—"

"Everything's taken care of. I promise I won't get in the way. I've got a reservation at a resort on Sanibel Island, and when you've got a few minutes, we'll get a head start on our time together, even if it's a short walk on the beach, I'll take it. You said it all when you said we needed to fix what's broken, and I've decided that this can't go another day."

"And Mama was okay with you leaving without telling me first?"

"She actually encouraged me to come."

"What? There she goes again, sticking her nose where she shouldn't." His need to see me certainly won points, but also had me worried. Could he know about Bruce? Maybe not, he sounded more anxious than angry. "Honey, I know I may have had some urgency in my voice last night, but this is entirely unexpected and a bit putting me on the spot." I turned my back to Mrs. Van Buren and lowered my voice, hoping she wouldn't hear me through the open sliding glass door. "I can't ask her for time away when I'm only scheduled to be here for three more days."

"If you need to see your husband," she interrupted, "then by all means do."

Embarrassed and surprised that she'd heard, I turned toward her. "Hang on a second, Darrell."

She smiled and winked. "It's not like I'm going to fall over dead tomorrow."

"Darrell, I'll have to call you back?" I hung up and stood in the doorway to the balcony, my hand resting on the handle of the slider. The vast openness of blue-green from beyond Mrs. Van Buren's purple-scarfed head flirted with me, and for a second, I wanted to shut the door and run away from my responsibilities and obligations, jump right into that water and swim until I reached some other island—some other life.

"I am so sorry about that. My personal life has gotten in our way one too many times."

She tilted her head empathetically. "Don't be sorry, dear. One can't help life acting out its fated script, and quite frankly, I'm happy to have a part. I only wish I could help you in some way."

"Just sharing your story has helped more than you know."

She reached out a trembling hand until I walked over and touched it. Our relationship had deepened. We'd become friends.

"That must've been some talk the two of you had last night? So he'll be here when?"

"Around six tonight if traffic flows smoothly."

"Then please bring me the phone so I can call Stephen and make sure he has enough fish for one more."

"Are you sure?" I said. "We wouldn't want to impose?"

"Even-numbered dinner parties are always better, and I'd love to meet your husband. Now stretch the receiver over to me, but you're going to need to do the dialing, the base won't reach."

After she firmed up plans with Stephen, I called Darrell back and offered the invitation.

Answering after one ring, he said, "And you're absolutely sure I wouldn't be intruding?"

"Seems that way...just come with an appetite for fish. Hey, is that your other mobile ringing in the background?"

"Ah, yes, probably my substitute with some questions. So how about some directions on how to get there?"

"I never could understand why the college won't let you use one cell phone for everything."

"It's policy, Julia...now how 'bout those directions."

"Call me when you get to the Sanibel Causeway, and I'll give them to you then. Mrs. Van Buren and I were just about to get started." We said our goodbyes and I hung up. We rocked silently for a moment, her chair creaking more than mine.

"Are you still going to tell him about Bruce?"

I scribbled a series of circles on the front of my notebook. "Eventually."

"Yes, yes, of course, Miss Scarlett, think about it tomorrow. You know the longer you dwell on it the harder it'll be to come clean." She sipped on some tea Isa had brought up while I'd been on the phone. "It's really silly that Darrell should stay at a hotel. Give him the option of either staying with us or at Stephen's. I know Stephen wouldn't mind."

"That's very gracious of you, but I don't want to put anyone out."

"I wouldn't offer if I didn't mean it."

"Thank you, I'll tell him when he calls later."

"Good, now that that's settled, on with Chapter Five?" She took out a sticky note she'd used as a bookmark and found her place. "Let's see, we ended with Margie and Haley discussing the loss of the baby during her honeymoon on Jekyll Island. You'd think good things would be on the horizon for these two girls."

"I sure hope so."

Chapter Five
Summer 1939

Two years after Margie's wedding I finally graduated and Mother's apron ties let me loose—all the way to Atlanta. The streetcar that took me to work downtown likened to that of a mobile sauna. Rains from the night before reversed back toward the sky, creating humidity that glossed the faces that sat around me. I knew without a doubt why locals called their town "Hot-Lanta".

We passed Rich's Department store where two men stood on ladders in the storefront windows taking down red, silver and blue glittered stars as big as football players. They had had an exciting display for the Fourth, including a real canon from the revolutionary war on loan from a local museum.

The streetcar rattled and dinged onward, whizzing by Butler's Shoes, a barber shop, the movie theater and several other tall stone buildings that housed all sorts of businesses. As the massive, triangular Hurt building came into view, I craned my neck, not realizing my hat had grazed the woman's nose sitting next to me.

"So sorry," I said, embarrassed, but still looking at the skyscraper—not like those in New York City, but a skyscraper by Atlanta standards.

The young rosy-cheeked woman who looked about my age asked, "Do you like that building?"

"Yes," I said. "That particular building fascinates me— how it's built on a point in the center of downtown."

"Funny how they couldn't come up with a better name than Five Points for the heart of the city, but I suppose it *is* where the five major arteries of Atlanta intersect. You know my father helped build that building," she said proudly.

"You don't say."

"It took thirteen years to build those seventeen stories. I think someone from the Coca-Cola company put some money into it too. That's why that giant advertisement sits out front at the tip of the corner for everyone who passes through the intersection to see."

The sign, at least one story high, pictured a gal who wore a wide-brimmed hat. She held a Coke bottle just beneath her lips.

"I sure wish it was me about to sip that bottle," I said dry-mouthed. "It's just nine-thirty and already feels like a scorcher today." The streetcar's bell sounded about a block after the Hurt Building. "Well, this is me. Maybe I'll see you tomorrow?"

"No. My husband usually takes me into town, but our car's got a bum tire. It should be fixed later today. But my name's Suzie if I should see you around again."

"Nice to meet you. I'm Haley, and it was nice talking to you."

As I stepped to the wide sidewalk already bustling with folks either shopping or going here and there on business, I glanced at my dime-store watch mother had bought before I left Macon last month. *Nine-forty...good,* I thought, *early again for my third week at the bookstore.* Margie planned to meet me for lunch, and I couldn't wait to see her. Life had been lonely living in the big city. As much as I loved the excitement, it really wasn't for me. Other than Suzie who I'd just met, I'd only met my boss.

So far the storeowner, Mr. Brewer, had left me in charge most days, said he had a lot of politicin' to do campaigning for a seat on the county commission. You might think a simple bookstore owner wouldn't have the means to run for a seat, but how about a bookstore owner who owned the entire ten-story building?

"I like to stay in touch with the people," he'd told me when I interviewed for the job. "You can tell a lot about a person by what books they buy, and then I know just how to market my campaign to them."

Before walking in, I checked my reflection in the glass storefront and realigned my lavender derby-style hat, then stepped back and read the gold letters flawlessly written in calligraphy... "The Page Turner..." *Maybe I'll write a book some day that will be for sale under this very roof.* My writings hadn't amounted to anything more than short stories. Lack of time and an uncertainty that others would like my work had kept them from blossoming into more.

A string of three bells jingled when I entered, and Mr. Brewer greeted me without looking up.

"Good day, Miss Anderson," he said, patting his shiny bald head with a handkerchief. "Got another shipment of 'The Grapes of Wrath' in today." He tapped the large brown box on the dark wood counter.

I came right in and put my purse in a cabinet under the register. "Where would you like me to put them?"

He scratched his gray-stubbly chin and thumped his red suspenders. "On the table in front of the window, between Hemingway's stuff and my lovebird's cage. And put a few at the register too, please ma'am."

"Is it alright if I close the store for lunch today while you're gone? Margie said she'd bring me an indoor picnic before her Garden Club meeting."

"Just remember to put the 'Be-back' sign out. I'm so glad Margie's mother told me about you. Mrs. Harris and her husband have been very supportive in my campaign. Just last week Mrs. Harris went to the other side of town to help get some colored folks registered to vote and passed out my flyers while she was there. Well anyway, I'm just happy I got a trustworthy gal to work my counter. The last one stole from me."

"Where are you headed today, sir?"

"I have a Q-and-A with the newspaper and should be back by three." He grabbed his hat and a blue and white seersucker blazer from behind the counter.

"Wish me luck."

"Luck!"

For a Tuesday, we were unusually busy—a small group of mothers with their bouncing toddlers browsed the children's section, a few gentlemen perused the periodicals, and then I noticed in the back of the store a dapper man, maybe in his late thirties, about the same age Papa had been when he left. He leaned with his shoulder to the wall, thumbing through several books in our mystery section, especially the Agatha Christies which I found a bit odd; a book on business or world events looked more up his alley.

While unpacking the new shipment of Steinbeck, I felt his eyes fall on my humid shoulders. Pretending not to notice, I continued setting books on the table where Mr. Brewer had directed me to do so next to the storefront window. He was about fifteen feet away, facing me, just behind a bookshelf that skimmed his clean-shaven chin. When he looked back toward the books, I stole a peek—his sloped shoulders filled a light blue suit with a red striped bowtie. The gray that streaked his black hair brought out smoky blue eyes that skimmed the book in his hand. He wasn't exactly the cat's meow, but handsome enough to take a second look. When I did, he smiled straight at me. Flustered, I quickly looked down into the cardboard box.

Before I'd left for the city Mother had said, "Almost twenty-one and you still haven't gotten past a third date. I don't think I'll ever hear the word, 'Grandma.'"

"You're the one that told me never to fall too hard," I reminded her.

"Take that comment with a grain of salt," she amended.

I told Mother, "Patience," with regard to the grandma comment. But truthfully, my own patience was thinning. All my friends were either married or on their way to the altar. She worried so about me being on my own, even if it was in Margie's parent's guesthouse. Allen and Margie had moved into their new home ten months prior, and Mr. Harris said I could stay there until I found a good apartment in town.

A different gentleman in a white suit plunked two periodicals and a newspaper on the counter by the register. He rang the service bell, causing me to drop two books to the floor. The dapper man looked at me, then turned away. I could tell by the gyration of his shoulders that he'd been amused by my clumsiness.

The bell rang again.

"I'm coming," I said embarrassed.

While ringing up the white-suited man, I glanced to see if the man with the smoky blue eyes still lingered. He did, now only about ten feet away, over by the window where I'd just been unloading books. He caught my eyes before I could dart them back at the register. A crooked smile gave way, his front tooth subtly overlapping the other. Our exchange got interrupted by the toddlers, at least six of them between the ages of one to four, all singing, or trying to sing, "Jack and Jill" while hopping on one foot—right there in front of him.

Next came the mothers all with books in hand needing some assistance. "Yes, yes, one at a time," I politely instructed. After helping the last of them I decided to muster up the courage to go help the man with his mystery selection only to find that he had become a mystery himself. He must have slipped out with the chaos of all the bouncing children. A disappointment.

Margie came straight at noon, looking fresh in cotton pastels and a white straw hat. I put out the "Be-back" sign and drew the retractable shade. Two stools from behind the counter and a book cart served as our table and chairs.

"No linens at this joint so this'll have to do," I joked. "What's in the picnic basket?"

"Leftover fried chicken, fried okra and apple pie…no a-la-mode, of course," Margie said. "It would've melted by the time I backed out of the driveway."

"How's the house? Did Allen ever get that pillar fixed? He was furious about that one little crack when I was over for lunch last Sunday."

"Someone's scheduled to fix it Friday," she said, opening a thermos. "I tell you, this first year we've been in our new house, there's not a week that goes by that we don't have to fine-tune something."

"You'll get the kinks out soon. I remember Papa telling his clients that it takes about a year to do so. Hey, guess what?"

"What?"

"A man came in the store today and looked at me."

"Don't be so surprised Miss Haley, you have lots of men looking at you."

"No, I mean he *looked* at me." I raised a brow.

She stopped unpacking the basket. "Why of course he did. With that porcelain skin and those emerald eyes, what man wouldn't look?" She poured lemonade from the thermos into two jelly jars. "So am I hearing that you perhaps returned this *look*?"

"Yes."

"Was he cute?"

"In a different way."

"How so?"

"He had some gray in his hair, but a handsome face… and sort of crooked teeth, not in an ugly way, but in a way that gave him character."

"Hmm, an older man…did you talk to him?"

"Are you kidding? Even if I'd had time you know how hard it is for me to talk to men."

"Well, if he comes in again, ask if you can help him find something…like a date."

I flicked a piece of okra at her. "The day I ask out a man is the day I eat chicken liver."

"Never!" we both said in laughter.

"Okay, change of subject. Allen and I have decided to try and have a baby again."

"That's wonderful!" I raised my half-filled jelly jar. "Here's to twins."

"Twins? One is all this girl could ever wish for. So is your mother still coming this weekend to help you with your apartment search?"

"She'll be here late Saturday morning."

"I insist ya'll come eat with us Saturday afternoon. Allen's been wanting to give his new custom-made barbeque pit a try. They just finished it yesterday; the bricks match the ones on the house. He's also got a fella coming from his Wednesday night poker group. Steaks sound good?"

"Whoa…yes, steaks sound good, but who exactly is coming over?"

"Oh, it's just a friend."

I knitted my brows at her. "Is he married?"

"No," she said, delicately nibbling a drumstick. "Nice, guy, though. He works for the Georgia Power Company, and we met him while building the house. He's an electrical engineer...went to Auburn, I think."

"Oh really? My Godmother Sylvie's husband, Ron, went to Auburn, too. He does quite well working for Florida Power and Light down in Fort Myers."

"I remember you telling me about your being there after your father left...that you used to play dress up with all her crazy hats. Wasn't she the one that came and stayed while your mother was sick?"

"That's the one. So you promise me this engineer lad isn't a set-up?"

"No set-up on my part."

"What can Mother and I bring to this non-set-up barbeque?"

Margie laughed. "Just your appetites."

Greeted by an arched trellis laced with red roses, Mother and I drove up the dogwood-lined driveway. Once to the house, it looped around a small courtyard where in the center sat a two-tiered fountain with a statue of St. Francis of Assisi gracing the top.

Mother still drove the old Chrysler that Papa had bought her, only now it was painted the same blue as the hydrangeas on Margie's front porch.

When we stopped, the tailpipe belched and Margie came out the large oak doors to the wraparound porch, waving both hands.

"You're early," she said.

"Haley needs to use the little girl's room so I sped along a little faster than usual."

"Mother!"

Margie laughed, "Oh please, Haley, it's just me. Allen's out back poking at his fire and his gentleman friend isn't here yet."

Mother's eyes widened. "Gentleman friend? Haley, did you know he had a friend coming?"

"Not now Mother, I've got to go to the bathroom." I leaped up the porch steps

"I'll fill her in," Margie said. "The closest bathroom is across from the study to your right."

"When I returned, Mother's smile shined bright enough to be seen in the next state, Margie surely having filled her ear with something about this man coming.

We first stopped in the foyer where Margie showed Mother and me an oil painting she'd had commissioned of the house. Still unframed, it leaned against the side of the staircase.

"I had the artist age the house a bit by painting in some ivy wandering up the brick. You'll also notice a swing hanging from that big magnolia off in the distance to the right of the house. I just know I'll have a child someday. Would ya'll like a cocktail? Allen has mixed drinks on the bar in the living room, and I have a batch of mint juleps in the ice box."

"I'll take a mint julep." Then I rethought the idea of too much alcohol mixed with meeting a new man, and added, "Lot's of ice, please."

"Anything cool without the bite would be good," Mother said, admiring the china hutch as we crossed into the kitchen. "That nagging cough has come back again."

"Do you want Allen to take a look while you're here?" Margie offered.

"No, no…I'm fine, really. So show me what you've done with the place. I haven't been back since ya'll first moved in last fall."

While Mother got the tour, I went out to the back porch where Allen was busy setting up the croquet course in the velvety grass just few yards out.

"Looks like fun," I said, stirring my drink with my finger. Then I noticed tall flames coming from a small brick structure. "And your barbeque pit can certainly hold some fire."

He mopped his brow with a tennis towel and walked over. "How are you, Haley? You look as fresh as the mint garnish in your drink. Is that a new sundress?" He kissed my cheek hello.

"Why yes, thank you. And you're looking sporty in those blue madras shorts. I don't believe I've ever seen your knees."

"Knobby aren't they," he laughed. "How's work at the bookstore?"

"Keeps me busy for now. I'd still like to be writing, but it doesn't pay the bills."

"Write on your days off."

"Oh I do, but it's still not enough time."

His eyes rose over my shoulder as the screen door opened with another visitor.

"Mr. Vandermar," he said, extending his hand. "Glad you could make it."

"Your wife pointed me out this way, said she was in the middle of a tour."

If I hadn't been holding onto the railing I would've fallen down the porch steps for sure.

Allen's smug smile indicated some scheming had been set into motion. "Miss Haley Anderson I'd like you to meet my poker buddy Mr. Harry Vandermar."

In front of me stood a man much taller than I'd remembered, with a crooked smile and early gray in his hair. Quickly, I found my poise. "Nice to meet you Mr. Vandermar. Shop at The Page Turner often do you?"

"Ah, that's where I've seen you," he said, giving a lousy performance at making it seem like a coincidence. "I was looking for a gift for my mother that day, but couldn't find the particular mystery she'd requested."

"Which one?" I continued the small talk while calming my nerves with a gulp from my cup.

"'Murder is Easy,'" he said.

"That one's sold out. But we'll be getting more soon."

I could hear Mother's cough nearing the screen door. "Excuse me for a minute."

Intercepting her and Margie before they got to the porch, I whispered, "Did you know that that was *the man* from the other day?"

Guilty expressions came over both their faces.

"You both knew?" I said, tossing my hands in the air.

"I knew nothing," Mother said, "until Margie filled me in earlier. He's a little old for you, but seems quite the catch."

"I had no idea he'd go down to the store for a sneak peek." Margie put her arm around me, a mischievous smile dancing about her lips. "But you haven't had a date since you came for our Christmas party, and when Allen mentioned bringing his one single friend from poker over for dinner, I thought who better to join us but you."

"It's so hard to be mad at you Margie." Shaking my head, I blew out a sigh. "Come on...let's go play some croquet."

Coughing again as we walked outside, Mother said, "I'll sit up here on the porch and watch you kids play. Feeling a bit tired this afternoon."

Allen looked at me with concern and after handing me a mallet asked, "Has she been coughing a lot lately?"

"I don't really know. We see each other about once a week."

Leaning his mallet against a pine tree, he walked to the porch. "Do you mind if I feel your forehead?" he asked Mother.

"Go ahead, but I promise you it's nothing," she waved.

He placed the back of his hand across Mother's head, then to her cheeks. Margie and Harry watched closely from the foot of the stairs, both fiddling with their mallets.

"Does she feel hot?" I said.

"A little, but it may be from the weather. Margie, go grab my bag for me, please dear. It's in the study on the sofa. I'd like to take your temperature just to make sure and listen to your lungs if that's alright."

"I appreciate your concern, Allen, but I promise it's nothing. Now quit making a fuss over me and go play. Jeesh... there's nothing I hate more."

"But..."

"I insist," she barked politely.

Allen and I walked down the stairs and he said under his breath, "Keep a close eye on her and let me know if anything changes." Once to the center of the yard, he called out, "Okay, who goes first?"

"The ladies, of course," Harry said, tipping his cap at me.

Mother liked his answer, raised her iced tea, followed by a nod of approval.

I'd been set up for sure.

Downtown, the white glow of the Paramount Theater's marquee read, "Now showing...*The Wizard of Oz*." Never did I think such an imaginative piece of literature from my childhood would come to life, and in color at that.

Harry held every door open for me, stood up when I left the table at the restaurant, and let me pick where to sit at the theater—a true southern gentleman.

After the show he asked me the most peculiar question.

"If you could be any character from the *Wizard of Oz*, which one would best suit you?"

"Hmm, that's a tough one," I told him as we walked through the city lights. "Maybe a little bit of the Tin Man and a hint of the Lion."

"I thought for certain you'd pick either Dorothy or Glenda the Good Witch."

"Not always who we appear on the surface, huh? How 'bout you? Which one would best suit you?" I nudged his arm with mine, both of us walking with hands in our pockets.

"Certainly not the Scarecrow seeing I graduated at the top of my class...probably the ole' Wizard himself."

"Why's that?"

"Because I like to help people see their strengths, even when they don't think they exist." He opened the door to his convertible and let me in.

"And what strengths might you see yet to surface in me? Anything yet?"

"Why this is only our first date, Haley, but from what I've learned about you tonight, there is a confident woman locked in there somewhere, but something is holding her back."

"How can you tell?"

"Because you chose the Tin Man and the Lion. We can't get very far without love and courage...with courage comes confidence. How can we ever feel passion if we don't have the courage to seek out our dreams."

"Okay, Mr. Wizard, I like how you put that. When you get to know me better, please tell me when my confidence gets unlocked." *Oh my, did I just refer to the future with a man on the first date?* I shook off the thought, and instead enjoyed the summer air blowing at the scarf in my hair. For the first time in my life, a date didn't make my palms sweat or get me all tongue-tied. Harry's grounded nature enticed me, and I easily saw him as an anchor in my future.

"One more lap up and down Peachtree?" he offered under the stars.

"I would say yes but the lady in me needs to get home; perhaps another night?"

He put his hand on mine, our first romantic contact of the night, and smiled knowing I'd just agreed to another date without his having to ask. "Alright then, another night it is."

He pulled up to the curb of my new apartment and let me out. We strolled down the sidewalk to the cute place Mother and I had found the previous weekend. Flower box planters hung from the windows, each giving the two-story building splashes of color during the day. My unit sat in the middle of the building on the second floor accessed by a set of brick steps.

The silence of the midnight hour broke as his loafers plodded up after the clicks of my high heels. When we reached my doorstep, all became quiet again—so quiet I feared he could hear my thoughts, teetering whether to let him kiss me. To my surprise, he bent down and planted a tender kiss on my forehead. That was all.

"I had a nice time," he said, fiddling with his keys. "Allen was right when he said you were genuine."

Nothing about him threatened or bothered me, but nothing sent fireworks ablaze either. Oddly enough, that sat well with me, and at that moment I realized maybe a safe harbor rather than a passionate river was what I'd been looking for all along.

Chapter 12

Mrs. Van Buren stopped reading and blew a puff of air toward her brow. She struggled to take off the purple warm-up jacket that clung to her boney shoulders.

"Need some help?"

"Please. That blazing sun is getting hotter by the minute."

"Better?"

"Yes, thank you. Just drape it over the back of my chair. Now shall we go on to Chapter Six or do you need a break?"

"No break," I said, sitting back down, "but before you turn the page, I have a few questions."

"If you don't mind I'd like to hold off with the questions."

"Just one? It's about Margie's house. Did it really have a fountain out front with St. Francis of Assisi, because my house has a fountain out front with the same saint? Now I can understand that many people like to put him outside seeing that he's the patron saint of animals and all, but the likeness of Margie's house to mine, with the dogwoods and——"

"Questions later, let's keep the flow going."

Before I could put forth my suspicions that Margie's house had an uncanny resemblance to mine, she jumped right back into the story...

Chapter Six

From the kitchen window of my scantly decorated apartment, Margie and I sipped hot tea while watching hundreds of Atlantans make their way toward Peachtree Street.

"Hard to believe Governor Rivers encouraged all this," Margie said, face pressed against the glass. "God almighty... Germany's invaded Poland and it looks like Hollywood has invaded Atlanta," she laughed, setting her teacup on the windowsill. "Those four men down below have swords at their sides and guns pointed up in the air... the whole kit n' kaboodle. I sure am glad you invited me over to see the excitement from up here. I hate crowds. If you didn't know there was going to be a parade for the *Gone With the Wind* premier you'd think the city had traveled back in time with all those people dressed up in Civil War period dresses and uniforms."

I pressed my forehead against the window, too. "Governor Rivers came on the radio again this morning reminding everyone that most stores and streets off or near Peachtree Street would be closed today. It was nice of Mr. Brewer to give me the day off even though he said he'd be in getting the store ready for the book signing tomorrow. I can't wait to meet Margaret Mitchell."

"Plus you had to come help me decorate my Christmas tree, or should we call it a centerpiece since it's only two feet high." I placed the twig-like tree on top of the kitchen table and used a red-cloth napkin as a tree skirt. "It's not much but it's mine…now where are those cute little elf ornaments you brought over?"

"On the folding chairs in the den. Quite the decorator-on-a-budget touch with the bedspread draped over them," she teased as she followed me to my makeshift sofa. "I wish you'd let me and Allen help out and buy you some proper furniture."

"What? You don't like my end tables? Why they're only made of the finest cardboard boxes in town," I said, and brushed my fingers across one of the crochet doilies. "Come on back in the kitchen so we can decorate my pathetic twig. Then maybe we'll venture down to the parade."

"I don't know, Haley. It's awfully crowded and really cold out there today."

"Would've gotten a better tree but I'm saving some money to get Mother a nice one when I go up next week. Harry's coming, too."

"Things must be getting serious between you two."

"As serious as I'll allow. But Mother says she really wants him to come, even made a special phone call last week just to make certain that I'd ask him. One thing's for sure about Harry, he's really been there for me where Mother's illnesses are concerned. She's always encouraged me to find a man who'll put my needs first, and he certainly does do that. What more could a girl want?"

"To be in love? Trust me Haley if you don't feel that ping in your heart for Mr. Harry Vandermar, it'll never work."

"You know my heart's had a steel armor around it since Papa left. I think it's incapable of feeling a ping. Mother's that way too. She's not had more than a social date since he left."

"How's she been feeling lately?"

"Worse than when I saw her at Thanksgiving. All the flu bugs that've been going around seem to want to set up camp in her chest."

"Is Sylvie still there?"

"Yep, she's been there for ten days now."

"I still don't understand why your mother didn't call for *you* first?"

"She said she didn't want to pull me away from my job… said that they'd need me at the bookstore during the seasonal shopping time. But I told her I'm coming December 22 whether she likes it or not."

"That's a week from today. Sylvie's a good friend to stay with her this long."

"They're close like me and you. You know I'd be there for you any time you needed me no matter what." I topped off the tree with a foil star. We hugged and watched it sparkle.

"Hey there's your telephone. Maybe it's Harry."

"Or Sylvie with an update on Mother."

I ran to the cardboard end table and answered.

"Hello…"

"How's Rhett and Scarlett?"

"Hi Sylvie, they're not here yet. The parade doesn't start for another hour, and they'll be coming down Peachtree, a few blocks from my house."

"Listen, Haley, I don't want to alarm you but your mother's not well at all. She stopped eating and drinking and taking her medicine about three days ago...made me promise I wouldn't tell you. But at this point, I feel morally obligated to break my promise. She's fading fast and you need to get over here, and I mean now. Can you do that?"

"What are you talking about? I spoke with her two days ago and she said she'd just eaten some banana pudding you made her."

"Well she's full of beans. If you can't find a ride, I'll come get you myself."

"Hang on a second, Margie's over and I'll ask her." I covered the mouthpiece with my hand. "Mother's really ill and has had Sylvie holding back information about her condition."

"Why?"

"I don't know, but can you drive me? I'd ask Harry but he's in meetings till three."

"You bet 'cha. I'll call the hospital and see if Allen can meet us over there after he gets off work. Maybe he can help her."

"Sylvie, we'll be there in a few hours, four o'clock at the latest."

As I packed a small suitcase I remembered about work the next day. "The Page Turner! I'm supposed to be there early tomorrow morning."

"Oh, dear…Miss Mitchell and the book signing. Call Mr. Brewer and tell him the situation. He's a kind man. I'm sure he'll understand."

I put my suitcase by the front door, and then telephoned the store. "No answer. Can we just go by there on our way out of town?"

"It won't be easy with this crowd, but I think I can get my car down the alley behind the store."

"Great, let's go."

Once to the alley I flung open the heavy door of Margie's white Buick, knocking over a trashcan.

"Careful there little lady," Mr. Brewer said, having just stepped out the back door with his pipe.

"Oops, sorry about that."

"No need to show up for work today, Haley, we're closed for the parade."

"I know. It's my mother."

"She alright?"

"I'm afraid not. My Godmother Sylvie called and said she's stopped eating and drinking. I may need to take tomorrow and Monday off, too."

"I guess I can manage. You know Miss Mitchell will be here tomorrow morning signing books from ten to two."

"I know, and I do hate to miss it, but under the circumstances I have no choice."

"Of course not, I'll put aside a signed copy for you. How 'bout that?"

"That'd be swell. I'll call and keep you posted."

"Drive safely and watch out for all those movie star fans," he said, waving us off with his pipe.

Midway to Macon we stopped at a Texaco station for gas, Cokes and to use the phone booth.

"Did you get a hold of Harry?" Margie asked as I returned to the car.

"Yes. He's going to try and get by the hospital to see if Allen can get off early so they can ride together."

"Good," Margie replied, us both watching the attendant squeegee the front windshield. "If all goes well they should only be a few hours behind us. I know how you must need Harry right now."

"It certainly helps to have his support, but your being here is just as good if not better."

Before I knew it my childhood home stood before me. The large maple tree and the azalea bushes were naked from winter's wrath, and the wind blew the porch swing wildly. I'd never remembered the house looking so cold, uninviting.

A paralysis came over me while we sat idle in the drive-way, the Buick purring beneath my wool skirt and overcoat. When Margie cut the engine and put the keys in her pocket-book, I still couldn't move.

"Penny for your thoughts?" she asked.

"I have a whole piggybank's worth today. I'm scared to death at the thought of losing her, but mad as hell that she kept me in the dark. She's never done something like this before."

"Of course you're scared, and I'm sure her reasons for keeping you in the dark about her illness are for your own good. You know how mothers don't like for their children to worry about them." Her buttery leather glove squeaked when she patted my shoulder. "Ready?"

"No, but let's go anyway."

We entered through the backdoor to the kitchen and Sylvie stood at the stovetop, red-dyed ringlets bobbing beside her green-button earrings as she stirred what smelled like chicken broth.

"Thank goodness," she said, patting her chest. "I thought you'd never get here."

We hugged tightly, the spoon in her hand dripping broth on my coat.

"That's a good sign if you're making broth, right?" I asked.

"No, dear, I'm afraid I'm just making a cup of hope here. I still offer her something morning, noon and night, even though she refuses. Ya'll come on in and let me get those coats for you."

"Harry and Allen are coming, too," I said, handing mine over. "They should be here by six or so."

"Harry *and* Allen?" Sylvie put a hand on her hip. "Don't be thinking your mother's going to let Allen look at her. She won't even let me put the mustard plaster on her anymore...doesn't care, says 'why help a hopeless case.' Maybe you can talk some sense into her cause I sure can't."

"Is she awake?"

"No, she just went back to sleep about fifteen minutes ago. But she knows you're on your way and she's madder than a wet cat that I told you to come."

"Too bad," I said. "We'll just have to wait till she wakes up. Hot tea anyone?"

After an hour's worth of tea and reminiscing about all the summers I'd spent at Sylvie and Ron's place in Fort Myers, Margie reminded me of something I'd promised to show her years ago.

"I can't believe I never showed you Papa's rendering of The Breakers." I took her hand, pulling her along like I'd done the first day she'd come to the house. "It's upstairs in my closet."

"Keep it quiet up there," Sylvie said as we exited the kitchen toward the stairs.

When we got to the top, an orange glow came from Mother's door at the end of the hall. "Wait for me in my room. I want to peek at her real quick like."

Taking baby steps down the hallway, I stopped at the one framed photograph of my family, just the three of us, taken the Easter before Papa left. Mother either hid or threw out all the others that showed his face. I can still picture our neighbor Mrs. Baker crossing over our lawn that morning, pieces of grass sticking to her pink high heels. "Wait a second Mr. Anderson," she called out, reaching for Papa's camera. "Let me take it of all ya'll together." She squatted down to me, and straightened the daisy corsage pinned beneath my Peter Pan collar. "Why you and your mother look as fresh as this spring day in those bonnets and yellow dresses to match. Now sit right there on the steps…and Haley, sit on your Papa's knee. There we go…say cheese."

The look on me and mother's faces, so relaxed, secure and happy. Naïve faces. I kissed my finger and placed it on the picture.

The closer I got to Mother's room, the slower my feet moved. Would she look so different than what I'd seen while visiting during Thanksgiving? Mother's figure, always soft and petite, couldn't possibly have gotten any thinner, could it? At least she was up and around then, shuffling from room to room in a tattered polka-dotted robe, still holding onto her will to live.

My palm gently pushed the door open. She laid there like an old faded rag doll, an arm stretched out on each side of her deteriorating frame. A brown lampshade threw tea-colored light against the white sheets, and the wavy hair I'd always seen pulled in a bun spilled around her pillow and down to a chest that strained for every breath.

This was the fourth time Mother had battled pneumonia and I could clearly see that her scarred lungs were about to give out. I quietly closed the door back to a crack and joined Margie in my bedroom where she hovered over the dresser, twirling her finger around a small velvet drawstring bag. I knew what was in the bag. Mother must've been snooping through my drawers when she was up at some point and left it out.

"What's in here?" she asked.

"Go ahead and open it."

She tugged at the sides and poured the contents onto my bed.

"That sure is a fancy bag for a game of jacks."

"I was playing with them out on the front porch the day Papa left. I swore I'd never play again until he came back."

"And you've kept them all this time?"

"Yep." I scooped them up and placed the bag on the dresser. "Now let me show you that rendering." I reached to the back of my closet, behind old coats and party gowns. "I hide it back here because Mother doesn't know I have it. She thinks he took it with him."

"Wow, it's like a dream palace with those towers on each end, the palm trees and the Atlantic Ocean in the background."

"If I ever do fall in love, that's where I want to go with him."

"I don't blame you."

"Ooh, the doorbell. I bet that's the guys."

Just as we entered the hallway, a meek voice came from Mother's room. "Haley…is that you?"

"Yes Mother," I hollered down the hall. "Shoot, the doorbell must've woken her. Go tell Harry I'll be right down."

This time when I walked in, her arms were crossed and her eyes slit into a wicked glare.

"I told Sylvie not to call for you," she said. "I didn't want you to come and see me like this."

Approaching her bedside with caution, I said, "Don't be mad with Sylvie. She did what any humane friend would do and called the last of your flesh and blood to come be with you." I sat beside her. "What's this I hear about you not eating or drinking?"

"Never you mind about that." Her eyes widened over my shoulder toward the door. "Well hello there, Harry." She sang, a renewed energy noted in her tone. "Don't be afraid, come in and have a seat there on my vanity stool. You're looking quite handsome today, isn't he Haley?"

"Yes Mother."

The three of us, no more than three feet away from the other, exchanged an awkward circle of glances.

"I came straight from meetings and didn't have time to change out of my suit and tie."

"Where's Allen?" I asked.

"He's down talking with Sylvie."

"No doctors up here," Mother waved off. "If Allen wants to pay me a social visit then that's fine, but he's not touching me." Frail flannel-clad arms crossed over her chest once again.

"Mother, he may have something that can help you."

"No help," she said, directing her attention back over to Harry. "Do me a favor, son and open that left side-drawer to the vanity."

Harry swiveled around and opened the drawer.

"See that metal throat lozenge case?" She struggled up to her elbows, pointed, and then collapsed back to the pillow.

"Yes ma'am."

"Take it out for me and open it."

Harry popped open the small container. "Looks like a nice ring Mrs. Anderson."

"Ring?" I said, puzzled.

"Please call me Joyce, and yes it is. My engagement ring...I've got no use for it now."

Plotting eyes glanced over at me, and Harry's leg uncrossed and began to bounce at the knee.

"Mrs. Anderson, I don't mean to be disrespectful, but why would I want to see your engagement ring?"

"I'm giving it to you as a gift."

"You're doing what?" I said.

"Haley, dear, he needs my blessing," she rasped, "just in case I...well, you know...die."

I looked back at Harry. "Have you two already discussed something without my knowing?"

Harry hesitated, but then gave an impromptu, "Uh, yes, as a matter a fact we have."

Mother nodded at him with approval.

"You have?" I doubted. "When have the two of you spoken without me around?"

"Doesn't matter," Mother snapped.

Overwhelmed with embarrassment, I got up from the edge of the bed and headed for the door.

"Wait!" Harry shouted.

The vanity stool he'd been sitting on tipped in his rush to catch me. I stopped in the doorway, still facing the hall, his breath on my neck.

Softly, he said, "If you walk out that door I'll never be the same. I know I may not be the young man you'd set your dreams on, but if I can't have you in my life I'll just become that empty soul you saw at the bookstore last summer. This is your chance to let that confident woman come out that we talked about on our first date. She's ready, Haley. No more working at The Page Turner, you can stay at home and write all you want. Let me take care of you."

I turned around and faced him. "What about love?"

"You know I love you."

"But this isn't appropriate," I said, raising my voice so Mother could hear.

She threw a hand across her forehead. "For the love of God, let me go out peacefully knowing that you'll be protected."

"Such a forward gesture, Mother...so unlike the lady you've taught me to be."

"A lady would not interrupt a proposal."

Harry tamed my wagging hands in his. "I'd planned on asking you sooner or later. It may as well be sooner."

"That-a-boy," Mother said in a loud whisper. "Well..."

He cleared his throat and took the ring in his right hand, looking back at Mother first who gave him a nod toward the floor.

"Oh, yes...of course." He went down on one knee, Mother smiling from the bed behind him, satisfied with her puppeteering. "Haley, I know without a doubt that I love you and want to spend the rest of my life with you. Please, marry me?"

My attention habitually went to Mother whose sunken eyes blinked in slow motion beneath brows that arched with anticipation.

How could I let her down when she may only have days to live?

Kneeling down with him, I first shook my head yes so Mother could see my answer. Then, reluctantly, the words passed over my lips, "Yes, Harry."

"Then it's settled," Mother said, using what energy she could muster to clap her boney hands together. "Now go on back to Atlanta so you can start planning your wedding. Sylvie has everything under control here with me."

Sylvie had come up the hall and stood just behind us. "I have what under control?"

"You have me under control. The kids are getting married," she announced. "They have a heap of things to do other than look after me."

"Married!" she gasped. "Is that why you're both on your knees?"

Harry stood and then helped me up.

"Mother gave him her ring from Papa," I said to Sylvie. "I've never been so embarrassed in all my life. And now that this wonderful thing has just happened, she's in a rush to get us out of here."

"They don't need to be here," Mother insisted, the emotion wearing on her. "There's a wedding to go plan. And they'd better hurry up before I die."

Sylvie slowly moved toward her.

"Joyce, this has got to stop! Why don't you just read her the letters?"

Mother winced in a failed effort to sit up, and then moaned, "Shut your mouth Sylvie. You'll rob her of the happiness she deserves. Remember…ignorance is bliss."

"What letters?" I sent Mother a penetrating stare and walked toward the bed.

"From your father," Sylvie blurted out. "They're in a large manila envelope under the mattress, opposite corner from your mother."

"Sylvie you promised me," she pleaded.

"You've taken this too far, Joyce, wanting to sacrifice yourself to hide the truth. Never in my life would I have thought you'd be so selfish."

I wedged my hand under the mattress and snatched it out. "Sylvie, Harry...I need to be alone with my mother."

"I was only trying to protect you," she said.

Unlatching the worn metal prongs, I pulled out two letters in their original envelopes, each postmarked from Utah. One was dated November 10, 1929, just weeks after he'd left; and the second was more recent, December third of this year. My neck and palms began to sweat. I opened the one marked from 1929 first, recognizing his handwriting on the yellow-lined paper.

My Dearest Joyce,

It's been just over two weeks since you asked me to leave and rightly so, knowing how it must have hurt you to find me with Ginger that day.

We've now traveled to Salt Lake City where she has a brother who'd like me to help design a church for his new ministry. He has graciously opened his home to us both, giving me time to design and build a house. As much as I know this hurts you, I must be truthful. Ginger and I plan to marry once our divorce is final.

The mountains are like giants here, making those in Georgia look like foothills. I know Haley would enjoy seeing them, which leads me to the key reason why I am writing. I want to have summers with her. The thought of never seeing her plagues me terribly. I don't blame you for wanting to punish me, I deserve it. But taking away Haley? She never did anything wrong.

Once I get the house built she could come overnight by train. I hear the summers are pleasant, and I'm certain she'd enjoy a change of scenery between school years.

Being angry with me is expected, but don't deprive Haley of a relationship with her father.

Whatever you decide, I will always send what money I can, starting with the fifty dollars that's enclosed. Please know that I did and still do love you, just not in the way that you needed me to.

Love,
Lester

"But you told me he left because he didn't love you as much as you loved him, and that he wanted more children that you couldn't give him. All these years you let me assume that he didn't want to see us!"

"He had an affair, Haley…a blasted affair!"

The energy to be angry drained her already depleted body, but I had to know.

"Who was she? I mean, where did he know her from?"

"If you must know, she worked at the print shop where he had his blueprints made. One Tuesday around lunchtime when you were at school I'd forgotten to take my lunch to the college with me that day. When I came back for it, a car was parked at the curb with 'Print Shop Specialists' marked on the side. I thought nothing of it at first, remembering the store owner had told me they'd changed their pick-up and delivery times to noon."

"Yeah, I remember Mr. Johnson's son always coming by our house with those deliveries. He used to come just before dinner and always have a butterscotch candy for me."

"That's right. His name was Jed, nice young man. Anyway, so I figured it'd be Jed inside the house with your papa. As always, I went in through the backdoor, and the first thing I noticed was a purse on the kitchen counter next to the cookie jar. I'll never forget it…mint green with a white flower clasp. Their giggles foolishly wandered from the study."

"What did you do?"

"First I watched them through a crack in the door. I couldn't believe it. She ran her fingers through his beard and kissed his lips without him twitching, like he expected it. Then he said, 'Not, here, wait till later at our special place.' Never in the thirteen years that we'd been married did he look at me the way he did her."

"I'm so sorry, Mother."

"So I flung open the French doors in one swift motion, called them every word I'd been taught not to say, and then told him to leave and never come back or I'd tell you the truth about what kind of man he was. The last thing he ever wanted was for you to look down on him." She held her chest, letting out timid, almost fake coughs.

"I can understand your jealousy, but that wasn't fair."

"Love isn't fair," she whispered through cracked lips. "As wrong as it was, the only way I could hurt him the way he'd hurt me was by taking you away. This pitiful part of me wanted to show him that I meant business, you know, make him shake in his shoes at the thought of never seeing you again. I thought surly he'd leave Ginger and come groveling back to me some day, but he never did. What I did was vindictive, a horrible act of jealousy, and I know an apology won't buy back the time you lost with him. For that I'm truly sorry."

"His actions were certainly almost unforgivable, but I need to see him. You can understand that, can't you?

"I understand, but I can't condone it. If you love me..." she turned her head, letting out three bass-curdling coughs, "you'll put it away. It's best we leave things the way they are. Knowing that you're reading about your father just makes me suffer more." Sweat dripped past her temples.

"I'm not stupid, Mother. It's postmarked twelve days ago."

"Please...you'll only hurt us both."

"I'm already hurt."

I took out the letter. A check enclosed fell to the bed.

"What's this?"

"A check to you from your father...that part of the letter is yours, but the content is mine. Let me keep one last piece of him to myself," she begged.

We shared a silent gaze.

I began to put the letter back in the envelope, and when I did, she inhaled a gulp of air, a long sigh gurgling out as she rolled away from me toward the wall. Quietly, I took the letter back out.

To Ms. Joyce Anderson:

Though we've never met, I feel I already know you. Lester spoke of you and Haley often over the years, especially Haley. He regrets not having been able to watch her grow up, and we both regret her never meeting our three sons, her half brothers: John, Scott and Nathan.

Lester made several offers to have Haley come out and spend summers with us, all of which you refused. I know the bitterness you hold for us, for me, is harsh, and I have a feeling after what I'm about to tell you it will be even harsher. Lester was on a construction site four days ago. A crane hoisting some framework for a roof gave way and took his life. Workers at the site believe his death was instant so let's hope he didn't suffer.

He has left Haley some money, just over $5,300, in his will. I know in the past, other than simple birthday cards, you have refused to let Lester contact Haley, but this time, it is your God-given duty to tell her that she's lost her father. After Christmas, I will find a way to contact her myself to make sure she received this money. That's what Lester would have wanted. She will find out everything sooner or later, but I think it would be best if she heard these things from you.

The funeral is scheduled for December eleventh at Spring Valley Christian Church, the church he helped my brother design and build when he first moved out here. I can understand if you don't want to attend, but please encourage Haley to come. Her brothers and I would love to meet her.

With Sympathy,
Ginger Anderson

When I finished reading, she still faced the wall. I walked around to the side of the bed so she had to look at me.

"You coward," I accused, waving the letter in her face. "You'd rather die than fess up to all of this. And here I was feeling sorry for you, wanting to do anything to make *you* feel better...even saying yes to a man I don't love."

"It'll keep you from getting hurt."

I got down on my knees, inches from her face. "Maybe I wanted to take that risk, but now you've deprived me of that, too."

Mrs. Van Buren closed the book and tapped the cover.

"Like they say... 'that's all she wrote'."

"That's it? What do you mean that's it?" I said feeling gypped. "Did you ever get to go to The Breakers Hotel in Palm Beach? And what about the lighthouse passage you read to me yesterday before we drove out there...that was about you and Stephen, right?"

She blushed. "Yes."

"When you laid next to him under the lighthouse, did you..."

More blushing. "Let's just say the lighthouse got an eyeful that night. But I couldn't write any further about me and Stephen. Some things are too raw to put onto paper."

Her head tilted down at the old leather binder. She let out a sniffle.

"Can I get you a Kleenex?"

"Thank you, dear, they're over on the desk."

I walked the short distance to her desk and picked up the box. "It's empty."

"There's a travel size in the right hand drawer."

Just as I began to open the drawer the old woman moved faster than I'd ever seen her move.

"Wait!" she cried, reaching toward me, tripping over the slider track on the way.

But it was too late. There, sitting on top of all the drawer clutter, like it'd been thrown in there last minute, was a black and white framed photo of a very familiar young lady wearing a cap and gown.

"Why do you have a picture of my mother on her high school graduation?"

"You weren't supposed to see that," she said from the floor, putting the hand that had just reached for me over her hip in pain.

"Do you need me to get Isa?"

"No," she said abruptly, "just help me to the sofa where I can stretch out, and please bring me the phone. Stephen needs to be here, and then we'll explain everything."

Chapter 13

I watched Mrs. Van Buren's distorted finger try to dial Stephen's number.

"Damn-it!" she cursed. "My fingers keep slipping from these little holes. Could you dial for me?"

I knelt beside the sofa and dialed the numbers she recited. When it began to ring she held the receiver to her chest.

"Would you mind giving me a minute alone?"

"I'll be in the bedroom when you're ready." As I walked out of the sunroom, taking one last look at the photograph lying on the desk, my thoughts began calculating the characters of her story, all of them real, all of them kept secret. Grandma Peg was more than just an acquaintance.

Cracking the door behind me, I flopped onto the bed and stared at the daisy trim near the ceiling, the fan overhead dizzying my already whirling mind.

I've got to call Mama.

My purse sat on the pillow beside me, and as I fished around for the phone, I tried to figure out how a picture of my own mother had found its way into Helen Van Buren's hideaway.

After hearing about Margie and Allen's Buckhead home in the last few chapters, there was no doubt in my mind that that house was Margaret and Ashton's home—the house my grandmother had willed to me. Did Mama even know that Mrs. Van Buren and Grandma Peg had been friends, and if she did, why all the secrecy? Had Mama's picture been sent with a graduation announcement years ago? If so, why was it framed and hidden in a drawer? Exchanging pictures of your kids with a best friend is commonplace, but an 8 × 10?

The anxiety to know the answers made my stomach synchronize with my already spinning head.

Once I found the phone, I turned it back on—it'd been off since slamming it shut on Bruce the night before. Three missed calls showed on the display. I dialed for voicemail service...

"You have three new messages," the automated voice stated.

The first message was from Bruce when he'd tried to reach me while we'd been at church. The second, from Darrell, in his attempt to get a hold of me before he'd called Mrs. Van Buren's land-line to tell me he was on his way down to Florida. And the third had come just minutes ago. It was Bruce again.

"Hey darlin', I'm gonna be tied up here overnight so we'll have to set aside another time to rendezvous. I remember the old broad saying something over lunch yesterday about a doctor's appointment on Monday. I'm not giving up on you."

Before I could even punch in Mama's area code, Mrs. Van Buren called out from the sunroom.

"Stephen's on his way," she said. "I want to show you something before he gets here."

"Be right there." I threw the phone on the bed. "Damn it," I whispered to myself. I'd hoped to speak with Mama real quick before she'd summoned me back to the room.

"Ooh," I said, noticing a blue ice pack on her hip.

"Isa heard the thump of my fall and checked on me. She brought me this and some ibuprofen for the pain."

I stayed about three steps away, too nervous to sit. The sight of her in that purple warm-up suit stretched across the sofa...she had to be miserable. But I still wanted to yell out, *WHY, WHY, WHY was that picture of my mother in your drawer?!* In some way I felt betrayed. To think I'd shared everything with her, and she'd hidden this huge link of common interest. As much as I wanted to scream out my questions, I hesitated, not wanting to send this delicate woman back into the shell she'd been confined to for decades. We'd come so far together.

"Are you sure you're up for this right now? I have so much to ask."

Her heavy lids closed for a moment, and she let out a descending sigh. "Sweet Julia, I'm old and tired and ready to let go of all this." She took her hand off the icepack and waved it in a circle as if the gingerbread house had held captive all her reasons for hiding. A smile crept over her face. "Once I let go, for the first time in seventy-five years...God, has it been that long since Papa left…" she shook her head, "seventy-five years since I've been free to simply enjoy being. Do you understand what I mean by that?" Pure desire sparkled through her transparent green eyes.

"I think so."

"I've been accommodating everyone else all my life…even feeding my readers what they wanted to read rather than a real story with raw, twisted emotion like the one I've been telling you." Her eyes fell to my tapping foot. "I know you're antsy for my explanation about your mother's picture, and I promise it will come soon. But you need to hear the rest of the story."

"One quick question."

"Yes."

"You said the real name of your college roommate was Margaret, right?"

"Yes, she preferred the nickname Peggy, but I always called her Margaret because that's how we were first introduced and it stuck."

"And in your book, Margaret is portrayed as Margie, correct?"

"Yes."

"Do you recall Margie's, I mean, Margaret's Buckhead address in Atlanta? As you know I live in Buckhead, and surely I've passed her home at one time or another."

The chatter and smile above her chin diminished. "West Paces Ferry Road," she answered, eyes drifting out the open slider toward the gulf.

"My house is also on West Paces Ferry…interesting coincidence."

The room went quiet for a moment until a ripple of wind grazed the wind chimes and drifted in across the sofa. Slowly, she looked back at me, the purple scarf flapping with the light breeze coming in through the sliding glass door. "I think you know that it's no coincidence."

"The descriptions of those young dogwoods lining the driveway…those are the now giant dogwoods that line *my* driveway; and the brick barbeque pit out back…it's still there, crumbling around the corners, Darrell just cooked a brisket on it last weekend, but the fountain with St. Francis sitting on top…that's when I knew it had to be a sure thing. Why didn't you just tell me about your relationship with my grandmother when I first got here?"

"Because I needed you to listen with unbiased ears. Like I said before, reporters and entertainment news broadcasters bugged me for years to do an interview. I didn't feel I could trust them. They're always molding stories into what sells. But one Sunday while reading your column it dawned on me how to go about it. I'd told Isa, 'We'd better get a biography completed before I turn to dust,' and I tapped the newspaper page with your column and said, 'Why not Margaret's grand-daughter. She'd be perfect for the job.' Isa agreed and a few days later called your house."

Another strong breeze whirled about outside. I noticed my notes flapping around, still on the rocking chair. I walked to the balcony and flipped the note tablet shut, brought it inside and tossed it on the coffee table. "This interview has taken a personal turn, and everything from this point on is off the record."

"Only if it bothers you," she said with a shrug. "Trust me, dear, think of the series of events that I've laid out for you as a wall of dominos, each of them little black confessions tumbling down in precise order. Soon, you'll see where the last one falls. But you have to let the others precede it in order to understand why the biggest secret was kept under lock and key. Understand?"

I nodded and finally sat down in the overstuffed chair to her right. "You said you wanted to show me something before Stephen got here. What is it?"

"Would you mind getting my cane? I left it lying against the balcony railing."

She propped up to her elbow and unscrewed the ivory handle.

"Here," she handed it back to me, "turn it up-side-down."

"Up-side-down?"

"Go ahead."

When I did, something made a zipping sound, and a diamond necklace poured out of the end. I couldn't believe the number of diamonds embedded in the white gold that ran the length of the choker. And then I gasped at the teardrop diamond pendant that clung to it…at least four carats!

"It's spectacular."

"Here, put it up to the light," she said, grabbing hold of it. Light reflected off the stones, and iridescent dots danced around the room—over the curio cabinet filled with angels, across the bookshelves lined with her work and then to her desk where Mama's picture lay still without answers.

"I can see why you keep it hidden. It must be worth a fortune."

"I don't care about the monetary value. It's the sentimental value that's dear to me."

"Did Stephen give it to you?"

As she nodded yes, his footsteps slowly came up the staircase.

"I hear someone's got a lot of explaining to do," he said somewhat jovially, removing the white golf cap that hid his silver hair. He smelled like grass and his cheeks were red with afternoon sun. "Got here as fast as I could. Had to bow out at the sixteenth hole, but after what I hear you found," his warm eyes consoled me, "I knew I needed to come right away. Plus Helen told me she had a nasty fall in the midst of your find." He tapped the icepack on his way to the desk where he placed his cap beside Mama's picture. He picked it up, "Beautiful isn't she?" He admired her tenderly. "And you look like a blonde version of her." He noticed the diamond necklace in Mrs. Van Buren's hand. "I'll never forget the weekend I gave you that."

"The best and the worst weekend of our lives," she whispered, touching the scar on her cheek.

He rolled the desk chair over and wedged it between me and Mrs. Van Buren, the three of us less than an arm's reach from one another. For a few seconds, no one said a word, and the distant surf made our silence unbearable.

Mrs. Van Buren tapped Stephen's knee and said, "You know I told Julia about the lighthouse?"

"Should I blush or was she discreet?" he laughed.

"She was very discreet," I said, picturing a youthful couple on a blanket under the stars.

"That was in October," Stephen said, eyes glazed. "The nights are still warm in October. We went for a swim, too... did she tell you about that?" he raised his eyebrows.

"Discrete, Stephen....remember?" She wagged a finger at him. "Anyway, by December, we decided we wanted to go away overnight together...to the Breakers."

"It was her dream to go there," he said. "She never went with Henry...said it was sacred ground for someone that made her heart ping."

"What can I say," she smiled, "it finally happened."

"I'd been meaning to take some diamonds to a storeowner over in Palm Beach. A ritzy hotel like the Breakers had many upscale shops blooming in the streets around it. My wife Paula, though she didn't deserve the title, simply thought I'd gone on a business trip, which I did, but I brought along a business associate," he winked at Mrs. Van Buren.

"And I'd told Henry that I was going with my Godmother Sylvie to the east coast for some weekend Christmas shopping...even made a point to call her for our monthly chit chat the day before Stephen and I left, never thinking she'd call back on Saturday afternoon and invite us over for supper."

"She didn't."

A nod yes. "Henry answered, and you can imagine his suspicions once he realized I'd lied to him."

"Did he suspect you were...well..."

"Having an affair?" she finished. "He did after he went through my desk and called every phone number I had scribbled on my day planner, the hotel's number included. It was written on Friday's page, the day we'd left. I'd called the hotel to find out about proper attire for their grand ballroom dining. I'd wanted to look perfect for Stephen. Henry knew I loved that place, yet I'd always come up with some lame excuse why *he* couldn't take me there."

Stephen rolled the desk chair closer to her. "Long story short...the first night we had there was glorious, like something out of one of Helen's novels. But by Saturday night, Henry found us..."

"...in the lobby," Mrs. Van Buren continued. "We were admiring the Christmas tree before dinner and out of nowhere he appeared like a bad dream."

"What'd you do?" I said.

"After almost wetting myself I came clean and told him the truth, even as much as I knew it would hurt him. But I was confronted with a choice...*my* choice, to either live a loveless marriage with Henry, or live the life I wanted with Stephen. Henry and I had gotten married for such wrong reasons."

"How was your wedding anyway?"

"Wedding? Ha! More like a forced union," she said. "We'd rushed it for Mother. Two days after he'd asked me, we tied the knot right there in her bedroom with Pastor Davis presiding. She drank one glass of water each day so she could be there, then stopped after our I-do's. By Christmas Eve she was gone."

"I'm so sorry," I offered.

"Not as sorry as I was," she said. "I found more letters from my father addressed to me that she'd hidden and forgotten about. They were just simple hi-how-are-you letters, but they would have made his absence more bearable. I had to sift through so much stuff in that old house, most of which I got rid of, but for some crazy reason, I had to keep that old blue Chrysler that Papa had bought."

"Yep, she's a jewel now," Stephen said. "I love driving it."

"So back to the lobby...what did Henry do when he found you two together?"

"He didn't make a scene like you'd think. Instead his blue eyes smoldered at Stephen as he grabbed my arm and escorted me through the poinsettia filled lobby. The plush red-velvet gown I wore got caught in the lobby doors on the way out. Henry quickly tore it free, causing a slit right up to my knee. I continued on without a fight. He at least deserved some explanations which I'd planned to give him once outside, but he gripped my arm all the way to the car. I had no intentions of leaving. It was there that he told me about Sylvie calling him and how he'd gone through my desk to figure out where I was."

I turned to Stephen, "So Helen gets taken out from under your wings in the lobby of this glorious hotel and you didn't dispute it?"

"Being a gentleman, I didn't want to cause a ruckus, so I dashed back up to the room, got my car keys and took the route I knew they'd take home— State Road 80 through Clewiston and La Belle."

"Didn't you tell me Paula was from La Belle?" I asked.

"That's right. Small dot on the map, daughter of the town's lowlife conman," he reminded me.

"Pretty outsides, devilish insides," Mrs. Van Buren said with a snarl. "We'll get to Paula later."

"I didn't catch up to them until Clewiston," Stephen said. "Henry tried to outrun me. Now I don't know how well you know Florida, but Clewiston is near Lake Okeechobee where the gators are plentiful. You see, one of these gators had sat himself smack in the middle of the road. When Henry swerved to miss it, the gator moved too and he still hit it. The car flipped and landed in a ditch, wheel-side up."

Mrs. Van Buren's hands shook as she laced her fingers together.

"Is that how you got the scar?" I asked.

"Not from the gator, thank God," she began, "but from my face smashing into the windshield."

Stephen continued. "Henry was unconscious, but Helen wasn't. I moved them both to the backseat of my car."

"I just remember Henry's head resting on my lap," she said, "and I used his handkerchief to wipe the blood from his eyes."

"We decided to find a doctor I knew in Clewiston rather than going to the hospital...a Dr. Lipscomb. I'd custom made some jewelry for his wife recently and knew where he lived."

"Wasn't it late to be knocking on doors?" I wondered.

Stephen scratched his head. "Maybe ten o'clock. His wife was in bed, but the good doctor was out on his porch having a smoke. He jumped in the car straight away after seeing Henry and Helen's condition. He directed us to his office in town. But by the time we got there Henry'd stopped breathing."

"I was hysterical," Mrs. Van Buren put a hand to her scar.

"And for good reason," Stephen assured me. "The gash in her cheek went through to the inside of her mouth. Kept spittin' up blood, too. We left Henry in the car while I quickly carried Helen to Dr. Lipscomb's exam table. He gave her something to calm her nerves, and while stitching her up, I told him everything that had happened that night as well as about our affair. He said he understood, but was hesitant to lie to police about what'd happened. I convinced him to agree to a story, but it cost me an arm and a leg."

"I call it the million-dollar-story," Mrs. Van Buren added.

"You gave the good doctor a million bucks to cover for you?"

"It would've seemed like that much back then, but it was probably only a quarter of a mil. He wanted it in diamonds which worked out nicely for me—easier to hide on the books and at the bank."

"So what was your story?" I asked him.

"That he'd gone out for some late night fishing at a small dock on Lake Okeechobee. On his way back, he came across the accident and I, of course, was never there, and it was he that drove them to his office."

"Did Sylvie ever question where you'd gone?" I wondered.

"Never," Mrs. Van Buren answered. "And weeks later, after I'd decided to sell the Fort Myers home and begin construction on this one, she didn't pry as to why or ask what had happened the night of Henry's death. I think she had a hunch, but she took it to the grave."

"Wait a minute," I said confused about the houses, "I thought you and Henry built this house."

"No, after Henry's death, I took the money Papa had left me out of savings. What a hurried ordeal that was...building this house in time for our special arrival. There were only a handful of homes on the island and at the time were accessed by ferry...no bridges yet. I offered a $1,000 bonus to the builder so he'd get it done in six month's time. I couldn't take the constant condolences that came after Henry's death, and the guilt was more than I could bear. Going into hiding couldn't come soon enough. I figured if I spread it thin, I could live off Henry's life insurance policy for a few years while I made something of my writing."

"She refused any money I tried to give her," Stephen said.

"Well you sure succeeded at writing," I boasted, then turned to Stephen and asked, "So why didn't you just divorce Paula? You'd said she'd purposely gotten pregnant with Josh so she could marry her way into the good life."

"Not that simple," Stephen gripped his knobby knees. "Like father, like daughter. Paula could blackmail and con her way into whatever she wanted. She was ruthless."

"Huh?" I didn't follow.

The room got really quiet again.

"Horrid woman," Mrs. Van Buren said with a twitch. "Six weeks after the accident, I realized I was pregnant. I knew it was Stephen's."

"Oh my God," I said, recalling she'd told me she couldn't have children.

"Several days before the Breakers Stephen and I were in the office at his family's jewelry store planning our trip. Unbeknownst to us, Paula had come in and overheard everything."

"And she didn't confront you?" I asked.

"No," Stephen said firmly. "This was like gold to her, something to pull out of her bag of tricks when she wanted something from me, whether it be a diamond broche or cash to spend on a trip to Europe with her jezebel-of-a-sister. It was also her ticket to stay married to me so she'd remain included in the social circle that came with *my* name. To this point, she knew the only reason I'd kept the marriage going was for Josh's sake, and I had told her that once he was old enough for school, he'd get his education in South Africa and only spend summers here like I'd done as a boy. Her days of teas and crumpets at the country club were numbered, and she knew divorce was in her future. But once all this happened, she had me by the balls, knowing that if I divorced her she'd ruin not just my reputation, but Helen's and the family business'."

"Okay, so Paula knew about the affair, but wouldn't your word against hers have been sufficient to kick her out of town and out of your life? *She* was the one from bad blood."

"Remember I had Josh to think about. He was only two at the time, and later, come to find out Paula had more than just words to use against us."

"Huh?" I was lost.

"She came to me first with her twisted-blackmailing plan," Mrs. Van Buren began. "She knew I'd run to Stephen with her threats, sealing her assurance that he'd never divorce her. It was after I'd begun construction of my home on Captiva Island. For months I'd managed to go without running into that woman, but one day our buggies bumped at the supermarket. 'Mrs. Van Buren,' she'd said, dripping with bitter kindness, 'why I had no idea you were expecting, and the poor dear will grow up fatherless. How terrible you had to lose your husband in that dreadful car accident.' An intense hate cut the air from her dark eyes. 'Let me fix something special for you,' she offered, 'and bring it over tonight.' I thought I was going to throw up right there on her leather pumps."

"Don't tell me she came over," I dreaded.

"She showed up that evening with a dish full of blood pudding...the grossest dish I'd ever seen," she shrieked. "I can still see those brownish-red plump sausages oozing with pinkish grease. And just as casual as a day in the park, she said, 'It's full of the protein and iron *Stephen's* baby will need to be healthy.' Then she added, 'And if you think for one second he's going to leave me for you you'd better think again. I'll have both of your reputations smeared all over this town and maybe even have you put in jail; then that poor baby will be off to an orphanage. Recognize this?' She shoved a brown stiff handkerchief with Henry's initial's up under my nose. 'I found it under the seat of Stephen's car the Sunday after he'd come home from what he'd told me was a business trip to Palm Beach. That was about seven months ago...isn't that about how far along you are, dear?' She spoke to me as if I were a child, all soft and sickly sweet, and when I reached for the handkerchief that I'd mopped Henry's brow with that hellish night, she snatched it back. 'I know it was just a car accident, but there are many who would believe otherwise if I insinuated as such. It was only a matter of time before Stephen threatened to leave me. I just didn't think it would take him seven months, though. When he came to me yesterday, declaring his love for you, I showed him this,' she waved the handkerchief. 'And then I followed you around today, determined to see your swollen belly with my own two eyes. Worked out nicely how we bumped into each other at the Piggly Wiggly. Oh, and I have pictures too. Private investigators are expensive, you know. It's a good thing my husband gives me a large weekly allowance.' She pointed a slender finger in my face. 'You'd better hope that baby never crosses paths with me. It'll be sure to get an earful.' And then she smoothed over her dress and slithered out the front door."

"It was a miserable marriage," Stephen said with a shimmy, "if you want to call it that."

"What about the handkerchief and the pictures...did you ever find them?"

"She'd had them in a safe deposit box just north of here in Sarasota where her sister lived," Stephen told me. "And since her sister, the co-signer, had already died, I claimed the contents last May after Paula's death."

"How did you know she had a safe deposit box?" I asked.

"I didn't," Stephen answered. "When I sold the condo to move over to Josh's place, I noticed two safe deposit box keys in her jewelry box. We'd only had one box that I knew of.

After several hours of sifting through her things, I found a bank statement from the bank in Sarasota. All I had to do was show them the death certificate, prove that I was her husband and they let me right in."

"You wouldn't believe all the stuff that was in there," Mrs. Van Buren's eyes bugged out. "But the most incriminating would have been the two black and white photographs—one of Stephen and me at the Breakers holding hands in the lobby, and the other was of Stephen carrying me into Dr. Lipscomb's office. The private investigator had tailed us from the hotel."

"So that's how Paula knew everything," I confirmed. "Her PI had been on your tail the whole night. I can't believe you never noticed."

Stephen shook his head. "With all the commotion that night, a UFO could have landed on the roof of my car and I wouldn't have noticed."

"Point well taken," I said.

"What else was in the safe deposit box?"

"Fifty-thousand in cash, several pieces of jewelry and the handkerchief," Stephen said.

"What'd you do with everything?"

"I polished the jewelry and sold it to a dealer in Miami; the cash went into my bank account; the pictures are in my dresser drawer; and the handkerchief...Helen, you want to take it from here?"

She reached for the ivory handle to her cane. The T-shaped grip unscrewed at one more place, and rolled inside the base of the "T" was a brown spotted handkerchief, the initials *HJV* at the corner.

"Henry John Van Buren," she said as she handed it to me.

The stiffness had softened, and I rubbed my thumb over the black monogram.

"I know it seems sick, me carrying around a necklace from my lover and the blood-stained handkerchief of my dead husband, but I couldn't part with either."

I handed it to Stephen and he folded it long ways three times, and then rolled it up like a fat cigarette before putting it back inside the handle.

"How pregnant were you when you moved to this house?" I asked.

"Eight months." Mrs. Van Buren held her stomach. "That's when Constanz and Isa came. Living on an island accessed by ferry, I wanted a midwife here at all times."

"I thought you'd told me that you couldn't have children," I reminded her. "Was the baby still born?"

She and Stephen looked at each other. Stephen said, "You should be the one to tell her."

"Tell me what?"

Mrs. Van Buren reached for me to come closer. I got up, wedged passed Stephen and knelt between the sofa and coffee table.

"On October the fifth, a healthy girl came into the world. My best friend and her husband waited right here in this very room for the good news."

"My grandparents were here?" I said, beginning to put the pieces together.

"Yes, Margaret and Ashton," Stephen confirmed. "We didn't want our child to ever come anywhere near Paula, and in order to give our baby the proper upbringing she deserved, we decided who better to adopt her than a couple who'd wanted a baby more than anything in the world, but couldn't conceive."

I looked at Stephen, thinking about Mama's name, Stephanie. "Was she named after you?"

"Yes."

"Does she know about all this?"

"Oh, yes," they said together.

The betrayed feeling started to return.

"But we had to keep quiet because of Paula." Mrs. Van Buren reached out and stroked my hair. "I've wanted to meet you for so long. I looked forward to your column every week because that was like my weekly visit with you."

"If I hadn't stumbled across Mama's picture, when had you planned to share the rest of the story with me?"

"By Tuesday night at the latest," she said with a promising stare. "Stephen and I had already arranged for Darrell, your mother and the twins to fly in Wednesday afternoon."

"They all know about this?!" I said, rising to my feet.

"Settle down, child," Stephen guided me back to my seat. "Helen called your mother the day you flew down here. It was then that she gave her the go-ahead to tell Darrell and the twins about coming down here, but they knew to keep it a surprise."

"So Mama and the boys are going to be here on Wednesday? Hell, why not tomorrow since the cat's out of the bag. Is there anything else I should know? Or is my mother being your child and that fact that the rest of my family found out about all this before I did all there is?"

They both stared at each other while I had my huffy time.

"The boys and Darrell don't know yet," Mrs. Van Buren said. "All they know is that they're coming down on vacation. You can tell Darrell once he gets here, and we'll share it with the boys later…and Josh, too. That's why he's flying in tomorrow. It'll be like a family reunion."

"Josh doesn't know about any of this either," Stephen informed me, "but I don't think he'll be surprised. He couldn't stand his mother and always suspected I had someone else."

"But why is Darrell coming three days early?"

"He must have another urgent matter to discuss with you," Mrs. Van Buren said with caution. "If your mother knew about Bruce maybe Darrell found out, too."

"What! My mother knows about Bruce?"

"Don't be mad, Julia, she only keeps in your business because she loves you."

"You've talked to her about this?"

"I've spoken to your mother almost every other day since she learned to speak. Don't worry, she swore me to secrecy and asked that I not pry on matters about Bruce unless it came up. But aren't you glad it did? What a snake that man is."

Embarrassed, I said to Stephen, "You know about Bruce?"

"We share everything," he said, tapping Mrs. Van Buren's arm. "But don't you worry, no judgment passed here, and if that bastard ever comes within feet of this house I'll personally see to it that he won't be able to ever do it again."

I rubbed my temples, trying to recall anything that got passed me over the years. And then I remembered. "Mama talks regularly to someone she refers to as her godmother. I've never met her, or even seen a picture of her for that matter. She says she lives in Maine and is confined to an asylum. Can I suspect that I have no godmother in Maine?"

Mrs. Van Buren cornered her eyes to Stephen. They both nodded yes.

"And I bet it's you she came to see every fall."

"Yes, dear," she confirmed, "in October. We both celebrate our birthdays that month. I don't know if you remember me telling you about the place I kept in Atlanta during the height of my career, but I spent summers there. I told business associates that it was so I'd be closer to my publisher in New York, but it was really so I could see your mother when she was a little girl. Margaret let her spend weekends with me, and if anyone asked where she'd gone, Margaret would make up something about her sleeping over at a friend's house."

"That must've been so hard."

"More like heartbreaking," she sighed. "Every time our weekend was over I'd spray a little of my Shalimar perfume on her wrists."

"Did you get to see her, Stephen?"

"Very seldom. Sometimes I'd make a trip up there…tell Paula I was out of town on business. It's heart-wrenching not to be with your child. That's why we were so blessed to have Margaret and Ashton adopt her."

Looking at the two of them holding hands, my heart went out to them. How could I be angry? They'd given up their togetherness to protect *my* mother.

"Your selflessness is like none I've ever heard," I said tearfully. "And it's only now that you can freely be together?"

"Never too old to start over," Mrs. Van Buren said with a gleam.

Glancing at the wall clock, I noticed it was five o'clock. "Darrell's going to be calling any minute. But what I don't understand is if he does know about Bruce, why didn't he sound mad?"

"You'll find out soon enough," Mrs. Van Buren said, "I think 'Fur Elise' is ringing from in your bedroom."

Chapter 14

Without checking the number, I assumingly flipped open my cell phone.

"Darrell?"

"No sugar it's Mama."

Hurt and angry about her keeping the truth from me, I remained silent.

"Hello...Julia? Are you there?"

"As close as we are, and never one word about you being adopted. You could've at least told me that much."

Her French-manicured nails tapped the granite counter-tops in the kitchen, and then I heard what sounded like a long pull off a canned soda.

"For Christ's sake Mama, say something."

"How much has she told you?"

"Everything, I think."

"About Stephen?'

"Yes, and Paula."

"And the handkerchief?"

"Yes."

Her throat rumbled. "Ooh, that wretched woman."

"So I've heard," I said.

"You have to understand, I gave my word not to tell so to protect us all."

"Did Daddy know?"

"No, and you know how close we were."

"Well lo and behold, Miss Busybody herself has held onto a secret for more than an hour. Hear the trumpets roar."

"Don't you dare sass me about this Julia Ann. Do you have any idea how hard this has been for me? I've wanted to scream it out on several occasions, especially to you, but couldn't for fear of jeopardizing not only Helen and Stephen's reputations, but my adopted parents and maybe even yours and Darrell's. No telling what Paula was still capable of. She knew about you and your career with the paper. She made sure she knew everything about everyone...that bitch."

"Mother!"

"Cussing comes easy when I think about her. Jesus saved me going on twenty years ago, but there's no saving that woman, and as hard as I've tried, there's no forgiving her either."

"But after several years had gone by it would've been impossible for that stained handkerchief to pin anything on anyone? I think you all could have come forward and called Paula on her bluff. Henry died in a car *accident*."

"Anything's possible, but they never wanted to take that chance. We all agreed to never challenge the likes of Paula Donovan. No telling what else she had up her sleeve."

"How could Stephen bear to live with that woman for so long?"

"The love and devotion he had and still has for Helen got him through. Paula may have taken Helen out of his arms, but never out of his heart. I've never been one to say I was happy about a death, but when Helen called me with the news last year, it felt like a fortress of hell had been lifted off all our shoulders. I couldn't wait to hang up the phone and go tell you. But then to my dismay she insisted, 'Don't tell anyone yet...we're waiting to see if we can find Henry's handkerchief just in case she's boobietrapped some post death mayhem for us.' It took till about two months ago for Stephen to sell the condo in Fort Myers, and it wasn't until then that he went through everything and found the safe deposit key."

"Yes, he told me how the box was at a bank in Sarasota."

"But Helen still wanted me to keep quiet. She insisted on lining up a plan where she could tell you the story on *her* terms, you know, make sure you understood the course of events so that you could make fair judgment on all that had happened. And what better way for her to do that than to summon you down to do an interview for her long awaited biography. It just sounds like you pieced everything together a little sooner than she'd expected."

"It was hard not to when your senior portrait showed up in her desk drawer."

"You weren't snooping through her things, were you?"

"No Mother, I was getting a tissue for her, and when I opened the drawer there you were. The second my hand hit the knob, she must've remembered that she'd thrown the picture in there. She about broke a hip trying to stop me. I don't think she was ready to tell me everything yet. That was about an hour and a half ago."

"I see. What went concealed for almost a lifetime took only ninety minutes to expose. How awful it was for them, their whole lives spent apart with the exception of a few carefully planned encounters, and all for that pitiful woman who epitomized self-indulgence."

"She wouldn't say a word after I found your picture until Stephen came over, and then the two of them explained everything. I've never seen two people so in love."

"Like you and Darrell on your wedding day?"

I didn't answer. Misty-eyed, I pictured Darrell in an ascot draped around his long tan neck, the late morning sun shining in stained glass windows above the altar. The *ping* in my heart returned at the recollection, and I realized the power of love far outweighed the forces of lust. God how I still loved him.

"You alright, sugar?"

An overdue bout of tears burst out. "I know you already know about Bruce. Mrs. Van Buren told me today. It just happened, Mama. I never wanted to hurt anyone."

"Oh, Julia, I wish I was there to wipe your tears. Marriage can be tough, that's all there is to it. Mistakes do happen; it's part of being human. And don't for one second feel like you're the first woman to have ever had an affair. Most of the women in our very own neighborhood have either thought about it or gone through with it, including me."

"What?! I knew about Daddy's affair, but not yours. Who was he?"

"Some things are better left in the attic hidden under a big black tarp for no one else to see."

"Well, I need the largest sized tarp they've got. Bruce isn't quite the charmer I thought he was. He's turned out to be real trouble, Mama."

"I know."

"You know?"

"Helen calls me almost every day and we spoke last night before she went to bed. She told me all about his daddy, Luke Crawly. I can only imagine the clout he has being one of those real estate moguls on the East coast. I looked up the article myself, and it looks like this man was at the helm of something really big in the world of drugs. Probably has enough money to pay off anybody to do anything for him. I have to tell you sugar, I'm worried for your safety. You picked a bad seed for sure."

"Do you think Bruce's real reason for coming down here is drug related? Or do you think he really just wanted to be with me?"

"What do you think?" Mama's voice indicated that I already knew the answer.

"My sixth sense says it's his father, and I think his pursuit of me, and his made-up story about doing a piece on baseball spring training has got to be him covering his tracks."

"Where is he now?"

"He said he was going over to see some old friends in Miami today, but insisted on calling me later tonight in hopes that I'd see him. He won't leave me alone—to the point where it's creepy. But about two hours ago, he left me a message that he'd be tied up in Miami till tomorrow. I told Mrs. Van Buren that it sure is funny how the article on his father mentioned that the feds began their investigation about eight months ago, listing Atlanta as one of the cities tied to the ring. Bruce came to work for the paper eight months ago. Coincidence?"

"I don't know, but it all sounds dangerous. Don't take his calls."

"Do you think Darrell knows about him? When he called about coming down here he sounded oddly eager to see me, but not angry. Maybe he's playing with my mind."

"You know Darrell's not like that. He just wants to see you. But I must confess that I did have a heart-to-heart with him last night and questioned him about his love for you after which I suggested the idea of his going down there."

"*Mother...*"

"I had to. I knew that if he went at least then Bruce might leave you alone and it'd give you and Darrell a chance to talk. Helen was the one that suggested it. But don't worry, I didn't dare tell him about Bruce, but I did point out to him that you'd been feeling neglected."

"When did ya'll have this little powwow?"

"Late last night after the twins had gone to bed, apparently neither of us could sleep because we bumped into each other during a midnight fridge raid. He got out the ice cream, and I heated up the hot fudge. Over our bowls of guilt, I just flat out asked if he still loved you. That question led to an hour's discussion about how unhappy you've both been. Sometimes I think men are blind when it comes to emotion. I almost had to get out the dry erase board next to the telephone and diagram out a timeline of events that led to your present state. But once I opened up his eyes to how serious ya'll's rift had become, he said something peculiar"

"What's that?"

"He said, 'It's more than just a rift.' So then I put the idea in his head of going down there to see you. And wouldn't you know I heard the coffee beans grinding at five o'clock this morning. When I went downstairs, there he was with an over-packed duffle bag sitting by the back door. Now it's up to you on whether you tell him about Bruce or not, but I think in the long run being honest will test the true strength of your marriage. Wouldn't you want to know if he'd had an affair?"

I wouldn't answer, still trying to get over the fact that my own mother and Helen Van Buren had schemed together to bring my husband down here.

"Well…would you want to know or not?"

"Don't know," I said, wondering if ignorance would be bliss.

"Nothing brings the human soul more grief than having to hide a secret. Did Helen tell you about how her mother hid the real reason why her father had left her when she was just a girl? Then she manipulated her into marrying Henry before she died. Helen did it for her mother, not herself, and paid dearly for it."

"Yes, she told me all that. I don't understand how she let herself make the same mistake her father did by marrying simply to accommodate someone else."

"Sometimes we follow one of our parent's footsteps without even realizing it."

"So are you saying I'm duplicating something you or daddy did by having an affair?"

"No, I'm saying that I don't want to see you have to carry the burden of keeping a secret like all the damn generations before you. It's emotional torture and it's time this family shakes all of its skeletons out of the closet. Wouldn't you agree?"

"But what if I tell Darrell about Bruce and he leaves me?"

"Would you leave him if he'd had an affair because you'd neglected him at some point during your marriage?"

"Is there something *you're* not telling me about Darrell?"

Hesitation and more tapping of her nails to the counter. "The only thing I still can't explain is why he didn't take his Confederate uniform the other day when he went to meet the Brothers for a campout. And then there's the mileage discrepancy I noticed on his odometer that I told you about. Maybe it's time you question him about that."

"I thought you didn't want me to."

"I can change my mind. So you never did answer me about whether you could forgive Darrell if he'd had an affair too."

"Maybe," I said, gritting my teeth, envisioning *the act* of him with another woman.

"But you'd agree that it's better to know than to not know?"

"Now you're contradicting yourself. You just told me that you and Daddy's secrets are under a black tarp in the attic."

"Look, I never said he and I didn't divulge them to each other."

"Really Mama, I want to take your advice, but the last time I took it all I got was a hundred dollar charge on my Visa from Victoria's Secret and a dagger in my libido."

"Julia, I'm going to say this once so listen closely. In the end, you have to make the choice. If you don't plan to work things out, then yes, it's a secret you could maybe live with. But if you're going to spend the rest of your life with this man, you can't hide things from each other. If you do, all intimacy will be lost. Could you live with yourself without ever telling him? Some people do, claiming that telling would be selfish and why hurt the other person. But it's *you* that you really have to take care of first. Now, Darrell knows that the boys and I will be down there Wednesday, so consider yourself with three days to wash out the sheets you've slept in and make right for your future."

"You make it sound so dirty."

"Wasn't it?"

"Okay, enough about that. So now that the cat's out of the bag about Helen Van Buren being your birth mother, why not tell the boys yourself?"

"Because Helen wants to."

"What about the interview?"

"You can always tidy up the biography later. This is about family now. But she really does want you to be the one to write it."

"Alright then Mama I've got to go. Darrell's calling on the other line which means he's getting close and needs directions."

"Love you, sugar. Stay strong and do what's best for Julia."

A trail of white dust kicked up as Darrell's luxury pick-up approached Mrs. Van Buren's cottage. He had just missed Stephen and Isa who had gone to retrieve the fish fryer from Stephen's place. Dinner plans had been relocated due to Mrs. Van Buren's hip's reluctance to move further than a few inches at one time.

I stood at the top of the porch steps and watched him get out, the late afternoon sun streaking rays through banyan branches above him. His sandy brown hair had appealingly curled up at the ends from the humidity blowing through his open windows. The rest of him looked good, too. An old pair of Levi's fit loosely around his slender build, and a yellow polo shirt brought out the amber in his eyes. My heart pounded and the anxiety of all that needed telling made my head sway like the ferns hanging on either side of me. I didn't run right out to him, but stayed anchored on the first step and gave a gentle wave.

"Glad you made it."

"What an awesome place she has here," he said walking toward me. "But finding it was like something out of one of those reality TV shows. It's really hidden away."

My arms stayed folded, tears suppressed, until he wrapped a bear hug around me. I set my hands loosely on his hips. The familiar essence of sandalwood in his cologne mixed with a day's worth of sitting in leather seats made my throat close up and eyes water. *How could I have been so stupid?*

"I've missed you." He pulled away, tucking a loose strand of hair that a breeze had blown in my eyes back around my ear. "Why the long face?"

"Too much to handle in two days," I said, tugging his hand so he'd follow. "Come in and I'll introduce you to Mrs. Van Buren once she wakes up. She's upstairs in the sunroom. Isa and her driver, I mean, her boyfriend," I muffled a laugh, "Stephen, have gone to pick up his fish fryer and the fish he caught yesterday. We were going to eat at his place, but Mrs. Van Buren hurt her hip earlier."

"Nothing serious, I hope."

"Nothing that would prohibit her from eating and socializing; she really wants to meet you."

"Is that so," he grinned proudly.

"Go ahead and get your bag out of the truck and bring it inside. I'm sure it's okay that you stay here. We're more like family than you could ever imagine."

An odd look came askance. "I don't know Julia, are you sure?"

"I'm positively positive. She insisted, now come on." The gulf breeze dried up my tears, and I temporarily swallowed the lump in my throat.

&2&

An hour later, Darrell had gotten the CliffsNotes version about my unknown family members, the most riveting detail of course being the true identity of Mrs. Van Buren and Stephen being my grandparents. His reaction was one initially of shock mixed with a hint of pleasant surprise, much as mine had been.

Once Isa and Stephen returned from retrieving fish frying accoutrements, Darrell had the pleasure of hearing more details of decades past from Stephen over a cold beer at the kitchen table. I helped Isa get dinner started.

By the time we had the fish battered and ready for cooking, Mrs. Van Buren "yoo-hoo'ed" from upstairs. Isa checked on her, and shortly returned to report that we'd be dining outside on the balcony.

"I was able to get her from the sofa and outside for pretty hour," Isa informed us, "that's what she calls the time of day just after sunset. But she says to send you two up immediately for introductions." She waved Darrell and me toward the staircase. "She's sitting outside in the rocker. Oh, and she said to bring up a bottle of chardonnay." Isa reached to the back of the fridge, pulled out a bottle and handed it to Darrell.

"Just call us when dinner's ready and we'll help bring everything up," I offered.

"Don't worry about it," Stephen said, carefully lowering breaded pieces of fish into popping grease. "Just take up this stack of plates and forks along with the wine, and Isa and I can manage the rest." He placed the stack in my hand.

When we got to the top of the stairs, Darrell let out a cleansing breath.

"You're not that out of shape, are you?"

"Just got a lot on my mind."

Mrs. Van Buren sat angled, mostly toward the beach, the orange and deep purple sky as her backdrop. The chair rocked lightly, her cane pushing it to-and-fro between the slats of wood in the balcony floor. I hollered out a hello, and she craned her neck around to see us.

"Ah, Darrell I presume," she said, her smile half hidden by the purple scarf. "I'd waltz over and greet you, but my hip won't allow it."

"Of course not," he said, stepping quickly with the bottle of wine in hand through the sunroom and out the open slider.

"I'm assuming Julia's filled you in on our special relationship while I've been napping."

"Yes ma'am, she has," he said, extending his hand.

"No handshakes," she reached out her arms, which slightly trembled, "only hugs for family."

Darrell bent down and hugged her like she was a carton of eggs, the wine still in the grip of his left hand. "It's a pleasure to meet you. I hear ya'll have had quite a day of storytelling."

"Yes we have. How 'bout opening that bottle. There's a corkscrew and some glasses in the bookshelf cabinet next to my desk."

Darrell opened the bottle and filled three glasses, then placed the bottle on the bistro table where I'd laid the stack of plates and forks. "How's your hip?"

"Painful, that's why I could use a couple of these," she tapped the glass, "and I am worn slap out from all this story-tellin' which is why after dinner I insist ya'll take a bottle of my good wine that I keep hidden under the bar downstairs to the shore and enjoy the full moon soon to be dancing out over the gulf. A perfect setting for intimate conversations..." She raised a serious brow my way.

"Sounds like a good plan," Darrell said, sitting in the rocker to her left.

While they continued getting to know one another, I set the table, rehearsing ways to bring up Bruce. I didn't know if I should come right out and say, *I had an affair,* or if I should lead up to the events that caused it, and use the *you-left-me-no-choice* excuse.

Mrs. Van Buren and I locked eyes during the midst of this contemplation, her fair green gaze arching over Darrell's rocking shoulder. She concluded our silent exchange with a quick smile and nod of confirmation. The gentle look was one of compassion. She knew what I was thinking and that what laid ahead was going to be painful but necessary.

Stephen and Isa came up with the food, and at Mrs. Van Buren's request, Darrell helped scoot her to the table to spare her the struggle of having to switch from the rocker to a stiff bistro chair.

"Oh, it'll be fun to rock and eat," she said, placing a napkin in her lap, the wine seeping to her head. "Darrell says he's been teaching American history going on sixteen years," she directed at Stephen. "You should take him over to Josh's house and show him his Flintlock musket from the Revolutionary War."

"Josh is your son, right?" Darrell asked.

"Yep, my one and only...son that is." He patted Mrs. Van Buren's hand. "I'd take out the musket and show it to you, but he keeps the damn thing locked in a glass case, and I have no idea where the key is. He'll be back in town tomorrow."

"That's okay, just looking will be plenty exciting for me, and then maybe Josh will let me handle it once he's in town."

Isa extended the basket of cheesy corn muffins and asked, "I'm not sure if you'd enjoy seeing it, but I have my father's rifle from World War II. I know we were on opposing sides, but if you're interested in antique weaponry, I'll dig it out of the foyer closet later."

"Sure, that'd be great. Is it a Karabiner 98k?"

"Why yes it is."

"Those were standard issue for German soldiers back then. Do you have the magazine for it? They're worth more with the magazine."

"Yes, but I took out the bullets and put them in my jewelry box. Don't like the idea of a loaded weapon in the house."

"Me neither," Mrs. Van Buren seconded, her wine glass swaying. "You hear about so many of them going off for no apparent reason. With my luck, it'd be aimed upstairs toward my desk and get me right in the ass."

"Helen!" Stephen said in a correcting tone. "Watch her wine intake tonight Isa."

Darrell and I smirked a laugh at one another.

"Where does Josh keep his musket on display?" Darrel asked.

"In the billiard room," Stephen answered.

"Billiard room?" Darrell pouted a lip at me. "I've been trying to talk Julia into converting the formal living room into a billiard room."

"Not again," I said, recalling the ridiculous argument we'd had about a month prior.

"No one ever sits in there," he tried to reason. "It'd be fun for me and the kids, wouldn't you agree Stephen?"

Stephen raised a palm. "I learned long ago not to offer my opinion in domestic disputes. But we can shoot a game or two after dinner if you'd like."

I heard a slap of someone's knee under the table, followed by Mrs. Van Buren saying, "They have other plans. Isn't that right Julia?"

"Maybe tomorrow night after Josh is in town," Darrell said.

"Good thinking," Stephen agreed. "We'll play a little eight ball...that is, if it's alright with the ladies." His round eyes checked with his sweetie first.

"But only after we've had our talk with Josh," she said and then looked at me. "He still has no idea that your mother is his half sister."

"He'll be fine when we tell him about our past," Stephen said. "He knows we're fond of each other, there's no hiding that. And you know how he felt about Paula. He's known since he was a boy what she's capable of. Hell, look how she manipulated him into marrying her childhood friend's daughter—that no good whore from the swamps."

"Stephen!" Mrs. Van Buren smacked his arm.

"Well that's what she was. Paula practically did everything but say 'I do' for him. Josh still hates her for it. That's why he won't marry again." Stephen took a long sip of wine and cleared his throat. "So how long have you two been married?"

"Long time," Darrell said.

"Coming up on fourteen years," I confirmed.

"Gotta keep the communication open and the love always flowing," Stephen said, topping off my wine. "Never keep things from each other. Helen and I were forced to keep things from other people, but never from each other. We were up-front about everything, weren't we cupcake?"

"Stephen," she blushed. "Don't call me that in front of our guests."

Isa rolled her eyes, as if she'd heard them sweet talk hundreds of times before, them never aware she'd been only an earshot away.

How charming and reassuring it was to know that I too may blush when old and gray. Darrell's eyes connected with mine. He raised his glass and tapped it with his fork...

"Here's to having found the love of a lifetime." We all raised our glasses and toasted, Darrell simultaneously leaning into my ear and whispering, "There always has been, and always will be, one love in my life." He kissed my forehead. "Remember that."

If he did know about Bruce, he sure was going out of his way to make it extremely difficult for me later.

❦

After Stephen left and Isa went to help Mrs. Van Buren to bed, Darrell brought up his bag from the foyer to my room. We each grabbed a light jacket, and I slipped into some jeans. The evening air had chilled to a crisp sixty degrees.

Once to the shore, Darrell propped open two folding beach chairs and placed them on the wet sand close enough to where the gentle surf might lick our toes from time to time. A small cooler served as our cocktail table. Isa had filled it with a bottle of merlot and two of those plastic champagne glasses with removable stems.

"One for you…" he poured and offered, "…and one for me."

He overestimated the size of the glass and wine spilled onto the knees of his jeans.

"Shit," he muttered. "My attempt to be suave for my girl just backfired, huh?" He had a nervousness about him, almost like that of a first date.

"Sometimes flaws make us more likeable, approachable," I said, remembering our second tutoring session back at Emory. He'd scratched his cheek with a ballpoint pen he thought was clicked shut. Three long blue marks striped his face, and when we looked up at each other and I'd told him what he'd done, laughter took precedence over my studies. He tried to rub it off, making it worse—blue blush along his chiseled cheek. I laughed more, licked the tip of my thumb and tried to rub it off. That's when he grabbed my hand and kissed my palm, our focus going from American history to anatomy. Now look at us.

The full moon reflected off waves that softly lapped beneath our feet. I sipped my wine with closed eyes and squished my toes into the damp shelly sand. Followed by a gulp of salt air, I said, "Mama told me about your midnight meeting over ice cream last night."

"She did, huh." He grabbed my hand and placed a bare foot on mine. "Stephen said he'd take me fishing out in the boat early tomorrow morning, and then around noon while he goes to the airport to pick up his son...what's his name again?"

"Josh."

"Yes, while he's gone to pick up Josh, he said I could use his fly rod and do some shore fishing in front of his bungalow. Want to try it with me? He's got two poles."

"That's the same time that Isa is taking Mrs. Van Buren to town for a doctor's appointment. I was going to organize my notes while she was gone and come up with an impressive preface for her biography, show her that I'm still as serious as she is about writing it."

"Well if you change your mind, you know where I'll be."

He stroked my hand with his thumb, a worried pressure to his touch. I let go, breathed deeply. It couldn't wait any longer.

"Darrell, there's something I need to talk to you about."

His finger shushed my lips. "There's something I need to say first."

"Okay," I said, surprised yet somewhat relieved for the delay.

We both fiddled with the stems of our plastic glasses.

"Do you remember the year that the boys began preschool?"

"Of course," I said. "It was bittersweet."

"Well, the years that led up to that day, you were knee deep in either diapers or notes for writing your column, completely obsessed with trying to be the perfect mother and best columnist for one of the biggest cities in the South."

"I just remember feeling guilty for spending time away from the boys, and I hated that it was Mama that got to see their firsts. When the workday was done, every bit of leftover energy I had went to the kids."

"Exactly... which led me to feel a little bit...well, like I've made you feel lately."

"What...forgotten, neglected, cast aside?"

"Ouch!" He stabbed his chest with his thumb. "You make it sound so harsh, but yes, very neglected." He set the plastic wine glass on top of the cooler and began tugging at his wedding band.

"What are you doing?"

He placed it in the palm of my hand, the same palm he'd kissed all those years ago at our tutoring session.

Painfully eyeing the gold band, I said, "Oh my God, you know about—"

"Yes, I know that you've figured out that I have no Brothers of the Confederacy."

"What? No Brothers?" I said confused.

"You have to understand that she was just a random student that I was tutoring at the time. She came on to me! I'd planned for it to be a one time thing. It never occurred to me that she'd lied about being on the pill. I was going to tell you about the baby but—"

"A baby! You have a goddamn baby with this woman?!" I flew out of my seat and kicked it, the cold metal frame stinging my bare foot. "This pales in comparison to my issue," I mumbled, shaking my head.

"What do you mean?" he said, rising from his seat, looking down at me.

"Nothing," I crossed my arms and quickly reverted back to his ordeal. "Boy or girl?"

"A girl, Shelby, she's nine now and we just found out last spring that she has leukemia. That's why I took off Friday and told your mother I was going to meet the Brothers in the mountains. Shelby's mother had called that morning that I was supposed to drive you to the airport. She'd taken a turn for the worse. I had to go be with her."

"Have all those trips over the years been to visit Shelby?"

"Yes, and the other phone I have…the one that chimes like a bell?"

I waited for the next surprise.

"It's a direct line for Shelby or her mother to reach me, not the university. Her mother is remarried now, but we always agreed that I'd stay in Shelby's life."

"Why didn't you just tell me about all this when it'd happened?"

"If I had told you we wouldn't be here having this conversation because you would've slapped divorce papers in my face so fast there'd been no time for discussions."

"You don't know that," I said. He was right though. "This is too much." I sat down and drained my wine. "So she has leukemia?"

"Yes. And I should also tell you that those investments I made last spring weren't for some stock. The money went toward Shelby's treatment."

"How have you paid child support for all these years unnoticed?"

"Little bits here and there. Look, I tried to do the right thing for everybody, and this was the only way I knew how."

"But lying just imprisons everyone!" I turned to the silver-lined horizon, wanting to take a giant step off the edge of the earth. The lies we'd told to protect the other had melted away all sense of trust and integrity I'd held in him...in myself.

We stood side-by-side, silent, arms folded until a hand squeezed my shoulder. I knew he wanted me to face him, but I couldn't.

"Once I realized that there was a possibility that Shelby may not be around much longer, this overwhelming urge to tell you everything came over me like wildfire. I don't want to hide this anymore."

I shrugged his hand off my shoulder.

He continued. "And after having that talk with your mother last night—"

"Does she know?"

"Yes, I told her last night, but she swore not to tell you as long as I'd come straight down and tell you everything."

"And have you?" I finally faced him.

"Yes, Jules, I promise. Bottom line is that Shelby hasn't been responding to her treatment like the doctors had hoped. I needed for you to know about her, and the twins have a right to know, too. It's only fair that I tell them that they have a sister."

Empathy for his situation was slow coming, my own affair dangling off the tip of my tongue. I buried my head in my hands. *Telling him now should be easy after what he's done.*

But still the words didn't come out. I then knew how it felt to be deceived. He pried my hands away from my wet face.

"Leave me alone," I jerked. "I need time to think."

"I don't blame you for being mad...even hating me, but—"

"Shut-the-fuck-up and go away."

With hands pressed back over my face, I listened to his footsteps fade into the seagrape hedges behind me. Once I knew he was gone, my knees buckled. I fell to the wet sand, closing up in a spiral like the conch shells around me—a ball of hopelessness. I, too, had stuck thorns into our marriage. What's worse is that I'd played the coward for not telling him.

Chapter 15

*A*n hour went by while I sat in the damp sand, trying to digest what Darrell had told me.

A hundred painful questions raced through my mind. *Who is Shelby's mother?* left me breathless. At least my affair had only given birth to a dangerous situation.

Gathering up the chairs and cooler, I made my way toward the porch light which winked at me through swaying palms and banyans. Darrell was nowhere in sight, but his truck remained unmoved.

After setting the cooler and chairs down beside the front door, I quietly entered, firmly grasping the door handle so it wouldn't slam shut. The seat of my jeans was wet with salt water chilling me to the bone. A shot of brandy was a must before bed. As I walked through the living room toward the bar, something caught my eye leaning against the coffee table. It was a gold-framed piece of art. Walking closer, I noticed a typed note taped to it, faded keystrokes jumping about the page.

Dearest Julia,

> *Got Isa to bring out my old typewriter so I could write in bed—handwritten notes are a thing of my past. It occurred to me that I have yet to show you my symbol for survival...Papa's rendering of the Breakers...my castle of hope. The hundreds of hours spent studying this rendering, fantasizing about characters dancing about its renaissance walls, falling in love, were never wasted hours. I truly believe in happily-ever-after's, even if some take a lifetime to achieve. Isa said she saw Darrell walk in from the beach looking distraught. You did the right thing by telling him, Julia. Expect him to be angry, but don't lose hope. He loves you; that I can tell. You too deserve to find your happily-ever-after. Good night my dear granddaughter. Sleep well.*

> *Love,*
> *Your doting Grandmother*

The faded rendering of a castle set by the sea captivated my senses. I could feel the breeze from the simply sketched palms and taste the air blowing in off the Atlantic Ocean— the perfect setting for a night of romance. How horrid that a night of wonder turned into such a tragedy. Her secrets, all of them, began at this setting. She was now free from hers. I was the only one left. I should have told Darrell.

After drinking a shot of brandy in one swig, my achy conscience tiptoed through the kitchen and up the stairs, skipping the squeaky one at the bottom. When I reached the top, there on the sofa slept Darrell, fully dressed, his long denim legs hanging over the edge. He snored lightly, the corners of his mouth turned down with shame, guilt and worry, no idea that he wasn't alone in his expressions.

Monday morning the dawn of a new day, a life-changing day, seeped through a crack in the bedroom curtains of the daisy trimmed room. My eyes sprang wide open, thoughts instantly picturing Darrell's daughter, her illness, her likely bald head and withering frame. My anger had mellowed overnight, and I felt real concern for her, for him. He was hurting. The idea of telling him about Bruce would only compound his heavy load. Maybe it would be best never to tell him. That would be my punishment.

I walked out to the sunroom in my nightshirt to find an empty sofa; then I remembered his plans of an early fishing trip with Stephen. Halfway down the stairs, the faint melody of my phone began playing. I froze, gripping the handrail for a moment, something in my gut certain it was Bruce. *Just let it ring*, I thought, like Mama had told me to do. But curiosity took hold, and I ran back up the steps and to my room to check the number. It was him. I didn't answer, just stared at the display.

I decided to stay upstairs and get ready for the day. Breakfast could wait and I'd officially lost my appetite. He called three more times while I buttoned up a blue gingham sundress and fixed my face and hair. Then after the fourth time, I turned off the phone. His persistence became intrusive, frightening.

To my surprise, when I came out of the bedroom, Mrs. Van Buren sat alone rocking on the balcony in her usual spot, the turquoise scarf tied about her head just like the day we'd met.

"Good morning," I said and sat beside her. "You snuck up here like a mouse. I usually hear and feel the elevator."

"Something's wrong with the wiring in the blasted thing," she said. "It happened a few months ago and cost a small fortune to fix."

"It must've been painful having Isa help inch you up those stairs." I looked at her hip.

"A six-foot German woman has no problem carrying little ole ninety-pound me."

"She carried you?" I cracked up, envisioning the two of them.

"She'll be up in a few minutes with some breakfast. So what'd you think about the surprise I left out for you to see last night?"

"The rendering is amazing. I remember Haley describing it to Margie in your manuscript, but after seeing it up-close-and-personal, I couldn't help but think of how precious a gift that was from your father. It's been on quite a long journey with you."

"Indeed. Did you get my note, too?"

"Yes, and Darrell didn't look distraught last night because of what I failed to tell him, it was because of what he wound up telling me."

She stopped rocking. "You didn't tell him?"

"No, I couldn't after what he said to me."

"Oh...and what was that?"

"The gist of it is, years ago he had an affair that produced another human being."

"What!"

"Yes. Her name's Shelby. She's nine and she has leukemia." I continued on with the rest of the story.

"How'd this one get past me and your mother?"

"Mama just found out the night before Darrell came here. He 'fessed up over a midnight bowl of ice cream."

"Good heavens! So why didn't you go ahead and tell him about Bruce after hearing all that?"

"I couldn't. Don't know why exactly, just got to thinking about her cancer and how he said she might die. I hope you're not disappointed in me."

"Sometimes a situation presents itself unexpectedly. We can't plan for the situation, so when it happens, we act on instinct. Your instinct was not to tell him...not to hurt him anymore than he was already hurting. Now if you didn't love him you would have gone ahead and lashed right out."

"I do love him."

"I know you do," she said, reaching for my shoulder. "But sooner or later the truth has got to come out or else," she said, pointing to my heart, "this will ache forevermore. Listen to it, dear. It never lies."

"I can't wait to be able to sit here with you and Mama both. I'm actually glad you told her about Bruce."

"Oh? I thought you'd be angry with me."

"A little at first, but it felt good to get the truth out to her, too."

"'Nothing makes us so lonely as our secrets.'"

"I've heard that before," I said, the loneliness having closed in tight over the past several months.

"It's a quote from Dr. Paul Tournier of Geneva. And yes, it feels more than just good to get the truth out…it's exhilarating."

All was quiet at the gingerbread house except for a faint breeze grazing the wind chimes. I had fixed myself a pimento sandwich and gone to the balcony hoping to get some creative juices flowing and piece together an impressive preface for Mrs. Van Buren's bio. She and Isa had already left to Fort Myers for her doctor's appointment and weren't due back till late afternoon.

Shells crackled below as Stephen drove up in the old blue Chrysler. His white capped head leaned out the window.

"Darrell decided he wanted to take the boat back out to North Captiva for a look around," he hollered up to me. "If you'd like to join him he said for you to meet him by

12:30. Our morning fishing excursion proved to be a tease. Fish were jumping out of the water winking at us, but none biting."

"Think I'll pass on the fishing today," I said, leaning over the rail. "There's some writing I need to get busy with."

"I'll be back around three or so," he said. "Josh's flight is due in just after one o'clock. I'm taking this baby in for some gas and then by the hardware store on my way back. I promised Helen I'd fix that bottom step near the kitchen that's been squeaking. You need anything while I'm out?"

"Not a thing, Stephen, thank you."

"Alrighty then. Be back with your…I guess he's your half uncle, in a few hours." He tipped his golf cap in that gentlemanly way he always did and gave a wink.

"Look forward to meeting him," I waved.

I propped open the umbrella in the center of the bistro table hoping to minimize the noonday glare that blazed over my laptop. The curser blinked at me like a heart beating, waiting to tell all that I'd come to know. Two more days till I got to see Mama and the boys. I missed them terribly and couldn't wait. We would all share a long-awaited family reunion.

Just as I was about to strike the first key, the door off the kitchen slammed shut.

"Hello!" I hollered.

No answer.

"Darrell?"

Nothing…

Maybe Isa hadn't shut the door all the way when she'd left with Mrs. Van Buren.

With eyes settled back to the curser, I began to type... *Helen Van Buren exemplifies the true meaning of romance through her...*

I stopped again after hearing what sounded like a chair tipping over in the kitchen. Quietly rising, I slowly stepped off the balcony and through the open sliders.

"Darrell?" I said again, stopping at the curio cabinet full of Hummel Angels, their black eyes washing over me. Before I got a full view down the stairway, the bottom step squeaked.

"Who's there?" Walking closer, I looked down.

"Hey darlin'."

"Bruce?"

"Yes, darlin'."

"How'd you get in here?" I said.

"Doesn't matter, you didn't answer my phone calls. That wasn't very nice of you."

His ocean blue eyes looked wildly at me, and in what seemed like slow motion, those alligator boots came creeping my way. I walked backward until my rear hit the overstuffed chair.

"You shouldn't be here," I said, nervously sitting on the arm of the chair. He came closer, his knees brushing against mine, tobacco and beer reeking from his wrinkled white button down.

He tapped the tip of my nose with his thick finger. "I thought you understood that I decide when it's over, darlin'. You've gotten all uppity not answering my phone calls."

His hands slithered around my waist, gripping my hips. He thrust me off the chair toward him. I withdrew.

"You used to like that." He forced me closer.

"You're drunk and you really shouldn't be here. They'll be back soon—all of them."

"These walls have ears and eyes, and I know this house's every breath and heartbeat."

"What do you mean...ears and eyes?"

"We've had this place bugged for years."

"We? Who're we?"

"Now don't you worry your pretty little head about that. But we know everything...about the necklace in the old goat's cane, the handkerchief, and I can assure you that my Great Aunt Paula would be proud if she were standing here today."

"Oh my God...your grandmother was Paula's sister... the one from Sarasota where they found the safe deposit box?"

"That's her. Now listen here," he said, untying the grosgrain ribbon around my waist. "I promised her before she died that I'd do my best to get you pregnant; 'Taint the bloodline,' she would say." He continued running his fingers from button to button, till he groped me between the thighs. "My mother deserved Paula's fortune when she died, but Stephen had the will changed...had her sign something that she thought was a tax form, but what it did was leave Paula's side out of the inheritance. Mother got nothing. I got nothing!"

"But your father—isn't he wealthy?"

"Now you know as well as I do that he's come into a little trouble with the feds. I overheard your...what was it ya'll called it...Nancy Drew'n. You know more about me than I think I know about myself," he said somewhat amused.

"You didn't go to Miami to visit friends. You went there to see to your father about business, didn't you?"

"That's none of your goddamn business." His open palm met my cheek.

"Darrell's here and not far off either. He'll hear my screams," I said, trying to get to the balcony so anyone could hear me.

"None of your neighbors are home, and what I need to do won't take long." He pushed me to the sofa and fell on top of me. "I do believe when we all had our lunch together last Friday Mrs. Van Buren said something about a one o'clock appointment in Fort Myers today. That leaves me enough time to make one last deposit. You know for the last six months I've poked holes in every condom we've used. Damn if you ain't barren at the ripe ole age of thirty-eight."

"Get off of me," I pushed him. He stumbled toward the elevator.

"One last time in an elevator might be nice."

Knowing it was broken, I let out a muffled laugh.

"What's so damn funny?" His palms slammed against the elevator door causing the angels in the curio cabinet to rattle. Staggering back toward me, he tripped on his booted feet. His head met the glass coffee table. It cracked

"Goddamnit!" he shouted, holding his right temple. Blood trickled down his scruffy cheek.

Eyeing the stairway, I quickly stood and walked around him.

"Where in the hell do you think you're going?"

He gripped my ankle. "You're really scaring me."

Holding the table for leverage, he rose. "Fuckin' liar."

"Liar? I've never lied to you about anything."

"Not you…my father. I was jipped because of Stephen and Helen, and now I've been jipped by my own fuckin' father. Just over a million dollars. It's mine! The son-of-a-bitch says he mailed it to my crazy-ass mother. He said I don't deserve it. I was supposed to have played pro ball, you know. He'd counted on that for me, for him."

"Your mother? I thought she was at a psychiatric facility in Jacksonville."

"She is, but she's still got a PO Box and only he knows where the key is…goddamn traitor."

"Did you ask him where it was?"

He gripped my throat with a bite. "Of course I fuckin' asked him. You think I'm stupid?'

"Please, just leave me alone." I gasped for air as his pressure eased. "If you go away now, it'll be our secret. I promise, I won't tell anyone."

"Give me some credit here, darlin' I'm not that stupid." His hand bit my neck again, sending me to the floor near the elevator.

"I told you it's not over till I say it's over."

He ripped my dress the rest of the way open, unbuckled his pants and pried my legs open with his knees.

"I say when it's over."

His thrusts ripped me apart. Lying there like a rag doll, my eyes fell to the curio cabinet full of angels, their innocent faces longing to help me.

God help me…forgive me, I mumbled along with desperate cries for Darrell.

The air went black, numb and bitter until a burst of red sprayed about the room covering my torn sundress, the walls and the curio cabinet.

Bruce's disfigured head fell to my shoulder, and when it did, Darrell stood behind him, his eyes filled with rage. An old shotgun stayed steadily aimed in his hands. His face began to crinkle with disgust at what he'd done.

"Oh my God—I think I killed him."

I shimmied out from under him, his gored head plunking to the floor. No sign of a pulse when I checked his neck.

"His name's Bruce, right?" Darrell asked, looking for confirmation as he drug the body next to the stairs.

"Yes. I can explain."

"You don't have to." He helped me up. We stood silently side-by-side studying the lifeless body before us. "When I let myself in the front door to come up and see if you wanted to go out in the boat, I heard voices... talking...threatening you. When I got far enough up the steps to see who it was, it all came together for me. The way he'd looked at you at your office Christmas party last year—like he'd already had you. I remembered what Isa had told me about her father's Karabiner 98k being in the foyer closet, and that she kept the bullets in her jewelry box. I got the gun and loaded it, and when I got to the top of these stairs," he pointed behind him, "he was on you...all over you. You were whimpering *my* name. I had planned to pull the trigger...miss him, you know, scare him. I didn't mean to kill him."

"We should call the police," I said.

"No!"

"Yes, this is forced entry, and I feared for my life. That gives you the legal right to shoot to kill. You saved me from God knows what else he had planned."

"Maybe we can clean this mess up, bury him…like it never happened. Let people assume he went missing."

"Is that what you want? For us to have the burden of living with another secret for the rest of our lives? Captiva Island has held captive its last secret. Now call the police."

He pulled his phone from his back pocket and dialed 911.

"And Darrell…"

"Yes."

"Look at me."

"Yes…"

"I love you."

He swallowed hard, took me in those familiar lanky arms and let out a long sigh.

"I love you too."

Epilogue

A year has passed since my interview with Mrs. V—correction—with my grandmother and a galley of her biography sits in my hands. *Owning Your Heart – The Helen Van Buren Story.*

After the police had investigated and questioned Bruce's death, Mama and the kids flew home and Darrell and I had driven the scenic route home across State Road 80 through La Belle and Clewiston and on over to Palm Beach, home of The Breakers. The accident flashed through my mind as we made the drive: the gator, the flipping car—the birth of so many scars.

Secret-free at last, I thought as we drove past streets lined with orange groves. Or was there still one secret left?

I had yet to tell Darrell about Bruce's plan to impregnate me. The horrific thought of carrying his child had me all twisted up inside. Darrell made a beeline to the very next roadside drugstore. I used their minuscule bathroom. Darrell followed me in, his back pressed against the bathroom door, our legs touching while I peed on one of those test sticks. Two pink lines meant you were pregnant, and one meant you weren't.

One line appeared. Overwhelming relief followed for both of us.

After that, our journey continued to The Breakers where we spent one night in an ocean-side suite. The rendering didn't hold a candle to what actually being there did for the senses. The rustling of palms combined with the ocean's distant hush instantly put me at ease as the valet opened my car door.

That night, we ate in their grand dining salon. I felt them there with us...Stephen and Helen...dressed to the nines, dining on lobster, prime rib and champagne, all a half century ago. The circular room haloed soft light, brushing lovers, including ourselves, with passion for the evening—his touch once again made me shiver.

The manuscript, a confession of what Helen Van Buren thought would stay sealed forever, now belonged to me. A new responsibility I now had being the keeper of this aging treasure.

"You choose what to do with it," she had told me during our goodbyes on her front porch. "Listen to your heart and soul. Let them guide you."

I listened. I chose. Like she'd told me before, "Sometimes life is way too messy to make good fiction." That tattered binder will remain my symbol of hope...hope to never give up on finding genuine happiness, no matter how long it takes.

I keep the binder in one of those glass cases, a lot like the one Josh kept his revolutionary war gun in. We hung it in the office over Darrell's desk.

His daughter Shelby has hair again. She spends every other weekend with us. The boys helped me paint the guest bedroom pink and we stenciled butterflies on the wall to symbolize her rebirth. The acceptance of her came easy for Dylan and Ryan, but I am still reaching. She favors her mother who actually resembles, of all people...me.

No charges were pressed for the death of Bruce Crawly. His rental truck had been found a half mile up the road from Mrs. Van Buren's place. Not only had Mrs. Van Buren's house been wired, but Josh's guest house where Stephen had been living was wired as well. We all wound up staying at Josh's that last night, Mrs. Van Buren's place having been filled with local authorities due to the fatality and of course, the rape.

Helen Van Buren, in all of her glorious eighty-seven years, had the sparkle in her eyes of a newlywed. Just last month, she and Stephen were married at the Chapel by the Sea. Of course we were all there in the first two rows reserved for family only. The rest of the church was filled with press. She revealed herself to the world with a bang—photos, white gown and all. Stephen even managed to carry her, at least for a few steps, down the aisle on the way out to her old blue Chrysler. Isa and I had decorated it with tin cans, streamers and wrote "Just Married" in white shoe polish on the skinny windshield, and on the shiny bumper, in red lipstick... "Happily ever after knows no age."

And so let it be told that on an island where pirates once held fair maidens captive, a cleansing breeze of truth blew from banyan to palm and freed us all from the loneliness that only secrets know.

෨෯

Acknowledgments

To my immediate family (Melanie, Christy, Emily, Michael and my dad, David, who hears me from above), I give bear hugs and sincere gratitude for their support and patience while I was writing this story. Your suggestions and insight helped push me to the end.

And a big thank you to Larry Myers of VanMeter Publishing who took me under his wing like a literary drill sergeant and helped bring out the best of my writing.

Also, thank you to all my other valuable sources of information and editing for *Captiva Isalnd*: Connie Buchanan (editor); Susan Holly (editor); Jim Ponce (Historian at the Breakers Palm Beach); Susan Welsh (Department of Communications at Wesleyan College); Julia Munroe Woodward (1930s Wesleyan alumni); Ray Harris (Florida Department of Transportation — road history); BookSurge; Amazon; and the world wide web.

And last, I'm thankful for the many friends, family, neighbors and friends of friends who took the time to read *Captiva Island* while still in its adolescent form. Your honest feedback and reviews helped give me the courage to finally let it go.

A Note about the Author

After receiving a Bachelor of Arts in Journalism from Auburn University in 1991, Kathy wrote for several publications including the *Pensacola News Journal,* the *Gulf Breeze Sentinel, Climate Magazine,* and *Guide to the Emerald Coast* (all located in Northwest Florida). Her most recent work can be found in *Entrée Magazine,* Naples, Florida.

In 2003 she took to novel writing as a hobby while raising her two children, Michael and Emily, and working on her Florida Teacher's Certification. Two manuscripts were born as a result, *Oakwood* and *Captiva Island*—the latter making its mark as a semi-finalist in the 2008 Amazon Breakthrough Novelist Contest.

Kathy currently works as the communications manager at a private country club in Naples, Florida, a place she has called home since 1993, and couldn't ask for a nicer setting in which to raise Michael, Emily and their fat cat Max.